Dead White Male

Paul Wiebe

KOMOS BOOKS

Upland, CA

A Komos Book

This is a work of comic fiction. Any references to historical events, to real persons, alive or dead, or to actual places, are included only to give the novel the false sense of reality that is the hallmark of farcical satire and that only a cretin would take as literal truth. Names, characters, places, and events that appear herein are either brainchildren of the author or are mentioned for his own subtle but harmless reasons; their resemblances, if any, to counterparts in the real world would be totally coincidental, though they would not surprise him.

An earlier edition was published by greatunpublished.com, 2001.
ISBN: 1-58898-375-7

Printed in the United States of America on acid-free paper.

Cover art by Stan Waling.

Publisher's Cataloging-in-Publication
(Provided by Quality Books, Inc.)

Wiebe, Paul, 1938-
Dead white male : a novel / Paul Wiebe.
p. cm.
LCCN 2002094711
ISBN 0-9718599-2-2 (pb)

1. Reincarnation—Fiction. 2. Fantasy. I. Title.

PS3623.I373D43 2003 813'.6
QBI33-1260

KB
Komos Books
991 Saint Andrews Drive, Ste. 138
Upland, CA 91784

This is for Bill and Millie Unrau.
Great storyteller, great cook.
Champion laughers. Grand pair.

Contents

Yet who would have thought the old man
to have had so much blood in him?

—Shakespeare, *Macbeth*

Dead White Male

Part One

1

A Pair of Star-Crossed Lovers

HE STOOD BEFORE THE DOOR of the principal's office, hesitant.

He tilted his head back slightly, adjusted his trifocals, squinted through the narrow slab, and read the new nameplate announcing the new occupant as MS. PENNI MODE, ED.D.

He took a large white handkerchief from a rear pocket. He unfolded it and wiped off the dewdrops that were beginning to form on his great white dome. He carefully refolded it and put it back in his pocket. Then he reached into his watch pouch, extracted the gold-plated timepiece he had inherited from his grandfather, thumbnailed open its worn cover, and checked the hour. Two forty-one: exactly on time.

He snapped the cover shut and slipped the watch back into its pouch. He closed his eyes, took a deep breath, and knocked.

"Come in," called a low feminine voice.

He reminded himself of Rule #1 for actors: relax. He counted to three. Then he made his grand entrance, taking pains to close the door behind him.

Ms. Penni Mode sat posture-perfect in a chair behind her desk. She was dressed in a dark-blue shoulder-padded business suit and was wearing a pair of fashionable steel-rimmed glasses. A small frown broke the surface of her wrinkle-free face as she vigorously made checkmarks on the papers arranged neatly before her.

Oh yes, he remembered. Faculty evaluation time.

"Sit down," she said without looking up at him. She pointed at the guest chair with the eraser end of her pencil.

He carefully sat down, shoehorning himself into the narrow chair. He hadn't been in this office for several weeks, since Ms. Mode took over for Henry Constant. He discreetly glanced around. Everything was changed. Instead of an old oak desk, there was this new steel one. Instead of a big soft padded guest chair, there was this mobile model on wheels, built for persons of more modest proportion. Instead of a red carpet beneath the chair, there was this slippery sheet of plastic. Instead of a sign on the wall advising ONE DAY AT A TIME, there was a poster with the message, THINK GLOBALLY—ACT LOCALLY. And instead of old standbys like *Lord Jim* and *Fathers and Sons* and *Hard Times,* the bookshelves now held new and unfamiliar titles like *Building Robust Competencies: Linking Human Resource Systems to Organizational Strategies* and *Beyond American Graffiti: A Longitudinal Study of Writing and Learning at the Post-Primary Level* and *Agenda for the Third Millennium: Empowering the Disadvantaged.*

She finally looked up, resting her chin on her left wrist. "Mr. Budwieser," she said abruptly.

Henry Constant used to call him Ed, and he called Henry Hank. He would come in and philosophize with Hank during his free hour; no appointment necessary. They'd sit there in the office with their feet up on that solid oak desk, he and good old

Hank, drinking coffee and calling each other by their Christian names and wondering what the world was coming to. But a month ago, just before Easter, wise, dependable Henry Constant had passed away from a heart attack—possibly a complication from the cirrhosis—and the control tower downtown had replaced him with Ms. Mode, a freshly-minted young Ed.D. who had got the job, as the *Kirkland Bugle* reported, because of "her skills in personnel management."

She whipped off her glasses and flashed a temporary smile.

He thought it appropriate to smile back.

She leaned forward. "I thought we should talk about the future," she began.

He nodded and cleared his throat and began to search for a masterful sentence that would introduce the speech he had spent this past Memorial Day weekend formulating and revising and polishing and practicing in front of the bathroom mirror—the speech that would eloquently put forth his vision of the future for Language Arts at Sunset High; the speech that would begin with a declaration of his well-considered philosophy of education, formed by the experience of thirty-odd years; the speech that would subtly demonstrate his mastery of the Classics, those immortal works of outstanding merit, those monuments of the human spirit, those shining and infallible touchstones that had stood the test of time; the speech that would off-handedly remind her (in case she had not had time to look at his file) that he had spent ten long hard summers working on his Master's thesis on Shakespeare's tragic heroes; the speech that would proceed to inform her that with Henry Constant's sage counsel, he had been grooming young Bob White to replace himself as Chairman of Language Arts in three years, when he would turn sixty-two and would finally be eligible for Social Security; the speech that would go on to recommend that Bobbie, despite being just fifty-one and having just a B.A. and being just a mite weak in Greek tragedy and Shakespeare's later plays, as well as having just a slight stutter, was the perfect man (having spent the last five summers on his thesis showing the influence of Aristophanes' *The Clouds* on John Kennedy Toole's *A Confederacy of Dunces*) to step into his own shoes and continue the long venerable tradition that had made Language Arts the pride of Sunset High—in fact, the pride of the entire Kirkland School District, if they only had the good sense to recognize the gold mine they had on their hands.

But that masterful first sentence would not come. It was a prisoner in his brain, tied up in a knot of words and parentheses and dashes and semicolons.

Ms. Mode looked at him for a long moment, quizzically.

"I thought you should be the first to know," she went on, sitting back in her chair, "that next year we're planning to reform the Language Arts curriculum."

Oh yes. Curriculum reform. That was another thing he had intended to mention in his speech. He'd been planning to point out that for the last several years he had given a great deal of thought to the possibility of revamping World Literature, perhaps replacing *A Midsummer Night's Dream* with *The Tempest* and *The Cherry Orchard* with *Death of a Salesman.*

She stared at a space twenty yards directly behind him.

Nice eyes, he observed. Quite an attractive young woman.

"I've asked Ms. Greene to be in charge of this process," she said.

Not exactly beautiful, not quite in Dora's class, but still, quite attract—. . . . What? Ms. Greene, in charge? Ms. Candi Greene? Twenty-three-year-old Ms. Candi Greene? Bubble-gum-chewing Candi Greene? Little Candi Greene, still running around in her training bra? Candi Greene, B.A. (Women's Studies), who only had a *minor* in English? Candi Greene, who refused to teach *The Scarlet Letter* because she found it "ex*treme*ly offensive," who insisted on teaching *The Color Purple* instead? Candi Greene, whom Hank Constant just had last month admitted was his one big mistake? Candi Greene? In charge?

"As you may or may not know," she went on, "Ms. Greene is an expert in deconstruction."

An expert. In deconstruction. He nodded wearily. Yes. He'd heard rumors to that effect. And he knew all about deconstruction. He'd once read an article on the subject in *Newsweek.* He was well aware that deconstructionism was a dangerous theory, designed by overpaid ex-Nazi professors in Ivy League universities as a plot to deprive Western Civilization of its most priceless possession, the Classics. He was well aware that the whole point of deconstruction was to rid the world of some fanciful concoction called "phallocentrism," a word that wasn't even listed in his definitive 1974 *Webster's*. He was well aware that the deconstructionists would not be satisfied until they had left the cultural battlefield strewn with the castrated corpses of legions of so-called "dead white males," from William Shakespeare to Ed Budwieser.

"I just wanted you to be the first to know," she repeated.

"Thank you," he murmured. It was the only sentence that came to mind.

She put her glasses back on and briskly stood up.

He stood up too, like an exhausted jack-in-the-box.

She glanced at her watch. "If you have any questions," she said, "I'd suggest you speak to Ms. Greene."

Speak to Ms. Greene? Candi Greene, whom he had overheard jesting about his teaching method, in which he played the parts of the characters in the Classics he assigned his students? Who snickered openly when he told her about his extensive collection of costumes: Prometheus, Oedipus, Samson, Becket—not to speak of Julius Caesar, Mark Antony, Hamlet, Macbeth, Othello, and King Lear? Who actually LAUGHED OUT LOUD last week when he came into the faculty lounge attired in Shakespearean doublet and hose immediately after treating his English Literature seniors to a stunning performance of Romeo's part in the balcony scene of the greatest love story of all time? Whose jests "set the table on a roar," to quote Hamlet, when she asked him whether he was sure he was doing Romeo, whether he wasn't "really, like, doing Fatstuff, y'know, that *old* guy," referring in her crude, vulgar way to Sir John Falstaff? Who was incapable of understanding the fact that playing the parts of those heroic characters, in costume, was the finest way to bring the Classics alive? Who could not possibly grasp the truth that the one time a man felt no boundary between what he was and what he aspired to be was when he was "strutting the boards, holding up a mirror to nature," in the sublime words of the Bard? Would *he* speak to a snide, disrespectful young woman about her plans for *his* department, *his* project for the last twenty-five illustrious years? He would not!

Ms. Mode strode quickly to the door.

He followed her, another speech beginning to form in his brain.

She turned to face him. "I have every confidence in Ms. Greene," she said with a sweet parting smile.

He cleared his throat.

"Yes?" she said brightly, opening the door for him.

He paused for a moment in the doorway, to think. He thought of the past, of the thirty-odd years he had spent as a member of the Department of Language Arts, twenty-five of them as its leader. He thought of the present, of the ominous but clear challenge to Western Culture's most valuable asset, the Classics. He thought of the future, wondering whether posterity would forgive him if he failed them in this, his hour of trial. He thought of his preparation for this moment of crisis, of the ten long hot vacationless Kansas summers he had devoted to the study of Shakespeare's tragic heroes. He thought of Shakespeare's bust, standing guard over his office, and of Shakespeare's serene but observant eyes, monitoring his every action. He thought of Hamlet, "screwing his courage to the sticking point," and of that young hero's words as he prepared to wreak his vengeance on those who had robbed him of his patrimony: "Readiness is all." Then he thought of the faculty evaluation forms on Ms. Mode's desk, and of Sir John Falstaff's advice: "The better part of valor is discretion."

He left her office without another word.

So next year, he sighed as she closed the door behind him, Ed Budwieser, whose steady hand had guided the ship of Language Arts for the last quarter of a century, was to be replaced at the helm by a callow young woman who had not even been born when he was her age. Just as this year Hank Constant—dead white male Henry Duncan Constant—had been replaced by Lady Macbeth.

But was this all so tragic? he asked himself as he wandered out into the long dark empty hall. Or was it a blessing in disguise? His thoughts turned to the judicious advice he always wrote on the blackboard for the benefit of his seniors at the tail end of their last semester:

THERE'S ALWAYS A LIGHT AT THE END OF THE TUNNEL;

and:

LOOK ON THE BRIGHT SIDE.

As he considered his own wisdom, he felt a strange but unmistakable relief. The weight of passing Western Culture to the next generation no longer rested on his substantial shoulders. Now that for all practical purposes he was no longer Chairman of Language Arts, he was finally free to do what he had been hoping and planning to do for the last ten years: leave philistine, prosaic Kirkland, move to the West Coast, and compose his memoirs for the benefit of a distant posterity that would, in time, come to appreciate the fact that for thirty-odd years Edward Budwieser, Master of Arts, had wasted his fragrance on the Kansas air.

§

She buzzed around the patient, dressed in a tiny pink pant suit, armed with a line of floss.

"Open wide," she sang.

He opened wide.

She accidentally rubbed up against him.

He flinched.

"Relax, Rabbi Scheinblum," she said gaily. "I'm not going to hurt you. That's Dr. Digby's job."

He flinched again.

"Just kidding," she reassured him. "My job is to take your mind off the coming pain."

A major flinch.

She ignored this response and launched into her assignment. One of the questions she'd been asking people as she flossed them up for Dr. Digby was, what did they like best about Kirkland? If they were to name her the one thing they liked best about living in Kirkland, Kansas, one thing and one thing only, what would that one thing be?

They'd been saying it's a nice conservative town. Still too much crime in the streets, maybe, and it was getting a little too big, in terms of population, but basically it was still a nice conservative town, knock on wood. They'd been mentioning the friendliness of the people. They'd been saying Kirkland was the kind of a place where family values were allowed to shine through, which accounted for the friendliness. They'd also been saying it was one big happy church-going community where everybody was free to go to the religion of his own choice and there were no long-haired Socialists—she guessed that maybe now they were called Liberals (this brought an indisputable flinch)—and very, very few atheists, just a few long-haired philosophers out at the University, and nobody paid any attention to them anyway, except for maybe a few sophomores, who'd grow out of it just about the time they started applying for jobs in the appliance department at Sears.

She personally had to agree with those who said the number one thing about Kirkland was the friendly people. But that's not what she told the patients, oh no, she was there to serve, not to preach sermons, and in her book one of the best ways to serve was to make the patient feel comfortable before Dr. Digby came in and shot him up with novocaine, and it would go against this basic philosophy if she started him—or her, she guessed it was now him *or* her—if she started him out with a sermon from her own personal point of view. So she started him out with a question, then she flossed his uppers, which gave him lots of time to think about his answer: nice conservative town, the friendliness of the people, great family values, freedom of so many churches to choose from, these four being the most popular choices.

She withdrew the floss from Rabbi Scheinblum's mouth and stood back to admire her work.

"Now I'm going to let you rinse."

Rabbi Scheinblum rinsed.

Then she started out on the lowers, and encouraged him to give some careful thought to the question about the advantages of Kirkland as a place to live.

She was beginning to say, she said, that from her own personal point of view Kirkland's number one asset was its people. Where else could you find honest, friendly people like the ones they had over at church, as well as fine Christian gentlemen like Dr. Digby, who had a different religious persuasion but wasn't prejudiced against people from other denominations, just as long as they believed in God and . . . (she was going to add *Jesus* but then noticed Rabbi Scheinblum's yarmulke and changed directions) . . . and had their share of cavities?

Another question she'd become known for lately was, why would anybody in his right mind want to leave Kirkland of his own free choice? Why on earth?

She invited him to rinse again.

Rabbi Scheinblum rinsed again.

The usual answer, she said, is, beats me. She didn't even have to give them a few moments to think about this question, the answer just kept popping out of them, often before she'd got to the point of drawing blood. Over ninety percent of the customers gave that exact same answer of, beats me. This was no exaggeration. Ninety, ninety-five percent at least.

She paused, then went back in to clean between a pair of lower left molars she'd missed.

Ed was another story, of course. Ed was her husband of forty years, maybe she'd mentioned that last time, she usually did —mention it, that is. Ed, and Mabel, her twin sister, who had been on her mind lately, poor dear. Anyway, Ed was another story. Ed was *always* another story. He belonged to that rare five, ten percent who spend their time thinking of reasons why people in their right minds would want to leave Kirkland of their own free choice. When she had challenged him the other day to give her just one good reason—she was still talking about Ed—he ticked off ten in a row, one right after the other. Then what did he do but, he added injury to insult by taking off his shoes and socks and counting on his toes!

She withdrew the floss and came up with the punch line:

"And they say teachers are underpaid."

Rabbi Scheinblum smiled.

"There," she said, flushed with the success of her joke. "One last rinse."

He accepted the tiny cup of water she offered him and did one last rinse.

"Now," she said. "Would you like to answer the quiz?"

There was a long silence.

"What do you like best about Kirkland?"

"I . . . ," said Rabbi Scheinblum.

"It's the kind of a test," she encouraged him, "where there are no wrong answers."

Rabbi Scheinblum cleared his throat.

"Well?"

"Actually," he said, "next week I'm moving to Seattle."

"Seattle! . . . Why Seattle?"

He cleared his throat again.

"Oh, you've lost your job!" she sympathized.

"That too," he confessed. "Also . . . I'm getting a divorce."

Mildred Budwieser paused, then headed for the door. There she stopped. "Doctor will be with you in a minute," she said icily without looking back at him, “right after he’s done with his e-trade.”

2

Early Retirement

"WHO'S A FAMOUS ROMANTIC POET?"

Mildred Budwieser looked across the queen-sized bed at her husband. She was sitting up straight and he was slouching, which was bad for his back but he did it anyway, just to be contrary. It was Monday evening, and she was requesting help on the daily *Bugle* crossword.

"How many letters?" Ed stared straight ahead at the screen, where a family of four was approaching rapture over an improved version of a major brand of tacos. But he could not appreciate their ecstasy. He had had a bad day. That afternoon his boss of two weeks had mortified him by accusing him of being a dead white male. Not in so many words, but. And just twenty minutes ago, during "Jeopardy," his wife of forty-one years had humiliated him by pointing out that Alaska was not a continent.

"Eight letters," said Mildred with a yawn. "No—nine. Two words. The second letter is an O."

He fondled the mute button. The marvels of the electronic age made it possible for him to bring the voices of complete strangers like Pat and Vanna into the privacy of the Budwieser bedroom. The voices, as well as—here he fingered the power button—the images. And he had the advantage. He could see and hear America's Game, brought to him from the Sony Picture Studios; the stars of America's Game could not see and hear him, already in his pajamas at 6:41 and the sun still up. He could see the glitter of their set; they could not see the downscale bedroom, decorated by Mildred in muddy browns and faded oranges and dull greens and furnished with garage-sale knickknacks. He could see them award prizes for luck and skill; they could not see him sitting up in bed and eating a huge dish of ice cream and strawberries, or Mildred alongside him, working on her crossword and inserting popcorn into a well-creamed face.

He could turn them on or shut them off with the flick of a button. They were dependent on his whim. Power!

He released the mute button.

"Here's our next puzzle," said Pat, coming alive. "The category is THING."

"Oh," added Pat, laughing at his mistake. "It's our jackpot round. We've added a prize to the Wheel, called MEXICO. What's that all about, Charlie?"

Invisible but exuberant Charlie announced a trip south of the border worth 8,937 big ones. "You and your guest will fly to Acapulco," he promised in a confidential tone, "where you'll enjoy a week's vacation in a luxurious hacienda featuring tennis and golf every day and long romantic walks along the beach every evening."

"Make it knitting during the day," said Mildred drily, "and I start to get interested."

Make it cliff diving, thought Ed.

"And make it crosswords at night."

"Let's stick to the long romantic walks," he murmured. But he wasn't thinking of Mildred. He was thinking of a possible señorita. A certain . . . Beatrice, perhaps?

Mildred withdrew a buttered hand from her popcorn bowl and patted him on the arm. It was her way of reminding him that he was fifty-nine years old. She had to do that sometimes. Remind him that there's a time for everything, which was a Biblical teaching, a time for long romantic walks, which was when you were young, and a time for watching the children grow up and have children of their own, and to hope and pray the long romantic walks your children take will end up with long romantic walks down the aisle of decent Christian or even Catholic churches, here she was thinking mainly of Charisse, and of course there was also Cyrus to consider, when the subject of Cyrus crossed her mind it was a time to hope and pray he'd find somebody to take a long romantic walk *with*, but maybe she had nothing to worry about, maybe there was something a mother doesn't know about her son, as Thelma Blossum always liked to point out, just as there were things a sister, meaning her, Mildred, didn't maybe know about her own twin sister, meaning Mabel, who was in a safe place for her own protection.

"Let's go," said Pat. "Gloria, it's your turn. Spin the Wheel."

A big brassy woman in her late thirties with rainbow-streaked hair spun the Wheel. "C'mon," she said, "big money, biiiiig money!"

"Who you rooting for?" asked Mildred.

"The retired English teacher."

"You identify," said Mildred, patting his hand.

He withdrew his hand and wiped off the butter. "I *empathize*," he corrected her. *Empathy*. From the Greek, *pathos*, to suffer. He empathized, all right. He was like that philosopher's definition of God: "the fellow-sufferer who understands."

The Wheel landed on $300.

"Three hundred dollars," said Pat, and Vanna clapped.

Gloria would have a T.

Vanna gave her *two* T's.

"Six hundred dollars," said Pat, and the studio audience showed its delight at Gloria's good fortune.

Mildred announced that she was rooting for the hairdresser. A single parent, like their daughter Charisse.

Gloria leaned down and spun the Wheel again. "Okay, c'mon, big money!" she urged.

There was wild applause as the Wheel landed on the slice of pie marked MEXICO.

Gloria paused, then asked for an N.

Pat instructed Vanna to give her an N. Then he told Gloria to lift up the slice called MEXICO, which was hers to keep if she solved the puzzle without hitting a BANKRUPT. Gloria lifted MEXICO. Underneath was a prize for $500, which got added electronically to the $600, making a running total of—

"How do they do it?" Mildred was speaking to him.

"Hmmm?"

"How do they add so fast?"

"Computers," he explained. "How can you tell she's single?"

"She said 'hi' to her kids. She didn't say 'hi' to their father."

Gloria hung a major portion of her body over the Wheel, grasped it firmly, and gave it a powerful thrust. "Big, *big* money!" she said, pattacaking energetically while the Wheel slowed and finally stopped on a $900 slice. Big money, thought Ed; but not big, *big* money.

Gloria would have an R.

She'd have one, two, *three* R's, said Pat, clearly pleased with her luck.

"What'll it be, Gloria?" asked Pat.

Gloria stopped to consider her options.

"How do you know they both have the same father?" asked Ed.

"A woman can tell those things," Mildred said. They could, too. It always took men a lot longer to figure things out. Women had a natural gift for it. Maybe they weren't as smart as men in terms of figuring out how computers could add so fast, but they made up for it in the really important areas of life, like figuring out who had once been married to whom and why they had split up, or which children took after which parent.

"Well?" said Pat. He was tapping his cards, waiting for Gloria's decision. He wasn't irate, that wasn't in his personality, but he had a show to run.

Come to think of it, thought Mildred, women were also better at word games than men. That's why she enjoyed crosswords so much, and why her favorite program was "Wheel of Fortune." Men were better at things like cultural knowledge and world geography, which was why Ed's favorite program was "Jeopardy" and not the Millionaire show that he said was designed with idiots in mind and came on too late anyway. He usually got about thirty percent of the "Jeopardy" answers right, while she was lucky if she got even ten percent. Except that tonight she'd guessed the answer to final Jeopardy and he hadn't. Question: "Continent on which Mt. Kirkpatrick is located." Ed guessed, "What is Alaska?" and she had to point out to him that Alaska is not a continent. She had guessed, "What is Antarctica?" which turned out to be right but put him in an even worse mood.

Gloria wanted to buy a vowel. She wanted to buy an E.

Pat instructed Vanna to give the lady *four* E's.

"Who does Vanna remind you of?" asked Mildred as Vanna scurried about with a nice smile, lighting up four E's. "Doesn't she just remind you of somebody?"

"Charisse," he murmured. But he was thinking of Dora.

"That's exactly what I was thinking," agreed Mildred. "Except I think Charisse's better-looking."

"Mmm," he said, still thinking of Dora.

"Why do they have to *buy* vowels?" asked Mildred suddenly. "Have you ever wondered why they have to *buy* vowels?"

"Vanna needs the cash."

"Why?"

"To keep herself in strapless outfits."

She knew he was joking and that he didn't necessarily mean it. He was like that sometimes, for instance during "Wheel of Fortune" and "The Miss America Pageant." It was his way of comparing her to the younger, fuller-bodied women. She didn't mind, though, because he didn't really mean it. So she laughed it off.

"I'd like to solve the puzzle," announced Gloria.

"Please do," said Pat.

"EARLY RETIREMENT."

Vanna smiled and turned over the remaining letters to show that Gloria was right. Pat smiled and congratulated her on her skill. The studio audience identified, bursting into spontaneous applause.

Pat appeared behind Gloria and put his arm around her waist as if to comfort her. "Not bad," he said, tapping his cards and checking the invisible scoreboard. "So far you've won $3550 plus a trip to Acapulco worth $8937, which gives you a current total of $12,487. And," he reminded her, "we have another round coming up, right after this."

Ed pressed the mute button, got out of bed, and made the day's final trip to the bathroom. He got back just in time to hear Pat announce the addition of a space that can change the score in a hurry. It was the retired English teacher's turn. He immediately hit the new $5000 space, smiled vaguely, asked for and received a K, and spun the Wheel, which came to a stop on BANKRUPT, his second of the evening. Gloria profited from his misfortune, avoiding the BANKRUPT and LOSE A TURN spaces while picking up an extra $9400 by solving the puzzle.

The audience clapped and whistled. Gloria said "Yes!" and made a large fist with her right hand and dug it into the midsection of an imaginary opponent, "Yes!" Pat appeared on the stage with the contestants to console the losers and congratulate the winner. The aspiring actor who was waiting tables in the Valley while waiting to be discovered and who had won a total of $200 mumbled that he had had a wonderful time. The retired English teacher who had come all the way from Oklahoma and whose earnings totaled some nice parting gifts looked meek and perplexed but agreed that this had not been his day. The hairdresser bounced up and down but finally settled down enough to embrace the host.

Ed flicked off the sound with a flourish of his omnipotent finger. "Lord Byron," he announced.

"What?" said Mildred.

"Lord Byron," he repeated testily. "The famous Romantic poet. Second letter is O, nine letters."

She took several seconds to fill in the blanks. "It doesn't fit," she reported.

Several messages later Gloria was back for the bonus round. She selected the sealed card under W, for Winner, joked with her jovial host, patted herself on the green part of her pompadour in nervous anticipation, waited for Vanna to uncover all the R's, S's, T's, L's, N's, and E's, made several wise choices from the remaining letters of the alphabet, solved the puzzle, won $25,000 for a grand total of $46,887, said "Yes! Yes!" and put on another boxing exhibition, was immediately ambushed by two youngsters, and was asked (Pat speaking) who these people were, to which she replied that they were her children, Britney and Taylor, proudly adding that they were the two best kids in the entire world.

Ed exercised his control over these events by punching the power button to OFF. He then put the remote control and his empty dish on his night stand. Mildred yawned and put her unfinished crossword and #2 pencil and empty popcorn bowl on her own night stand. He leaned over and shut off the light. She turned over on her side and went to sleep.

But Ed remained awake for a while, lying there in his grey pajamas with grey piping and grey buttons, watching the last sunlight filter through the Venetian blinds and onto the mud-brown wallpaper, musing over the events of the day. . . .

Dead white male, was he? And what was wrong with that? What wouldn't anyone in his right mind give to be a dead white male if his name happened to be, say, William Shakespeare? . . . He knew Alaska wasn't a continent, obviously. Everyone did. What he had meant was, Mt. Kirkpatrick was located in Alaska, which was located in North America, which was a continent. Mt. Kirkpatrick wasn't in Alaska, of course. He'd been thinking of Mt. McKinley—the Scottish connection had thrown him off—but isn't everyone entitled to a minor mistake now and then? . . . EARLY RETIREMENT. Funny. Just what he'd been thinking of that very afternoon. Be free, quit teaching, get out of stifling Kirkland, move to the West Coast, and write his memoirs. Wasn't that what he'd always wanted? . . . There was always the problem of finances, of course. But if a dizzy dame with rainbow-colored hair and a mind to match could win $47K, then why couldn't Ed Budwieser, M.A., spend just fifteen minutes exposing himself to the masses—or why not Mildred, for that matter. . . ? Dead white male? Not quite, young lady. Tomorrow we awake to a new day.

§

"What are you reading?"

It was Tuesday, the day after Gloria had won a trip to Mexico. Ed was laid out on his stomach, naked on the bed, musing over a Help Wanted ad that had been clipped from the *Kirkland Bugle* and had mysteriously appeared in his box that morning. Mildred was giving him his late afternoon backrub and being curious about his reading material.

"Hmmm?" he said.

"I said 'What's that you're reading?' "

"Just today's mail."

"Looks like a Help Wanted ad," she observed, leaning over for a bifocaled look. "What's it say?"

"It says . . . let's see. It says Middle American Life and Casualty is a growing, financially strong company."

"Good for them! What else?"

"It says they're looking for an insurance claims representative."

"What are the requirements?"

"They need a person who's ambitious."

"And?"

"Creative, too."

"Keep going."

"A third qualification is an ability to deal effectively with other persons."

"Is that all? Isn't there something else?" She was being *ironic*—she knew that word from crosswords.

"The person has to be willing to move to Tulsa and learn the insurance business," he said. He paused to give her time to respond. She didn't. "Isn't that me all over again?" he continued. "Ambitious? Creative? Able to deal effectively with other persons?"

He was missing the irony.

"The only one of these qualities I lack," he announced, "is a willingness to move to Tulsa. It's too much like Kirkland." He paused. "You don't want to move to Tulsa, do you?"

She ignored his question and stopped massaging. "Where did you say you got that thing?"

"It was in my box this morning."

"And who do you suppose put it there?"

He didn't know.

"You must have some idea."

He had an idea, all right. Ms. Penni Mode. Who else could it have been? But he didn't mention his suspicion, just as he hadn't told her about yesterday's knock-down-drag-out philosophical argument with Ms. Mode over the importance of the Classics.

He wondered aloud if maybe God wasn't the guilty party. He meant this as a joke, of course, because he no longer thought of God as an actor on the world's stage—if there even *was* a God, which all the great minds of the last two or three centuries agreed was highly unlikely. But as soon as he made this facetious suggestion that God was the one who had put the ad in his box, he began to think that maybe there was a grain of truth in it. Maybe the ad was put there as a sign. Maybe God was trying to tell him something . . . ambitious, creative, able to deal effectively with other persons—at least, if they'd give him half a chance . . . and didn't God used to have the reputation of being omniscient (from the Latin, meaning all-knowing; having infinite awareness, understanding, insight)? Now the question was—just supposing for a moment that there was a God, and that He took a personal interest—the question was, what was God trying to tell him? Take the job and move to Tulsa? . . . No. That would be too obvious. Maybe . . . realize your fantastic potential out on the West Coast of Mexico?

"God would know better," she said with conviction, and went back to the rubbing.

"Hmmm?"

"*God would know better,*" she repeated.

This was probably true, yes.

Did she know what the trouble was with today's kids? This was the question he suddenly wanted to discuss. He was an expert on the subject. He, and Henry Constant, in the days when there was still a Henry Constant. They used to sit there in the principal's office, he and Hank, and philosophize about the trouble with today's kids. Not that they agreed on the solution, but they agreed on the importance of the issue. Hank's philosophy was that the problem traced back to, number one, the lack of discipline, and number two, the lack of respect for elders, not necessarily in that order, because they were both aspects of each other. His own philosophy was that kids today don't understand the Classics. They'd sit there in Hank's office with their feet up on that big oak desk, drinking decaf and having a friendly argument over discipline and respect for elders versus tragic loss of understanding of the Classics. That's what he found he missed most about Hank Constant, those friendly arguments. The trouble with Ms. Mode wasn't that she was a woman, Dora was also a woman and was pretty much of the same mind as he was, and the trouble with Ms. Mode wasn't that she got rid of the old oak desk and put a new steel one in its place, the trouble with Ms. Mode went much deeper, it had to do with a certain lack of respect for experience and wisdom, as well as a total lack of understanding of the Classics.

"Do you know what the trouble is with today's kids?" He had to repeat this question, because he couldn't remember whether she had answered it, or even whether he had asked it.

"They don't understand the Classics," she said with a sigh. Of course she knew. She didn't agree, but she knew. She herself thought the trouble with today's kids basically had to do with them not showing up in church more often, and she had once told him what she really thought about this topic, which was a mistake, because then he didn't speak to her for three days, except to help her on the crossword when a French or Latin or Old English word was called for. This had made a big impression on her, all that silence, especially with those rose bushes to plant and she'd needed his help, which is why she now knew that the trouble with kids today was their lack of understanding of the Classics. She didn't necessarily *agree*, but she *knew*. In fact, she'd go ahead and say exactly what she had on her mind right now, except that she didn't know if she could stand three more days of silence, which is why she didn't answer his question about the trouble with today's kids by saying the clever thing that had just popped into her mind, Oh I wouldn't worry, sounds to me like they'll make great firefighters, referring to the story she'd heard just that morning, about a bunch of students climbing out the window and down the fire escape while Ed was reading his class the story about Romeo trying to climb into Juliet's bedroom.

"When you stop to think about it," he went on, "thirty-six years is a long time to spend reading essays on what kids have done on their summer vacations."

She'd never stopped to think about it.

"Kids these days don't spend their summer vacations going to California and driving around Yosemite with their parents and climbing Half Dome and then coming back full of spiritual experiences to write about."

Now, she said under her breath, they go to Europe and smoke pot with their left hand and their significant others and come back saying it was a bore.

"Now they go to Europe and smoke pot on the Left Bank with their significant others and come back saying it was a bore," he said.

Left *Bank*, she corrected herself. What had he said was the difference between left hand and left bank?

"Thirty-six years is also a long time to spend flossing teeth," he hinted.

She stopped the rubbing and pulled a heating pad out from under the bed and turned it on HIGH and positioned it on Ed's lower back. "I believe we're warming up to the subject of self-imposed exile," she said, bracing herself. That was the way he always talked when the subject of leaving Kirkland came up—he'd say something about going into "self-imposed exile," like all the great writers did.

"What would you think about, say, the West Coast of Mexico?" he ventured.

"Are you sure Mexico even *has* a West Coast?"

He ignored her illiterate question. "Think of it," he said dreamily, "a picturesque fishing village on the Pacific Coast of Mexico."

"Writing our memories, I suppose."

"*Mémoires*," he corrected her. "Writing my *mémoires*."

"And what would dear old Mildred do?" she asked sarcastically. "Wait tables?"

"Oh no. You'd be too busy supervising the cook and butler. That's during the day. In the evenings we could—"

"Take long romantic walks, I bet." She was being ironic again.

"Right," he rewarded her. "And gaze out over the blue Pacific." He wasn't thinking of Mildred, however. He was thinking of Dora. Dora, or Beatrice. Or maybe both. "You have to admit, it sounds magnificent."

"The word I'd have used is *unaffordable*."

He sighed. "Didn't you read that article in the *Bugle*? 'Mexico: Luxurious Living on $10,000 a Year'?"

"Let's see," she said, pausing to take the heating pad off his back, "at that rate we now have the wherewithal for . . ."—she was doing the figures in her head—". . . about six months."

He groaned.

She'd scored a major victory.

She left him naked on the bed and went into the kitchen to pop a couple of TV dinners in the microwave.

He got up, stretched, yawned, put on his grey pajamas and greying white bathrobe, and went into the bathroom. Then he sat down on the commode, reached into his secret niche behind the bathtub, extracted Scarlett Blythdale's well-thumbed *A Peculiar Passion* from its secret place, and turned to his favorite passage.

. . . "They frolicked lightly, free of earthly care, among the wildflowers scattered about the gentle meadows, high, high above the wide serene Pacific. Suddenly she turned and, lifting her pert chin and gazing limpidly into his moody steel-grey eyes, took his rough hand and clasped it to her soft milk-white bosom. 'Darling,' she murmured, 'I'm so hap—' " . . .

Just then Mildred stuck her head through the doorway. "Soup's on," she announced, destroying his dream of ecstasy.

§

"Follow the smart money."

It was late Wednesday afternoon, and Ed was laid out in Dr. Digby's chair. Digby was pinching his cheek and depositing a dose of novocaine into the right side of his lower gum with a long silver needle, at the same time offering free investment advice.

"Incidentally," warned Digby, "don't try this at home."

He chuckled at his little joke and went back to the subject of investments, still brandishing his needle. "If you really want to carry through on this ill-advised retirement threat," he said, "you're going to need the wherewithal." He put the weapon back on the tray. "And on the subject of wherewithal, my advice in this tricky market is, follow the smart money." He stood back to let the novocaine take effect and to allow his wisdom to sink in. "When the smart money is in there buying Microsoft hand over fist," he went on, "that's the time to be *in* stocks. When the smart money is paring down the Microsoft portion of their portfolios, that's the time to be *out of* stocks."

"Try it," said Digby, scratching around on the old filling with a metal hook. "It works."

Ed didn't always agree with Digby on issues such as politics and religion and the Royals and the Chiefs and the economy and the educational system and America and what was wrong with them, but he couldn't argue with the wisdom of going with the smart money. It stood to reason. How could you disagree on the subject of investments with a dentist who uses Chivas Regal as a mouthwash?

Digby stuck his head out the door to catch the up-to-the-minute stock market report. "It's sure worked for me," he called from the hall.

Ed also couldn't argue with the fact that it had worked for Digby. There it was as living proof, the brand new jet-black Lincoln, sitting out there in the driveway blocking the view of his vintage '66 VW Bug. Today it was the Lincoln, last tooth it was the red Mercedes coupe for the current wife. Number three, he believed it was. Carole. He'd noticed that that was often the name the third wife comes equipped with. Carole, spelled with an extra E. Used to sell beauty products, Carole the Third did, before Digby dismissed Number Two and came riding to the rescue. Mildred would know for sure, about the numbering system. She was the kind of person who kept track of those things. Anyway, the root canals and porcelain caps in and of themselves weren't enough to cover the cost of keeping Digby's harem in German cars. There had to be another factor.

"My advice to you," Digby repeated as he set up the drilling rig, "is simple. Go. With the smart. Money."

Ed just wished Mildred were there to listen to this frank advice. It was her afternoon off, however. She was probably home that very instant, putting her medications out of the reach of the grandchildren.

"You ever read *Barron's*?" grunted Digby as he removed his fingers from Ed's mouth.

He came up to rinse. "'nce in a 'ile," he had time to lie before the fingers were back in there doing battle with the tooth. It was going to cost another bundle, this porcelain cap was, even though

Digby called him a preferred customer, on account of Mildred's being his assistant. But it was worth it, because of this invaluable advice.

"You happen to read this week's article on what the big boys are buying?"

He was frankly glad to have the latex-gloved hand back inside his mouth. That way he wasn't expected to answer, Doctor could do all the talking. If Digby would just tell him what it was the big boys were buying, he could make a killing. He could transfer the five grand in his IRA from that low-paying CD into the stock market and sit back and smile and watch his investment grow.

"Ascension Airlines was up to 10.63 at 2:40, Eastern," said Digby. "A candidate for a spectacular takeoff if I ever saw one."

Spectacular takeoff? Like, maybe triple the investment in a year? In two years it would, what? Grow ninefold? Not bad. Not bad indeed. And it wasn't as far-fetched as it sounded. He'd seen the headlines:

Homeless Man Found Dead:
Portfolio of Millions

and

Cat Woman
Leaves Pets
Huge Fortune

If a bum could do it, or a bag lady, why not a man of letters? . . . He wouldn't have to wait three years till he was eligible for Social Security. . . . Maybe he should send in that well-crafted letter of resignation? Then he and Mildred could spend August in

Mexico, browsing around amongst the upscale villas and checking the butler and maid servi—

"It'll be tender for about three days," said Digby, pushing a button to raise him from the dead. "If you have trouble sleeping tonight, don't hesitate to give us a call tomorrow morning and we'll see what we can do."

"Ascension Airlines, is it?" he slurred as he stumbled toward the door.

"Ascension Airlines, ASCALS on the NASDAQ. That's my bet for the future."

"Oh," Digby called after him as he was leaving. "Be sure and tell Mildred I missed her feminine touch this afternoon."

§

"*Early retirement* is now the buzzard word."

Mildred and Thelma Blossum stopped to catch their breath in front of Le Wanderlust, a travel agency in Kirklande Centre. It was early Thursday morning before work, and the two women were doing one of their occasional puffarounds, dressed in faded joggers and worn Keds and clutching tiny barbells to their chests.

"You know what *I* think about that subject," replied Thelma.

Yes, she knew Thelma's thoughts on the topic of early retirement. Letting a man stay home day in and day out was about the same as putting arsenic in his chicken noodle soup, in terms of effectiveness. If he was fooling around and had good coverage the arsenic might not be a bad idea, but otherwise it wasn't recommended, unless of course you happened to enjoy working your fingers to the bone in the checkout stand at Safeway. Those were Thelma Blossum's thoughts on the subject, always followed by "take it from somebody who knows."

They puffed on.

"And of course dear old simple-minded Mildred," said Mildred, trying to catch her breath, "dear old simple-minded Mildred always has to go and bring up the subject of wherewithal."

"What's he got to say about that?"

"Oh, he's got all kinds of ideas."

"That's men for you," said cynical Thelma.

They stopped again, this time in front of the first Security sign, which was advising safe mutual funds for retirement accounts.

"Ed's a ready source of answers," she went on. It took him all night to think of them, but he was a ready source of answers. "Yesterday morning he was up bright and early with another scheme. He had me going on 'Wheel of Fortune' and making a killing, winning fifty thou or so."

"Fifty thou?" said skeptical Thelma.

"I kid you not, those were his exact same words, 'Fifty thou, at the minimum.' I said 'How do you expect me to even get *on* the Wheel?' He said 'No problem, ask and it shall be given.' I said 'That sounds like wishful thinking to me.' He said 'It's mentioned in the Bible.' I said '*Where* in the Bible?' He said 'Look it up, it's in there.' '*Where*?' I said. 'Take my word for it,' he said, 'it's got to be in there someplace.'"

"Just between me and you and the fencepost, Sweetie," confided Thelma, "I think he's got the Bible and Shakespeare mixed up."

"It wouldn't be the first time. Anyway, I said 'How do you expect me to win big?' and you know what he said?"

"Luck?" guessed Thelma, beginning to move on.

"Nope."

"God's will?" guessed Thelma.

"Remember, he doesn't believe in God."

"Poor man," observed Thelma sympathetically.

"Guess again."

"He doesn't expect you to cheat!"

"Oh no," she said. "What he expects is for my talent at crosswords to carry over to the Wheel, he said I'd quickly learn how to hit the large cap slices on the big pie, and the letters would just automatically pop into my mind with the inspiration of the $5,000 slice staring me in the face. He said a total of fifty thou was a conservative estimate. That's right, fifty thou, I kid you not."

"It's not that I don't think you're good at crosswords, Sweetie, but—"

"Maybe he's right," reflected Mildred, stopping in front of Discount Merchandise to think it over. "If it's mentioned in the Bible, maybe I should try to get on the Wheel. Wouldn't that be something, winning fifty thou? What I wouldn't do with all that money. Put in a Jenn-Air kitchen, buy a treadmill . . . maybe that's what I should do, go on 'Wheel of Fortune.'"

"When you put it that way," said Thelma, "it's your clear Christian duty."

"I suppose so," sighed Mildred. "Anyway," and they started to move on again, "he came up with another idea this morning."

"Oh Lordy," groaned Thelma.

"This time . . . you listening?"

Thelma was listening.

"This time he's got a hot stock tip, he wouldn't say from where, and he wants to invest our total life savings in Ascension Airlines, which is poised for a take-off."

"'Poised for a take-off'?"

"Those were his exact same words, I kid you not, 'poised for a take-off.' I said 'Why haven't I heard about this Ascension Airlines?' and he said 'It's a secret, only the big boys know about it, they're in there buying it hand over fist.' "

"Big boys, huh?" said Thelma contemptuously. "He probably means the Catholics."

"That was exactly my suspicion. I said 'Over my dead body are you going to invest our nest eggs in something run by the Catholics, it's like pouring money down the drainage ditch.' So he said 'Do you have a better idea?' and I said 'I most certainly do, and it's called staying right here in God's country.' "

"And what did the neighborhood philosopher have to say to *that*?"

"You know what he thinks about God."

Thelma paused to reflect. Then, "What I'd like to know is, if he doesn't believe in God, why does he go around quoting Scriptures, and in the second place, why did he play Christ in that Easter pageant?"

"He says the Bible's just literature, and he thinks of Christ as a great literary character, right up there with Macbeth."

"He'll grow out of it," Thelma prophesied confidently as they got to the south end of Kirklande Centre.

"At the age of fifty-nine?"

"Lee Roy quit smoking at sixty-one."

"That's not the same thing."

"It's the same principle," said Thelma. "Take my word for it."

"You're probably right," said Mildred wearily as they headed for the parking lot. She had her doubts, of course, especially considering the fact that Lee Roy Blossum ended up with lung cancer anyway. But it was still comforting to think the day might come when Ed Budwieser would go back to the simple childlike faith he had had out in western Kansas and finally admit that God wasn't just another poet, if there was a God.

§

"So it's Mexico this time!"

It was Friday evening, and the Deuces, four pairs of Kansas cosmopolitans, were gathered around two made-in-Taiwan card tables in the Budwieser living room, their feet resting on the Navaho rug Mildred had bought at Mrs. Krzynzky's garage sale, drinking 99.7% caffeine-free coffee brewed from pure mountain-grown Colombian crystals. They had completed their monthly exchange of American coins, and the six guests were lining up to provide expert commentary on the late-breaking news that Mildred had just reported. Last night Ed finally realized his literary potential by composing a thirteen-page letter to Ms. Mode in which he announced his intention of taking early retirement and moving to Mexico to write his memoirs.

The six commentators were as miscellaneous as the Budwieser furnishings. Gary Leben had given up his position as a social studies teacher at Sunset High to pursue his dream of selling life insurance to the upper middle classes. Ann Leben, who cultivated the habit of reminding the others that she had come within three semesters of graduating from KU with a double major in Art History and French, now spent her mornings clerking in Le Frame Shoppe and her afternoons following the intricate story lines of "One Life to Live" and "General Hospital." Mark Ecclebury, a former chemistry teacher, had been lured away from the classroom by Corporate America and was now cashing in on his knowledge of the periodic table in the Kitchen Division of Godfather's Pizza. Karen Ecclebury was a dedicated homemaker, a mother of four, a grandmother of seven, and a collector of discount coupons. Dora Jiggers had grown weary of teaching Language Arts and was now realizing her potential as the attractive hostess of the most fashionable Tupperware parties in

Kirkland. Dave Jiggers, formerly a counselor to troubled marriages, now tended potted plants and watched the mailbox for his annuity checks.

So it was Mexico this time, was it? Gary was counting his hoard of pennies and speaking to Ed and smiling wickedly.

"Last year it was Palm Springs," Mark reminded everyone.

"Ah yes. Palm Springs."

"Living on a golf course overlooking the eighteenth green."

"Existing, I believe, on the earnings of a blockbuster screenplay on the death of a small town in western Kansas," recalled Dora.

Ed smiled bravely at Dora's reminiscence. Which would she have rather done, he wondered: peddled plastic dishes in Kirkland, or lived on a Palm Springs golf course overlooking the eighteenth green?

"How did *you* fit into that plan, Mildred?" asked Karen.

"I was supposed to be the one who served cocktails at his literary saloon," ratted Mildred.

"Doesn't she mean salon?" someone whispered.

"Do they have literary salons in Palm Springs?" someone else whispered.

Mildred leaned over and put her arm around Ed. This was to show him it was all in fun, this dagger in his back. "Oh yes," she said, looking up at him mischievously, "that was the plan."

"Weren't you scheduled to dress up in an evening gown every afternoon and make sure all the other writers had enough booze in their glasses?" asked Ann.

"That's right," answered Mildred. "Enough beverage to inspire at least five doublespaced pages of ecstatic thoughts."

"Oh, she's a card!" they said.

"Where does she come up with those gems?" they said.

"And two years ago it was, what, Malibu?" remarked Dave.

"Ah yes," they said. "You were going to live in a beach house, weren't you? Of course, this was before you were scheduled to win the Pulitzer—"

"—for that book on the poetry of Emily Dickinson—"

"—the one on the symbol of the feather!"

There was a chorus of "ha"s.

Ed smiled grimly. Was that such a bad plan? If Mildred would've let him carry through with it, just think where he'd be now. Collecting royalties. Living in a mansion high above the Pacific. Being interviewed by Barbara Walters. Strolling the beach with Dora and the mysterious Beatrice.

"And what was dear old Mildred scheduled to do out there? Weren't you an important cog in that plan, too?"

"He had me down for waiting tables until the Pulitzer people called with the good news," said Mildred. "And then I had a choice, . . ." and she paused for effect.

"A choice?"

"I could either divorce him for his woman problem—"

"Divorce?" they said. "The Budwiesers? You have got to be kidding!"

"Ed? a woman problem?" they said. "*That'll* be the day."

"—or go crazy," and she nervously waited for a response.

This time there was no comment. The Deuces were a sensitive crowd, especially when it came to the subject of Mildred's twin sister, Mabel, who had taken up permanent residence in Luneberger Manor.

"Either way, I was going to put him on the literary map."

Divorce her, he thought. Why hadn't he carried through on *that* idea?

"But the one that beats all, in my book," said Dora, "was the one where he was scheduled to move to Oakland."

He groaned privately. *Et tu*, Dora?

"Oh, yes," they said. "He was going to live down on the waterfront and write a novel on survival in Antarctica."

"Ha! Jack London the Second!"

"For a guy who's never been outside the state of Kansas. . . ."

Never outside of Kansas? They were forgetting about his trip to Dodge City—the one on which he had accidentally ended up in Atlanta.

"And how were you supposed to support him in Oakland, Mildred? Weren't you supposed to—"

"—oh, God, get this—"

"—wasn't it an occupation that required all your—"

"—all your—"

"—feminine wiles?"

Three Deuces were wild on the floor by this time, rolling over and over on Mrs. Krzynzky's former rug. Gary was down there, Dave was down there, Mark was down there, they were all making fools of themselves, just because he had once had the enterprising idea of having Mildred support him in the same way Sarah supported Abraham back in Egypt. What was so funny about *that*? He looked down disdainfully at the trio of losers lying there on the floor: three horizontal near-dead white males, putting in their last hurrahs.

Mildred smiled self-consciously and went into the kitchen for more decaf. Karen and Ann followed her out. Had they gone too far this time? they wondered. The look on his face . . . well, it worried Mildred, but then maybe this was no different from the other times they'd given him an old-fashioned ribbing about his visions for the future, which were harmless, Karen assured her, men's dreams always were, they were just ways of letting off steam, that's all—except, Mildred thought, maybe this time there was something else going on in his mind, because after all he'd had a rough week, what with the Help Wanted ad and everything, and this time he'd actually *composed* that letter of resignation he'd been threatening to write for how many?—twenty?—years, but of course he hadn't sent it . . . or had he? . . . No, as Ann pointed out, he'd said and done some strange things in his life, but he wasn't crazy enough to actually *resign* before becoming eligible for Social Security . . . was he?

And back in the living room, a life insurance agent, a counselor-turned-gardener, and a pizza cook, were still on the floor recovering from their bout of comic ecstasy. This left Ed and his lovely Dora alone at the card tables.

Dora turned to him and winked. "Oh, the fantasies of the male of the species," she said playfully.

"I wouldn't call them *fantasies,*" he said. "I'd call them *goals.*"

"Goals?" she laughed.

Sometimes Dora sounded just like Mildred. Didn't they realize that all those other visions of moving to the West Coast were prophetic of his real future; that things were just now beginning to fall into place—his investment in ASCALS was taking off for stratospheric heights (up three tenths of a point just yesterday!), he was beginning to outline his intellectual history—; that he was destined to leave stultifying Kirkland, move to Mexico, live high above the Pacific in an upscale villa with Mildred and the maids and butlers she would supervise, sleep late in the morning, work on his memoirs in the afternoon? And, in the evening, he would enjoy deeply gratifying trysts with Dora and the dark enigmatic Beatrice who was destined to show up in his life very soon.

Dora flashed a cryptic smile, patted him on the knee, stood up, and stretched the Wonderbra stretch he found so thought-provoking. Then she went into the kitchen for more coffee, picking her way gingerly through the maze of exhausted male corpses strewn about on the threadbare rug.

"It's a good thing he has you," she told Mildred as she entered the kitchen. "He needs a reality principle."

3

Molls

ON THE LAST WEDNESDAY AFTERNOON IN JUNE, while Ed was reading the copy of *Molls* he had bought at a garage sale, the phone rang.

Perhaps *bought* isn't the word. What had happened was this. The previous Saturday morning he had accompanied Mildred on her weekly bargain hunt, and while she was checking out the action in pant suits, he'd come across a stack of magazines—several copies of *Arousal*, a *Playmate* or two, and the *Molls*—items that he, with time on his hands and no Classics at his disposal, paged through, just out of idle curiosity. Mildred came over to him to share her delight over the discovery of a white pant suit, size six, which would have to be dyed pink and ironed and taken in at the waist but was otherwise just *per*fect. He became so enthusiastic over her purchase that he accidentally slipped the *Molls* between the folds of the pant suit, an oversight that went undiscovered until they got home and Mildred was on the phone to Thelma with news of her fabulous buy and he was continuing to admire that bargain when what to his astonishment should fall out of the folds of that pant suit but the copy of *Molls.*

And so there he was on that Wednesday afternoon, taking a well-earned break from his job search, languishing in the bathtub, looking at the pictures in *Molls* and enjoying a bottle of Mogen David, when the phone rang.

He sat up. It would be the travel agency, responding to his letter of application. He put the magazine on the floor and raised his well-knit body out of the tub. They'd be wanting to fly him to Santa Barbara in their corporate jet for an interview with the CEO.

He bounded over to the hall telephone and stood there for a second before taking the receiver off the hook.

"Hello," he said in his best baritone voice.

The caller wasn't the travel agency, however. It wasn't even the school board in Napa Valley, which was looking for a superintendent—an innovative, experienced, decisive team leader with strong fiscal management skills—and were offering a salary in the six-figure range. It was a Betsy Something from San Diego, who was taking a survey to find out what ladies of the house thought about her company's vacuum cleaners. He was no lady of the house and had never even heard of Banshee, Inc., but being a gentleman, he tried to accommodate her anyway. He informed her that the Budwiesers got their appliances from Monkey Wards.

"To tell the truth," she confided, "I get mine—I'm separated, y' know—from Sears. I just work for these people, I don't necessarily indorse their product." Ever since Arnold left, she went on, she'd had to work to make ends meet. Not that he left her, she pointed out, she was the one who filed. Arnold drank, she said in strict confidence, and in her book this was grounds for divorce, even if you were a good Christian and had been married for twenty-five years and had kids working their way through junior college.

"What a coincidence," he heard himself say. He was standing in the hall, dripping wet, staring down at the bathroom floor at the *Molls* cover, which depicted a darkly handsome mobster dressed in a wide pin-striped double-breasted gangster suit, wearing a black hat and dark sunglasses, clenching a gold cigarette holder between his teeth, and with a petite but buxom brunette hanging onto his left arm and a tall, slender blonde ensconced on his right.

"Rilly?" she replied. "Kids in junior college?"

"That, too," he lied.

He hopped over a puddle of water and stretched the phone cord into the bathroom. On the vanity top sat his newest costume: a black hat, a pair of dark sunglasses, and a plastic cigarette holder, in which was inserted an unlit Marlboro.

"You mean you're separated?" she asked.

"Did I say that?" he teased as he put on the sunglasses and inserted the cigarette holder between his teeth.

"It was more of a hint," she giggled.

He placed the hat on his head at a jaunty angle. Then he gazed intensely at the likeness of the brunette moll on the floor. Beatrice! "Been thinking along those lines," he said.

"Rilly!"

"Agnes drinks too, y' know," he slurred.

"Y' don't say."

"That's only part of it."

"There's more?"

"Well, yes. It's something. . . ." Here his voice got husky and trailed off.

"Problems, is that what I'm reading between the lines?"

He took a healthy sip of the Mogen David. “I don’t like to talk about it.”

“Mental, is that what I’m hearing?”

“It’s probably not as bad as I’m letting on.”

“Sounds like somebody I once walked down the aisle with,” she empathized.

“Misery loves company,” he said philosophically.

“Don’t it,” she agreed.

“Say,”—here his voice dropped half an octave lower—“what’s San Diego really like?”

“Oh . . . the weather’s great the whole year round, but it gets kinda boring.”

Boring? he thought. California? Well . . . it’d be an *interesting* kind of boring.

“And there’s lotsa rilly nice people, but you gotta consider the Mafia.”

“The Mafia?”

“The Mexican Mafia.”

He peered into the bathroom mirror. The Mafia! Mexican! He smiled to himself. He’d be in his element.

“What d’y’ think—it’s Betsy, ain’t it?”

“Right. Betsy Bandero. That’s B-A-N-D-E-R, like in candor, but add an O, like in dough ray me.”

“What d’y’ think, Betsy, would a Chiefs fan be accepted in San Diego?”

“Oh yes,” she said. “I personally don’t know of any Chiefs fans, but I presume you’d be treated like a human bean in spite of your bizarre taste in baseball teams.”

“Football.”

“Football? I was never rilly good on the different kinds of sports. Games is games, in my book. Say, what was that name again?”

"Ed Budwieser, that's W-I-E-S-E-R, I before E except after C, but my friends call me Buster." He was thinking of what he had once overheard his grandmother say to his mother: "He's all boy, why in God's name did you have to give him a sissy name like *Edward,* why not something masculine, like *Buster*?"

"Well, Mr. Buster," said Betsy Bandero, "if you're any indication, Kirkland, Kansas is the place to be."

"I'd have thought San Diego was."

"You might just be ri—. . . say," and her voice suddenly turned to a whisper, "I gotta go, my supe's lookin' at me kinda funny, but just don't y'all be surprised if some day rilly soon you get a call from the Kirkland airport and a li'l ol' Betsy Bandero person axes you to come pick her up."

"Not if I don't first—"

But she had already hung up.

He went into the hall and put the receiver back on the hook. Then he came back into the bathroom, dried himself with the purple king-size towel, leaned over the sink, and peered through his sunglasses into the steamy cracked mirror, admiring how the new costume brought out his darkly handsome features.

The phone rang again.

It would be the blonde moll. Dora.

He returned to the hall, stood beside the phone for a moment, and accidentally knocked the receiver off the hook. He fumbled around on the floor before finally locating it.

"Hel-lo-o," he said in a baritone imitation of Pavarotti.

Nothing. No answer.

Oh. Wrong end.

"Hel-lo-o," he repeated.

This time it wasn't a moll. It was Mildred.

"Ed?" she said. "Are you all right?"

"I was just singing in the shower," he sighed, and he began to remove his costume item by item.

"Oh. . . . I was trying to reach Target, I wanted to see if they still have that sale on panty hose, but I must've invertently rung the wrong number."

"In*ad*vertently," he mumbled.

"Say, what're you doing at home?" she suddenly chided him. "You're supposed to be out looking for a job, for goodness sakes."

At least she was being cheerful about it. A few weeks ago, when she'd found out that he'd actually sent in that letter of resignation, her sunny nature had disappeared behind a black cloud. She was *not* moving with him to Mexico, she insisted, standing there with her tiny hands on her tiny hips and practically screaming at him—or to Oakland; or to Palm Springs; or to Malibu. He *was* going to apply for the insurance job, plus any other job for which he was even remotely qualified. Well, okay—say, what did she think of him becoming a tour guide? he'd seen an ad on "making the world your work place." Did they pay salaries to tour guides? Of course. *Actual* salaries, not just tips? That was his understanding. Okay, if he was sure. Sure he was sure. That's all she wanted to know. He'd be gone several weeks at a time (he was thinking of places like Acapulco), would that create a problem? She thought she could handle it; when he'd been gone that summer to Atlanta, she'd done okay.

"I'm waiting for a phone call," he explained.

"From the pizza place?"

"Yeah." This was not true. He hadn't even applied for that job, which she'd demanded he do. He was overqualified. Instead, he put in for the job in Napa Valley. He was more of a West Coast kind of a person. Besides, after a year on the job he'd be in a financial position to move farther down the coast, maybe even all the way to Mexico.

"Oh good!" she said. She meant it, too. Maybe Ed was right, maybe there weren't just a whole lot of creative ways to deliver pizza, but he always said he'd like to travel, so he'd probably learn to actually enjoy it, delivering pizza, plus the fact that it was a very Christian occupation because of the service angle, as Thelma pointed out, maybe not exactly the same as delivering Meals on Wheels to the old folks, but more or less in the same category. She knew better than to mention this to him, of course, the service angle, because it would get him going on the fact that he'd spent the last thirty-x years of his life teaching the Classics and personal pronouns to the kids and what did it get him, not even a single thank-you, which was a subject she was tired of hearing about, that plus the subject of the upscale villa on the West Coast of Mexico and having hired help, which in *her* opinion was about as unchristian as you could get. But on the other hand, listening to him talk about it was a lot better than them actually *moving* to Mexico, as Karen Ecclebury had pointed out, and Thelma Blossum had said pretty much the same thing, she'd once said "Sweetie, just be thankful you've *got* a husband, job or no job, and having fantasies is just the way men are, in this world you've got to learn to take the bad with the good."

"I'll be home soon," she sang, "love ya," and hung up.

"Love ya," he mumbled into the dead phone.

He went back into the bathroom and stashed the sunglasses, the hat, the cigarette holder, the pack of Marlboros, the magazine, and the Mogen David behind the bathtub. He reached into the medicine chest and retrieved the mint mouthwash. He gargled. Then, with his head ringing from the busy phone, he went into the bedroom and flopped on the bed and rolled over on his stomach and closed his eyes and waited for Mildred to come home and give him his backrub.

§

Next Sunday morning Ed was in the choir loft of a newly-repainted, plywood-steepled church that had just recently taken down most of its Christmas ornaments. He was sitting there in the sweltering heat with the other choristers, listening to the sermon of the Reverend Dr. Tad Heedon, who had been extolled by the editor of the *Kirkland Bugle* as "the best and brightest of the new generation of spiritual leaders." Reverend Heedon was dressed in a clerical robe and a pair of expensive sneakers and was the proud owner of a ponytail and a pierced left ear, in which was inserted a jade ankh.

"Religion," young Rev. Heedon was saying, "isn't about long, sad faces. Religion is about joyful, happy faces."

Ed, who just the previous Friday had had his application for unemployment finally rejected, took quick stock of the other joyful, happy Deuces in the choir loft.

Mildred, dental technician, was working on the Sunday crossword puzzle.

Karen Ecclebury, homemaker, was inking in the O's on the church bulletin.

Mark Ecclebury, pizza cook, was studying a note he had just received from Ann Leben.

Ann Leben, aficionado of soaps, was coyly decoding the contents of a note she had just received from Mark Ecclebury.

Gary ("Ace of Spades") Leben, successful life insurance salesman, was dead to the world.

Dave Jiggers, retired marriage counselor, was analyzing the body language of several couples in the congregation.

Dora Jiggers, former English teacher, was listening to the words of the young minister; probably checking his grammar.

"Do you know how many times the word *joy* is mentioned in the Bible?" Rev. Heedon asked.

He paused to give the congregation time to guess.

"One. Hundred. And fifty. One. Times!" he finally revealed to his eager listeners.

Ed glanced over at Dora to see if their minds were running in similar channels. Dora glanced back at him. Not now, not in church, she seemed to be saying. His thoughts wandered back to the lead story in *Molls*.

. . . "Suddenly their glistening eyes locked. She touched the back of his hand. His rough but gentle hand caressed her golden hair. She fingered his white terry-cloth bathrobe. He gazed deeply into her hazel eyes and whispered secret provoking thoughts into her ear. Her breathing quickened; she grabbed him by his pajama lapel and pulled him down to her on the wild, primitive rug. 'Kiss me, you gorgeous hunk,' she implored him. He tipped her head back and kissed her passionately on her ruby lips. 'Again,' she begged. He kissed her again, this time placing his strenuous tongue between her willing lips. She pulled herself free from his powerful yet tender embrace and began to unfasten her—". . .

Mildred was clearing her throat. A signal.

What? he lip-synched.

She pointed a stealthy forefinger at his midsection.

What?

She pointed at her own lap.

Oh. His fly was open. He covered it with a Bible.

“If there was an Eleventh Commandment,” Rev. Heedon was saying, “and I know there isn’t, so you don’t have to phone me up this P.M. and say Tad, ol’ buddy, where in Scripture do you find the Eleventh Commandment—but if there was such a commandment, do you know what it’d be? . . . ‘*If it feels good . . . do it.*’”

Mildred put the crossword back in her purse. Tad Heedon was *such* a nice young man. He was absolutely *per*fect for Sue, who worked in Dr. Digby’s office as a receptionist. Everybody agreed they were one of the nicest young couples in Kirkland, except that some of the older and more conservative folks said his sermons were way too modern. She didn’t know about that, she never actually listened to them, you really didn’t have to, all you had to do was *watch* him preach to see how sincere he was, in fact they said he was once a football player and that after he made a score he’d get down on his knees in the end zone and actually *pray,* right out in the open, which told you just about everything you wanted to know about him. . . . Maybe they should have the Heedons over some Sunday for dinner, also invite Charisse down from K. C., maybe it’d rub off, maybe Charisse’d finally see what she was missing in terms of family life and finally get serious about somebody like Tad Heedon—not Tad Heedon himself, of course, just somebody *like* him, except for the ponytail and pierced ear—and it wouldn’t necessarily have to be a minister, just somebody with basic fundamental Christian family values, plus a competitive sal—

Oh. Rev. Heedon was praying. She hushed down her thoughts and covered her face in her hands and peeked through her fingers at the other Deuces.

Karen was chewing on the edges of the church bulletin.

Mark was stuffing a note in his pocket.

Ann was blowing her nose.

Dave was cleaning his fingernails.

Gary was waking from the dead.

Ed was dealing with his zipper problem.

Dora had her eyes closed and was listening to the prayer and whispering to God.

". . . and if there was a Twelfth Commandment," read the young minister from his prepared script, "we know what You wouldst have it be . . . '*Go for it!*'"

§

On the Fourth of July, the Tuesday after the Rev. Tad Heedon preached his well-received sermon on Commandment XI, what could be seen chugging over the wide plains just twenty miles west of Kirkland but a '72 Winnebago, trailing large puffs of black smoke.

At the wheel of that Winnebago was the new Ed Budwieser.

Sunday night he hadn't been able to sleep. He was taking stock. Examining his life. Taking an inventory of his most striking qualities. Here he was, he reflected, the former Sage of Sunset High: intelligent, enlightened, erudite, cultured, urbane, sophisticated, imaginative, even visionary; an astute observer of the human scene, an extraordinary thespian, full of creative potential; and unemployed.

He rolled out of bed, padded into the bathroom to drain off that last glass of Reunité, then creaked his way down the steps to his basement study. There, from the bricks-and-boards bookcase, he removed his copy of *Cruden's Complete Concordance of the Old and New Testaments*. He sat down on the musty rug, opened the musty book, found the word *joy*, counted the number of references to it (Rev. Tad had been correct: exactly one hundred and fifty-one), and began looking them up in his musty King James Bible.

But halfway through The Gospel according to Saint Luke, a deep slumber fell upon him. And as he slept, he dreamed an incredible dream. He was at the foot of a mist-shrouded Mount Whitney. A huge hand reached down out of that mist and presented him with a shining book. There was a great earthquake, and a mighty voice from heaven spoke unto him, saying, "Take it and read; take it and read." Then everything dissolved into nothingness—the peak, the mist, the hand, the voice, the earthquake. Everything but the gilt-edged book he was left holding. That book was *The Selected Poetry of Lord Byron.*

He did as he had been instructed. He reverently opened the book at random, found a stanza in *Childe Harold's Pilgrimage,* and read:

The race of life becomes a hopeless flight
To those that walk in darkness:
But there are wanderers o'er Eternity
Whose bark drives on and on, and anchored ne'er shall be.

What could this be but a sign? he asked himself in his dream. A clarion call to a higher, more noble purpose, a summons to join the elect, the tiny band of highborn spir—. . . .

He was awakened by internal groanings, urgent and sustained. Back up the stairs he frantically charged, knocking over two brooms and a dustpan. Into the bathroom he stormed. Unable to locate the light switch, he sat down in total darkness—on the vanity mirror. Damn Mildred! His hand quickly checked for signs of damage. Little harm done. He found the switch, brushed the shattered glass onto the floor, lifted the lid on the commode, and sat down again.

It was there, alone in the bathroom in the middle of the night, surrounded by shards of a broken mirror, that Ed Budwieser came to the most momentous decision of his nearly-three-score years. With the words of the Reverend Tad Heedon and Lord Byron ringing in his ears, he made a solemn vow. He would change his life, boldly and irreversibly and without compromise. He would cease his foolish toil and dedicate his life to the pursuit of joy. He would cast all that is petty and trifling behind him and grasp the unknown, the enigmatic, the forbidden. He would shed the mundane cares of a prosaic life and embrace the poetry of a vagabond existence. He would without further delay leave for the West Coast.

Thus it was that on the Fourth of July, Ed Budwieser found himself behind the wheel of a '72 Winnebago—the "Firecracker Special," as it had been advertised—attired in his Lord Byron costume, which Mildred had let out at the waist. He was alive, for the first time in many weeks: teeming with joy, gladness, and the wonderment of sheer being. All existence was like the wide ocean before him, begging to be crossed. He was on a pilgrimage; a quest; an odyssey. Snatches of poetry coursed through his teeming mind: "Up with me! up with me into the clouds!" and "Surprised by joy—impatient as the wind / I turned to share the transport—Oh! with whom / But thee. . . ."

. . . It was midsummer. They were sitting in a forest grove in the High Sierras, the two of them: he, Lord Byron, and she, "who walks in beauty, like the night"—the tall, tantalizing Dora. He had chosen for the occasion a pair of dark tight-fitting trousers and a loose, flowing white shirt, open to the waist. She had chosen to remain *au naturel*. They were drinking Madeira and engaging in earnest conversation, discussing the meaning of a difficult passage in *The Rubaiyat of Omar Khayyam*. In the foreground was an overturned picnic basket, from which loaves of French bread and wild strawberries had tumbled in casual disarray. In the background, bathing her feet in a sparkling brook, was his demure but voluptuous mistress, Beatrice, also known as Betsy, attired in a transparent gown.

Then the tableau came to life. Betsy stood up, stretched, languidly approached the others, seated herself on the grass next to them, and began to paint her toenails. Suddenly Dora reached over to him and gently pulled his head down onto her lap; she turned to Betsy and, calmly and without a trace of jealousy, wondered aloud how the two of them could best please their handsome lord. The dark woman responded wordlessly, kneeling in front of him, taking a wild strawberry and— . . .

What was that!

The bark listed to starboard, and he was forced to anchor it by the side of the road.

He got out to inspect the damage. A flat tire. Damn! Now what? Should he walk back to the nearest service station? And where would that be? He hadn't been paying attention. . . . Maybe he'd have to change it himself. Did the thing even have tools?

At that moment he noticed a car pulling up behind the disabled vehicle.

"You took the wrong road."

A woman was coming toward him, waving and calling.

"You turned left. You were supposed to turn *right*."

"What?"

"Didn't you see the sign back there—the one that points this way and says 'County Dump'?"

"County Dump?"

"Where do you think you're going?"

He blinked at the strange, irate woman who was questioning him. She was dressed in an unironed pant suit. She had her hair in curlers. She was his wife.

"I thought you were just supposed to be out for a test drive."

"Oh," he said. "I was." Yes. He *had* agreed to take it out for a test drive, he now remembered. She had doubted the wisdom of his purchase and had sarcastically challenged him to take the thing out for a test drive, just to see if it could withstand the rigors of their annual vacation trip to Kirkland Reservoir. She had insisted on following him in the VW Bug to make sure he wouldn't be stranded when the thing broke down.

"So hows come you're out here, twenty miles *west* of town? I thought the plan was to take the thing *east*?"

This was a good question. He didn't have an answer. Not one he would be willing to share with her.

"I was trying to avoid the rush-hour traffic," he explained.

"On the Fourth of July?"

Another good question.

"I think I have a flat tire," he said, pointing.

"I believe you're right," she said, nodding.

"Do you have any suggestions?"

She threw up her hands and took off toward the VW and opened the driver's door and got in and slammed the door and started the engine and turned the car around and spun off, redistributing small amounts of gravel in her wake and leaving Ed to guard the thing while she went back to the nearest service station to get help.

Why couldn't the man just concentrate on getting a job? she thought angrily as she drove off. Was that too much to ask? How did he think they were going to manage on just one salary? It wasn't that big to begin with, and she wasn't blaming Dr. Digby, times were tough, as Doctor explained to her and Sue Heedon whenever the subject of a cost-of-living adjustment would come up, it just seemed like people didn't have as many cavities anymore because of the fluoridation menace, and besides, there were his extra expenses, meaning the alimonies, which wouldn't be so bad except that Myrna and Ginny had gotten used to a certain lifestyle and couldn't be expected to just voluntarily start living on the cheap.

And then of course there was still their mortgage and the groceries and now all of a sudden the big liquor bill, plus the fact that Ed had gone out and sold those five hundred shares of Ascension Airlines stocks or bonds or whatever for a loss of a thousand hard-earned dollars plus the broker's fee, which Thelma agreed was stupid enough, but then to top it all off he'd gone down to Sudden Sam's on Eastcheap and bought that old relic of an RV with a toilet that didn't always work but a little refrigerator that did, for the booze, and without even consulting her.

But it wasn't any use bringing up the subject of money with him, because when she did all she got was a stare and a bunch of poetry by a crippled womanizing dead man and a reference to the number of times the word *joy* appears in the Bible, which he didn't even believe in.

She herself had always been happy with the old VW Bug, she'd told him when he showed up in the driveway with that thing. It didn't cost their total life savings, and it had always gotten them where they wanted to go.

"Yes," he'd pointed out to her about the Bug, "but it's got 150,000 miles on it."

"What about *that* rolling tomb? What kind of miles has *it* got on it?"

"Exactly 16,283 miles," he said proudly.

She could have sworn she saw a sticker inside the driver's door saying 198,000.

"That has to be a mistake," he said. "Sam guaranteed me this baby's practically as good as new."

She was sure he did.

"Anyway," he said confidently, "the tires are in excellent condition."

She was sure they were.

"And," he went on to explain, "the tires are usually a pretty good indication of the general shape of the engine."

She wanted to know where he got *that* idea.

"That's what Dad always used to say."

She wanted to know what a street sweeper in Dridge, Kansas would know about the general shape of engines.

He didn't have an answer to that. Which should have made her happy, it was always nice to score points against somebody with a college degree in Higher Things, but that time it didn't, because she was hoping against her better judgment that he was right about the tires and the engine, because if he wasn't . . . well. . . .

Half an hour later Mildred drove up in the bug, followed in a rusty pickup by a slow-moving youth named Slim.

Without saying a word, she got out and helped Slim jack up the Winnebago and change the tire. Then she wrote out a check to Slim, and he crawled back into his pickup and drove off.

"Follow me," she instructed Ed. "We're going straight home."

Ed picked up *The Selected Poetry of Lord Byron* and rose from the ground on which he'd been sitting. He climbed aboard the wounded bark, maneuvered her through a series of dangerous obstacles, and pointed her back on course.

. . . Betsy took a wild strawberry and pressed it gently but insistently against his firm lips. Slowly, slowly, his lips gave way to ever more urgent thrusts. She made a motion as if to withdraw—but no, he captured her delicate fingers with his strong white teeth. Again she pulled back, and again he held her inside him. Then she squeezed the strawberry, and the juice splashed against the walls of his mouth. Finally, her passion spent, she withdrew her fingers and laid her flaxen hair upon his strong broad shoulder, then placed her slender hand upon his robust chest. And when she had finished, she took his head in her lap; Dora placed another strawberry in his sensuous mouth. Then there, in the gloaming, the three spoke softly of their plans for life in Acapulco; of the poetry they would compose; of hurling their magnificent bodies from the high cliffs into the majestic Pacific, of which the poet John Keats had written, in 1816 . . . .

The engine sputtered and the ship slowly glided to a stop.

A quarter of a mile up the road, Mildred and the VW came to a halt, swung around, and came back. He closed his eyes, then climbed out of the Winnebago and prepared himself for a dose of deadly sarcasm.

"I have to hand it to old Rufus," she called from the VW. "He was absolutely right. 'As the tires go, so goes the engine.'"

It was a sentence she was to become extremely fond of in the days ahead.

"I thought Winnebago engines lasted forever?"

He was standing at the bow of his stranded bark, at the mercy of ancient Milo. Mildred, after locating Milo, had gone on home in her own cloud of smoke.

"Oh they do," came Milo's drawl from underneath the hood. "Problem is, this ain't no Winnebago engine. Looks like they took out the original and put a replacement in. This here looks somethin' like one a' them Phantom engines."

"Phantom engines?"

"The kind they used to put in lawn mowers."

"Lawn mowers?"

"*Riding* lawn mowers," explained Milo, coming up for air. "Ain't as bad as it sounds."

There was a long silence.

Ed finally asked, "So, where do we go from here?"

"My advice to ya would be, take it back t' town an' try 'n' getcher money back."

"It'll make it back to Kirkland okay?"

"That'd be my guess."

"Think it'd make it to the West Coast?" he ventured.

"Lemme put it to ya this way, Mr. B," said Milo, wiping the grease off his face with a red handkerchief. "Ya gotta helluva lot better chance a' gettin' to the West Coast by pushin' it than by countin' on this here piece a' shit."

§

It was Friday evening. Mildred was sitting in her living room with Gary and Ann Leben, treating them to some Selected Sayings of Rufus Budwieser while waiting for the other Deuces to arrive for a few games of pinochle. The Budwiesers had just gotten back from Ed's pilgrimage, she had informed them, their Fourth of July spent and her household budget absolutely *ruined.* She hadn't been able to get their money back—Sudden Sam's phone had been disconnected—so they still owned the Winnebago, which was parked out in the driveway with the gas gauge resting on E.

Ed was in the kitchen, spooning crystals into coffee mugs.

"Say Ed," Gary called out to his host, "I hear Ms. Mode's looking for somebody to teach auto mechanics."

"'As the tires go, so goes the engine,'" Ann called out. "You know how that translates into French?"

"How's this for the title of your next book?" Gary called out. "*The Wit and Wisdom of a Village Street Sweeper*"?

He was rescued from these crass barbarities by the doorbell.

He limped across the living room to the front portal, his face etched with the pain he still suffered from the injuries he'd received on his recent journey. Help had arrived at last. Help, in the form of Dora. His soulmate. The only other romantic in the group. The only one of them capable of understanding the infinite sorrows of life. The only one whose spirit truly echoed his own. The only one who appreciated the grand spirit of Lord Byron. The only one who. . . .

"What's that heap of junk outside?" asked Mark Ecclebury as he burst into the house, followed by Karen.

"That's Budwieser's Folly," explained Gary.

Ed limped back to the kitchen to boil water.

"Don't blame Ed," he heard Ann say. "He was just following Rev. Heedon's instructions. It felt good, so he did it."

The house was filled with coarse laughter.

"At least the good reverend practices what he preaches," observed Karen.

"What do you mean?" asked Mildred.

"Haven't you heard the latest?" said Karen. "Rev. Heedon ran off with Dora!"

"No!" said Mildred. "He didn't!"

No! thought Ed from the kitchen. She didn't!

"Yes," confirmed Mark, "they did. The word is, they're all out west. Dora and her boy friend—"

"With emphasis on the word *boy*," interrupted Ann.

"Dora and Tad headed for California, and after he read the note, Dave left for Colorado to sort things out."

"Did you hear that, Childe Edward?" Gary called out to the kitchen. "Dora finally ran off with the preacher."

There was no answer.

The Lebens spent the next five minutes assuring the Ecceburys how little they were surprised by this news. Mildred spent this time not believing a word of it. Dora and Reverend Heedon? She could see Dora running off with somebody, that was the easy part, but with Reverend Heedon? He and Sue were the perfect couple, plus the fact that he was only about half as old as Dora. It wasn't just that it was *hard* to believe, it was im*poss*ible. . . . On the other hand, maybe she was in denial. She didn't want to be in denial. They'd been telling her all summer, the Deuces had, that she was in denial as far as Ed was concerned, and she didn't want to be thought of as somebody who made a habit of being in denial. . . . Maybe Thelma could offer her some good advice on this point?

She excused herself and went into the kitchen to make a telephone call.

She found the kitchen empty, except for a whistling teakettle. Ed was gone.

She took the kettle off the stove and turned off the gas and went over and knocked at the bathroom door. No answer. She opened the door a crack and peeked in. Still no Ed. She looked behind the bathtub to see if the bottle had been tampered with. Not since she'd last checked. The dirty magazine was still there, too, plus the ugly black hat and the sunglasses and the smelly cigarettes. So down the basement stairs she charged, stepping over two brooms and a dustpan. She looked into his makeshift study, but all she could see were two items on the floor: a Bible and a book about how often certain important words like *love* and *family* were mentioned in the Scriptures.

She went back upstairs, past the brooms and dustpan, and into the living room and interrupted the bets they were making on how long the relationship between the older woman and the much younger man would last. She stopped to think that maybe she should call Sue Heedon to ask her if she needed a shoulder to cry on, but decided she could do that on Monday, at work. Then she gave the four Deuces the news: Ed was missing, and where did they suppose he was?

"I bet he's gone over to apply for Dora's old job," said Karen. She was being serious.

"No," Gary said. "I think it was for Reverend Heedon's job." He was not being serious.

"The Reverend Ed Budwieser," Mark said. "It doesn't come tripping off the tongue, but it has a ring to it."

"Also," Gary pointed out, "a salary."

"And he's already got the message down pat," Ann chimed in.

"'If it feels good, do it,'" the three said in chorus.

Would they be serious for once in their lives? Maybe they should call the police?

"And report that Ed's run off with another woman?"

Maybe she should call Thelma Blossum?

"Is she the other woman?"

She finally convinced them there was a problem, and they came up with a plan to call the police, but only after they had scoured the neighborhood to make sure Ed wasn't just out borrowing coffee at that time of night.

They wouldn't have needed to worry. When they got outside they found him in the driveway, walking around the Winnebago, gazing up at it and saying he couldn't believe it.

He explained that he'd just come out to get a breath of fresh air.

In the hot muggy night? She was beginning to *really* wonder.

§

The following Monday the Budwiesers had an argument.

It wasn't over the question of why he wasn't spending more time looking for a job, or over the question of why he had resigned his old job without consulting her or why he not only didn't want to talk about it, he didn't even want to *think* about it, or over the question of the liquor bill, or even over the question of whether *Molls* and *A Peculiar Passion* were Classics or just plain trash. Because after the Winnebago incident she had gotten Ed to promise to quit drinking and stop the new subscription to *Molls* and spend at least four mornings a week on the job hunt.

No. The argument was over a silly little thing.

It was over a Betsy Bandero.

That morning, ten days after their innocent telephone conversation on the subjects of vacuum cleaners and the relative merits of San Diego and Kirkland as places to live, Ed had received a follow-up letter from Ms. Bandero. It dealt with the subject of vacuum cleaners, but she gave it a personal touch by enclosing an autographed photo of herself.

He wouldn't have thought a thing of it, but Mildred called this photo to his attention.

"Well look what we have here," she said that afternoon after work as she was sitting at the kitchen table going through the stack of bills and other mail.

"What's that?" he called from his easy chair in the living room.

"A picture of Miss America, 1959."

"Oh, that." He'd forgotten to stash it behind the bathtub!

"Is this the San Diego floozy you keep talking about?"

"She's not a floozy, and she's not that old. She's younger than we are."

"I don't doubt it for a minute. What I want to know is, why did she include this picture?"

"It's probably company policy," he explained. "She works for a vacuum cleaner company, after all, and they're in the business of selling vacuum cleaners."

"I understand that," she said, coming to the living room and leaning against the door frame and waving the photo at him. "What I want to know is, why did Ms. Batsy Bandersnatch include this salacious snapshot?"

"Her name is Bandero, Betsy Bandero, and you call that salacious? It's just an ordinary picture. People who work for big companies do that a lot, add a personal touch to their correspondence. It's good business."

"Betty Grable incarnate, that's what she looks like to me. A brunette version of Miss Pin-Up."

"Really? I hadn't noticed."

"I think I can tell who is and who is not wearing an industrial strength bra."

When Mildred started throwing around words like *salacious* and *incarnate*, which she got from crosswords, and *industrial strength bra*, which she got from Thelma, he knew he was navigating dangerous waters. He knew she'd moved beyond satire, he knew she had arrived at hurt and anger, which meant the best strategy was to . . . well, he didn't really have a best strategy in this situation. All he could do was to continue to play dumb.

He was fairly successful, too. The real problem came later, when the phone rang and Mildred beat him to it.

"Hello?" said Mildred. ". . . Agnes? No, this is not Agnes, this is Mildred. . . . Yes he is, may I ask who's calling? . . . Oh you missed him, he just went out the door. May I inquire as to the purpose of your call? . . . Lost your job? I'm *so* sorry. . . . Thinking of moving to Kirkland, are you? . . . You sure you want to do that, Dear Heart? . . . Do you have any friends here? . . . *Besides* Ed? . . . No, we're not separated, we're getting along just fine, thank you. . . . No, I'm a teetotaler, but thanks for showing concern. . . . *Mental* problems? You must be thinking of my—somebody else. . . . Actually, we were thinking of moving to San Diego. . . . No, it's not the Mafia that bothers us, it's the preachers who. . . . Yes, that would be my recommendation, just staying put. . . . The same to you, Dear Heart."

She put the phone back on the hook and stared at nothing. She was thinking about the personal letter with the Miss Pin-Up picture and about the paraphernalia behind the bathtub, especially the booze, and about being confused in somebody's mind with Mabel, and about the Winnebago mistake, going west instead of east; also, some other thoughts, on the theme of how hard it was, being somebody else's reality principle.

Meanwhile, he was stretched out on the bed, staring at the cracks in the ceiling. He was thinking about going through life not being appreciated and not being understood and about being betrayed by one's former soulmate, if that's what had really happened, which he had reason to doubt, and about how a genius is often discovered many years later after his death and then has inspiring books written about his unrecognized greatness; also, some other thoughts, on the theme of how hard it was, being an older white male.

"Who was that?" he finally called, continuing to play dumb.

She came back into the bedroom and gazed at her husband of forty-one years, lying there on her Monkey Wards queen-sized bed, already in his pajamas, getting ready for "Jeopardy."

"That," she said, "was my lawyer. I get the house. You can have the Winnebago."

4

Camping Out

IT WAS A LATE EVENING IN AUGUST. The cicadas in the Budwiesers' trees had turned in their raucous banjos for the night, the squirrels were resting from a day of tag-playing, and the neglected '30s bungalow was bathed in the lustre of a quarter moon. Mildred was in the kitchen, dressed in a pink threadbare bathrobe, listlessly washing the day's dishes. Ed, wearing a pair of grey-on-grey pajamas, was sitting at his typewriter in the Winnebago, which was parked in the dirt driveway in front of the collector's edition VW Bug. He was printing a draft of a letter to his son.

Dog Days

Dear Cyrus,

Remember how we used to go camping? I was reminded of those times last night when your mother and I had a long talk about the good old days, etc.

We never actually made it out to the Sierras like we'd planned, but the back yard served just as well, didn't it. There weren't any bears and wolves out there, but there were the Blossums's ducks, which are still around (I can hear them now), even though Lee Roy is no longer around to feed them (Did your mother ever send you the obit?). I remember how much you enjoyed playing with our fine feathered friends as a boy.

Say, you've been missing out on a lot back here, besides the back yard birds and your mother's cooking and my sintillating (sp?) literary conversation. You're also missing out on watching your exceptional nephew and niece grow up. (Strictly speaking, she's your grandniece— have I got you interested? interested enough to write for more info? It's quite a story!) People are always stopping Charisse in the grocery store when she's in town and complimenting her on the kids' looks and intelligence. "They take after their grandpa," she says proudly. (When it's your mother's friends, she says, "They take after their grandma," that's how well-brought-up she is. In fact both of you were well-brought-up, your mother and I are proud of you, too, which is something maybe I should have ~~empathized~~ emphasized more.)

I call little Shaun "Buster," which is what they used to call me. Back in Dridge, we'd have had to tell everybody that Shaun's father was killed to keep America free, but Kirkland is a pretty liberal city (in spite of what you used to say!), so nobody thinks twice about Charisse being unmarried and toting around two exceptionally bright, nice-looking children (one of them is her grandchild, see above!).

It won't surprise you a bit to hear that Buster Jr. could practically recite some of Wm. Blake's "Songs of Innocence" when he was just thirteen months old. Your mother said I was jumping the gun by teaching him the Classics at so early an age, but that didn't keep your old dad from giving him his first literature lesson right after he blew out the candle on his first birthday cake! Now that he's two, he can practically recite "The Night Before Christmas" by heart. Your mother says aren't I rushing things, but you could probably guess my response. Right! I tell her if other parents and grandparents had taken the time to expose their children to the Classics, the educational system wouldn't be going to pot.

Speaking of the educational system, do you happen to remember Dora Jiggers? My colleague at good old Sunset High? She quit and left town, and there's a chance she's moved out there to the West Coast. I just mention her because you two might have a lot in common, both of you being originally from Kirkland, etc., and having found it maybe a bit stifling, etc. Anyway, you might keep an eye out and let me know if you run across her. But bear in mind that her last name might be Heedon by now. (It's a long story.)

Then there's Megan (your grandniece—see above). Talk about a nice-looking tyke! Clerks in the checkout line are always asking Charisse who the little one takes after, her mother or her father. You've got to hand it to Charisse, she handles this situation very well. She just says little Megan takes after her old granddad! You've got to hand it to the father, too, whoever he was, his genes didn't get in the way of an exceptionally strong blood line.

I'd have to say Megan's just as bright as Buster. Maybe even brighter. When she was only five months old, she'd already figured out that round pegs don't go in square holes. (She was way ahead of her great-grandma on that point, I'm sure you'll agree!)

I'm already poking around at garage sales for Megan's first birthday present. I'm looking for a puzzle map of the U. S. She'll point out where San Francisco is by the time she's eighteen months old, or my name isn't Ed Budwieser! Then she'll be ready for the spelling cards. (Does this sound familiar?)

I don't apologize for the high hopes I have for my progeny (from Latin, "progignere," through Old French and Middle English—the derivation is fasinating (sp?)), just like I had high hopes for you and Charisse. (Which you both lived up to, of course!) With the educational foundation they're getting, they should graduate from Harvard by the time they're eighteen. (You think I'm kidding, don't you?) Not bad for a couple of kids whose granddads/great-granddads (1) ran a street-sweeper out in Dridge, Kansas and (2) went door-to-door selling home remedies in Baggs of the same state!

Anyway, I thought I'd write to let you know I'm in the process of re-evaluating my most basic beliefs. That's something you and Charisse always encouraged me to do, remember (though not in so many words!)? I've come to the firm conviction that Time is the Great Healer. I'm also starting to read the book you gave me for my 50th birthday. Remember? "The Wisdom of the East." Maybe you can come home at Christmas and we can sit around in my Winnebago (!!!) and have a good old-fashioned philosophical discussion on the subject?

Speaking of Christmas, I hope you're not still holding that Santa Claus "adventure" against me. Maybe it's time I should explain what really happened. Your mother (!) picked out an Old Saint Nick suit for me at a garage sale and insisted (!!) I wear it to your school Christmas party. Then she volunteered me (!!!) to pass out the gifts to you and your classmates. I certainly haven't forgotten that disastrous (understatement of the year?) episode. I remember you telling me never, ever, to do that again. (You probably haven't forgotten it, either—but I hope by this time you've forgiven me. (Even though it wasn't really my fault. (Guess whose fault it was? (Hint: who was it was that served us beans and broccoli for supper? "Starts with an M, seven letters." (This is an official apology, in case you're wondering. (I've often wondered if that incident is what caused our "communications problem"?))))))

Your pal,

Dad

P.S. Say, how's the job situation out there? Do you happen to know of any positions available for English teachers who have a deep appreciation of the Classics? I'd even be willing to work part time. In fact, part time would be just about perfect! I could spend the rest of the time working on my memoirs, or maybe finishing that book on Emily Dickensen (sp?) I've been working on for the last fifteen years. I even have a title for it (the Dickenson book, not the memoirs!). "I'm Nobody, Who Are You?" (If this sounds familiar, it's because that's the first poem I had you memorize. "There's a pair of us, don't tell, they'd banish us, you know." Remember?)
P.P.S "How dreary to be somebody, how public, like a frog." My new motto!
P.P.P.S. Write some time, would you? It'd sure be great to hear from you! I'm still at the old address, except that instead of 3601, it's 3601 1/2. (It's another long story!)

P.P.P.P.S. I just hope you get this letter. The return address on your last postcard was a little hard to read.

5

Putting the Hurt behind Her

"WIVES WHO HAVE BEEN LEFT BY THEIR HUSBANDS FOR ANOTHER WOMAN": this was the theme of the "Mary Mudd Show" on the morning after Labor Day. Dr. Digby had invited Sue Heedon and Mildred into the TV lounge during lunch hour to watch several wives testify to the hurt and the pain a woman feels over a husband's sudden preference for a change in spouses.

"It's something you gals should identify with," Doctor had explained to his faithful receptionist and assistant. Sue Heedon nodded sadly and agreed that yes, the subject was certainly something she was an expert on, in fact if she'd have known they were looking for hurting women she'd have volunteered for the show, she certainly needed the money, hint hint. Mildred hesitated, however. As she pointed out to the good doctor, she wasn't really sure she qualified because it wasn't clear that there was really another woman involved and it also wasn't clear whether her husband had left her or it was the other way around. But

Doctor smiled and patted her on the back and reminded her that for all practical purposes it amounted to the same thing.

The four selected wives who had been left by their husbands were of four different minds on how to deal with the situation.

"Divorce him," advised Former Wife #1, an unemployed Ph.D. in Early Chinese Literature who had been exchanged for an M.A. in Sensitivity Training. "Divorce him, put the hurt behind you, and get on with your life."

"That's exactly what's been crossing through *my* mind," replied Mildred, nibbling on a peanut-butter-and-jelly sandwich.

"It's exactly what *I'd* do," agreed Sue, puddling around in her yogurt. "Except," she added, "he didn't leave a forwarding address."

"Have an affair of your own," advocated Former Wife #2, an unnamed paralegal for an unnamed law firm in an unnamed city. "Get on with your life," and she winked at the television audience, "there's lots of hungry men out there."

"That reminds me," said Dr. Digby, looking at his watch. "Time to catch a bite to eat. I've got a major repair job on a Number 15 at one."

"Have an affair?" said Mildred as Dr. Digby was leaving. "I couldn't see the point of it."

"I'm with you on that," agreed Sue. "Plus, it wouldn't look good for a pastor's wife."

"There's always that to consider, isn't there," nodded Mildred.

"Shoot him," recommended Former Wife #3, a well-landscaped secretary who had attracted a top-ten attorney to represent her and to negotiate a very nice advance on her story. "Shoot him, then get on with your life."

"Don't think I haven't thought about it," said Mildred.

"I don't know," disagreed Sue. "Like I said, the note didn't leave his address, plus the fact that it wouldn't look good for a pastor's wife."

"Start journaling," counseled Former Wife #4, who taught a class in creative writing at The Institute of Intimate Relationships and had written two best-sellers, *The Grieving Process in Four Easy Steps* and *Grieving for the Man Who Left You (and Good Riddance!)*, and was dickering with a publisher on a third. "Keep a journal of your innermost thoughts about your relationships. It's the absolute best way to put the hurt behind you and get on with your life."

"Now why didn't I think of that?" wondered Mildred.

"It's something a pastor's wife could do," agreed Sue.

Mary Mudd had *been* there, believe her she had, so she knew what these poor wives were going through. The one thing she wanted to emphasize, she said to her viewing audience as the credits rolled, was that if it happened to you it wasn't the end of the world, the important thing was—and the four expert witnesses all nodded their heads in agreement on this point—the important thing was that you should (1) put the hurt behind you and (2) get on with your life!

"That's good advice," said Mildred, wrapping up her uneaten peanut-butter-and-jelly sandwich.

"Terribly good advice," agreed Sue, replacing the cap on her uneaten yogurt.

Then Dr. Digby came back and the three went to work, Mildred helping the doctor repair the damage to the Number 15 and Sue billing its owner.

§

September 5

Dear Journal,

This afternoon Sue and I decided to have a girls' night out and get on with our lives.

We went to the Soup and Salad down at the Kirklande Centre and compared notes. I found out that Rev. Heedon had subscribed to "Playmate"! But he wasn't in the habit of making Byronic gestures and he never went into self-imposed exile, like the great writers such as Joyce Hemmingway. On the other hand, Ed never wanted to be a stand-up comic. (One of the few things he didn't want to be!)

After dessert we discussed how to be strong competent women in today's world.

Then we went over to Barnes & Noble and bought the book by Marliss Windell, Ph.D., "Grieving for the Man Who Left You." I'm following the instructions in Chapter One, "Getting Your Feet Wet," which is why I'm writing this. (I'm using Ed's typewriter while he's out. I just hope he doesn't mind!)

Mildred

P. S. I also asked Sue about the rumor that Rev. Heedon used to pray in the end zone after all his touchbacks. She said he played football, all right, but he only made one touchback and that yes, when he made it into the end zone he got down on one knee, but that was only to tie his shoe.

September 6

Dear Stranger,

Chapter Two is called "Wading Right in There," it suggests we write down our thoughts and remembrances of those who are nearest and dearest. Write them down like you're writing a letter to a stranger, it says, we're all strangers to ourselves. Which is why I'm writing to you specifically.

For beginners I've chosen Charisse as being nearest and dearest. This is only natural, since she's my daughter.

Here goes!

We named Charisse after Cyd Charisse. Actually, I was the one who named her, Ed wanted to call her Titania after the Queen of the Fairies in "A Midsummer's Night Dream," which was a play written by (guess who!) Shakespeare. But I wouldn't hear of it, I said if we called her Titania, people would think of her in terms of that ship that hit the iceberg, and I didn't want a daughter who was cold, I wanted a daughter who was warm and loving, which she turned out to be. Also, I wanted a daughter who could dance, which Cyd Charisse did in "Singin' in the Rain," which is my absolute favorite movie of all time. Anyway, it turned out she never learned to dance, but she still has men falling all over her.

People always say Charisse takes after me, because of the good looks, but in a lot of important respects she takes after Ed. Number one, she's very intellectual, and number two, she's prone to make mistakes. Number one and number two go together, just like in her father's case. Most of the mistakes she's prone to make spring from the fact that they think too much, Charisse and her father both.

The first big mistake Charisse made was back in the days when women were fighting their way out of the kitchen. She burned her bra, right in the middle of the Kirklande Centre. Actually, she burned my bra—she was only about twelve at the time, and she must've figured she couldn't make much of a statement burning a training bra. So she borrowed my bra and her father's cigarette lighter, this was back in the days when he smoked, and next thing you know she and some skinny lady professors with thick glasses were on the evening news explaining why they didn't want to be considered as sex objects.

Wouldn't you know, Thelma Blossum happened to be watching the evening news that night. Thelma and half of Kirkland. I thought I'd never hear the end of it. We're the only Budwiesers listed in the telephone directory and Kirkland is a very friendly town, so for about 24 hours I had to explain Ed Budwieser's philosophy of child rearing to the general public. That type of a thing can get awfully old, fast.

Charisse used to be in the public eye a lot. It seemed like she was always on television. When she was in high school, for instance, she was practically a regular on the Friday ten o'clock news. Every time Sunset High would score a touchdown, they'd have a shot of her and Bud Blossum holding up a sign. They weren't really cheerleaders, they were just witnessing. Which I guess you could say is a kind of cheerleading.

You can bet Thelma Blossum didn't have an awful lot to say about that. I'm not saying she doesn't believe in John 3:16, I'm just saying she's like me, she doesn't think it should be advertised to the general public.

Thelma also didn't have a lot to say about the cult Charisse and her son Bud joined when they were freshmen at

Kirkland State. At the time it didn't seem to be such a big deal, because Charisse was always way ahead of her age group in things like religious concepts. She was always the first to color between the lines in Sunday School and the one who sang loudest in the kiddy choir.

But somewhere along the line things must've gotten out of hand, because she and Bud Blossum got involved with that cult. At first we thought it was just a faith-healing group, and we need more of those, in my opinion, but then we read in the papers that those cults sneak into farmers' pastures and cut off the cattle's private parts. What does that have to do with faith healing? So we started to get concerned. I talked to Charisse about it and she said, Mom! What do you think I am? She didn't deny it, she just said Mom! What do you think I am?

Thelma Blossum said Bud didn't deny it either, so we knew we were on to something. This was the point in time where we went to Rev. Ripon and asked him to hire us one of those deprogrammers. He said they're very expensive, but I said money is no object. He said they're not always reliable and they can't guarantee results, so I said what did he suggest? He strummed his fingers together and looked up at the ceiling and suggested he himself could do it for half price.

That was money well spent, because Charisse and Bud Blossum finally left the cult. The problem was, they also left Kirkland State. Bud took up auto mechanics at the trade school and Charisse went to cosmetology school and learned hairdressing, with a minor in manicure science.

I talked to Charisse about this. I said why go downtown to cosmetology school when they're now teaching the exact same thing at the university? She said she knew it, but she didn't want to have to take classes in Plato and Shakespeare. I said she wouldn't have to take classes in Plato and Shakespeare, they now teach classes in the comic books of the '40s or the American male, everybody needs a good college education these days. She said oh Mom, nobody reads comic books anymore, that was in the olden times, and she already knew everything she needed to know about the American male.

Like I say, Charisse takes after her father, very intellectual. She has an answer for everything.

She's also like her father in the fact that she always wanted to move away from Kirkland. Which is okay, except that Kansas City is not the place to bring up children. Not in this day and age!

Sincerely yours,
Mildred Budwieser

September 7

Dear Stranger,

Speaking of bringing up children, Charisse is bringing up Shaun. He's our grandson.

I don't mind saying Shaun takes after his grandma. Not the grandma on his father's side, Charisse's not sure who that would be, because she's never been 100% sure who the father is. She narrowed it down to two, but she didn't demand any blood tests. She's too proud. She always figured she could take care of her kids by herself. I'm pleased as punch with her attitude. We're originally from small towns in western Kansas, Ed and I, so we have values like independence and family, which we passed along to our kids.

Shaun's last name is Budwieser, like ours, because Charisse is too proud to make a man marry her just because of some little mistake. Anyway, she admitted she was partly to blame, whether it was Mr. X or Mr. Y. She doesn't want us to harbor grudges against the X's and the Y's, because it would take away from our appreciation of little Shaun.

I have my own ideas about who they are. I have Mr. X down to be that hockey player and I have Mr. Y down to be the flyboy out at the air base, I forget their names.

Her father's probably right, I worry too much about who the other grandmother is, I should just pay attention to little Shaun. Just be happy he has our genes, he says, and let it go at that. This is good advice, except that when her father says we should be happy he has <u>our</u> genes, he's referring to himself. He thinks little Shaun's the spittin' image of himself, even though everybody else says little Shaun takes after his old grandma.

Ed's training little Shaun to be a genius. This doesn't worry me, what worries me is that Charisse seems to agree with him. When her father went out and bought a set of Winnie the Pooh books at a garage sale and started to read them to little Shaun when he was just old enough to sit up, Charisse took her father's side. I happened into the room about that time and said what's that you're reading and he said A. A. Milne, "Now We Are Six," it's a children's classic. I said it's not! and he said yes, it is. I said God, oh God, I'm not having this conversation, tell me I'm not, and he said little Shaun would never forgive us if we deprived him of his rightful place in the history of literature. Then Charisse said cool down Mom, it couldn't do any harm. That's what I mean by Charisse being on her father's side.

Little Shaun is just a good old average American boy. He's three now and he does most of the things Dr. Spock says a three-year-old should be doing. Except that he's a little late picking up on the purpose of the potty. He doesn't say much either, but his grandpa always points out that he's thinking and he'll probably start talking when he has something important to say, which is exactly how Einstein was. Perish the thought. Anyway, other than these little faults, Shaun is just your good old average American boy.

His grandpa has the boy pegged for being a man of letters, but I keep telling him that's gone out with the icebox. Besides, what would I say to Thelma if little Shaun turned out to be a man of letters? If twenty years down the road she asked me how's your grandson, what's he doing for a living, I couldn't very well say he's living somewheres in Europe, he's a genius and a man of letters, she'd turn right around and say oh, she was so sorry, I had her sympathy. If it's anything I can do without, it's Thelma Blossum's sympathy.

I have to admit I wanted a girl. If little Shaun had had a regular father, I would've said it makes no difference, you take what God gives you. But with Charisse being a single parent and everything, I just wish it would've been a girl. Girls aren't nearly as hard to raise in this day and age, and you have a higher chance of having them turn out normal. At least that's been my experience. Charisse was much easier to raise than Cyrus, plus she's turned out a lot better.

Yours very truly,

Mildred B.

Sept. 12

Dear Stranger,

Speaking of nearest and dearest, Charisse is also raising Megan.

We're very fortunate to have two grandchildren who take after us. Actually, a grandson and a greatgranddaughter. Megan's great-grandpa agrees with me on the point that Megan takes after us. At least he used to agree, I haven't talked to him for a week except to take him his meals and see how his new job is coming. Delivering pizza. Part time. We don't agree on which of us Megan takes after, though. Ed thinks it's her great-grandpa, but anybody with eyes in her head can see she takes after her dear old great-grandma. Same smile, same head of hair, and you can already tell she's going to have the same sensible attitude.

Charisse says she doesn't know for sure who Megan's father is, but she thinks its either a professor Felicity met at a poker game or a rock star. She's leaning to the rock star, though, she says that's what her woman's sense tells her. Number one, he was always coming to see Felicity at the time it happened, and number two, he was later arrested for possession. Her father said no, she was imagining things, it had to be the professor. I pointed out that English professors may <u>write</u> a lot about sex, but they never actually <u>do</u> anything about it. He didn't agree with me, but what else is new?

I don't mind saying Megan is the apple of my eye. That little tyke just <u>loves</u> her dear old great-grandma. She took to me right off the bat, right after Charisse brought her over. She likes her great-grandpa too, but it took her a while to get used to him. Babies are very sensitive to garlic breath, which puts her great-grandpa at a big disadvantage when it comes to who Megan takes to. I used to tell Ed to use the Listerine, he's stacking the deck in my favor, but he was always a very stubborn man. He said he didn't want to be loved for his appearance, he wanted to be loved for his intellect!

I said it's a good thing he didn't have to rely on his appearance, the only thing I wondered was, how was a little toddler supposed to love him for his intellect? He said Megan had his genes, pretty soon the laws of nature would take over and like would attract like. I said what if she turns out to be an ordinary, happy child? He said he couldn't imagine that. He was always absolutely sure his children and their children and grandchildren are cut from high-quality Budwieser cloth, they're all part of a big evolutionary leap, which no self-respecting Christian believes in.

The only thing that worries me about Megan is the fact that she's a couple of months behind in her development. The doctor says don't jump to conclusions, only time will tell if there's any permanent brain damage and he's seen a lot worse.

You can only hope and pray.

Yours V. T.,
M. B.

Sept. 22

Dear Journal,

I'm going to start calling you Journal. I feel we are no longer strangers.

I'm afraid we're only going to have the two grandchildren, unless Charisse decides to get married or have another baby, which she shouldn't, not at her age. I've about given up on Cyrus. I don't see him sending any grandchildren our way in the foreseeable future.

Cyrus was always a difficult child. All he'd do when he was a kid was stay in his room and read. I'd say why didn't he go outside and play with the other kids, get into trouble or something, it would be good for him? He'd say he was in the middle of a deep novel. I'd say what was he reading, one of Horatio Alger's books, or maybe a Hardy Boys mystery? He wouldn't answer, he'd just hide the book under the bedcovers and tell me to leave him alone, didn't I value his privacy? Which I did, but not to that extent.

When he wasn't reading he was always playing with his art collection. For instance, when he was in high school he bought a little plaster-of-paris statue. I said wasn't he too old to be playing with dolls? He said it wasn't a doll, it was a model of Michael Angelo's statue of David, the Jewish poet who is mentioned in the Bible as the writer of the Psalms. Well, I tried to be supportive, like a good parent, so I sewed David some underwear. Cyrus was well brought up, he said thank you. I could tell he didn't mean it, though, and the next time I cleaned up his room I found little David standing there in the altogether, like he had just taken a shower or was posing for a dirty picture.

That's the problem with being a parent, you scrimp and you save and you do little things for your kids, and they take it for granted. They don't even use the doll clothes you sew for them, all you get is a polite thank you.

I talked to Thelma about Cyrus. I said he takes after his father, except he's better-looking and has 20/20 eyesight. Also, he was always in much better shape, due to all those workouts down at the Y. She agreed with me, but she also pointed out that he's a Libra. She said Cyrus is a Libra and Charisse is a Gemini, which explains everything.

Cyrus didn't want to go to Kirkland State, he wanted to go all the way to K.U. He told us it was because of his allergies, but I overheard him tell Bud Blossum he found Kirkland stifling and he could hardly wait to get away from home. I don't have to say how much this hurt. The ironic thing is, Kirkland is actually a very liberal town. It's full of people like his father and me, who moved here to get away from stifling towns like Dridge and Baggs!

We finally let Cyrus go to K.U., but on one condition, which was that Kansas City would be the farthest east he would go. His father was willing to make it St. Louis, but I insisted on Kansas City, and I felt guilty about giving in that much. The other condition was that Cyrus major in accounting instead of art. He wanted to spend his life making little dolls, like Mr. Angelo used to do, but I stood up and insisted that if he was going to support a wife and family, he should get into a business that pays.

After he graduated, Cyrus wanted to move to New York, but I reminded him of his promise. He backed down and instead moved to San Francisco. I said that wasn't in the agreement, but his father wouldn't back me up on this particular issue, so I didn't have a leg to stand on. I said what about all those strange people? His father said what strange people and Cyrus said yeah, what strange people? I said you know, those, etcetera, but his father said he had no idea what I was talking about and Cyrus said he was a big boy now, he thought he knew how to deal with any strange people that crossed his path. His father happened to agree with him in this particular case, so again I was left without a leg to stand on.

Cyrus still lives in San Francisco, earthquakes or no earthquakes. He used to send us an artsy post card every Christmas, telling us he missed us and explaining that he'd fly home to visit as soon as he gets his CPA. As soon as he gets his CPA he'll probably also get married and raise a family, at least that would be my expectation. In fact, I wouldn't be surprised if he flew home with a surprise for us one of these days—a bride!

You can only hope and pray. And isn't that the whole point of Christianity?

Yours,
Mildred

P.S. I've often wondered if things would've turned out different if we'd have named him Fred, after Fred Astaire. That was my first choice, but Ed wanted to name him after another one of Shakespeare's characters from "A Midsummer's Night Dream." Surprise, surprise. But I wouldn't hear of naming a sweet child Bottom. So we had to compromise, we settled on Cyrus, after the Biblical king who invented the reaper.

10/28

Dear J.,

Then there's Mabel. The poor dear. Her biggest mistake was marrying that character in the first place. We all told her she'd be crazy to, couldn't she see they weren't meant for each other? We pointed out that what do a painter and a bookkeeper have in common? It would've been okay if he'd have been a house painter, which pays well and gives you weekends off for church and family. But somebody who paints pictures on canvas? Of sunflowers and of a naked lady sitting in an orchard with a couple of fully clothed businessmen?! It was all very tasteful, I've got to admit, except for the stuff he always kept hidden in the garage, which was nothing but s-m-u-t. But where's the market for tasteful pictures painted by a guy who dresses up like one of those Frenchmen, with a little black beanie and everything?

I'd have to say it was a good thing she finally left him, if she was the one who finally left. What choice did she have? It was either leave the guy or put up with all that trash. Forty years is a long time to spend living with a man who all he can talk about is moving to Green Itch Village. A guy who criticizes you for tiny little acts of Christian charity like freezing the garbage so the trash man won't have to smell it. I'm convinced he's what drove her off the edge. Ed always said it was in the genes, pointing to Aunt Myrtle, but I pointed out that the rest of us are okay. Thelma's convinced it was the affair with her boss and all the related stress, but I said affair? With Ron Rigby? Who in their right mind would have an affair with a mechanic with grease under his fingernails? She said it was in the charts for that time period (November) for a Pisces, and what other dark handsome man did Mabel have available? So I had to point out that she was brought up like me, Mabel was, in a Christian home that preached family values. She said don't worry, Honey, it wasn't her fault, if it's the stars that make you do it, you can't be held responsible.

I went to visit her yesterday. Mabel. I was going to tell her about Ed and me and Betsy Bandero and being called Agnes by mistake (whose, I wonder!?!?), but before they took me to the visitor's room I was reminded about not disturbing her, she was finally doing very nicely but bad news might set her back or send her off the deep end. So she and I ended up talking about the flower arrangement on the table and the things we used to do as kids.

The thing I remembered about what we did as kids was putting red white and blue crepe paper between our bicycle spokes for Fourth of July parades. The thing Mabel remembered most was sucking on worms.

We're twins, Mabel and me. That's the scary part!

M.

P.S. I think I'm going to return Mrs. Windell's book and try and get my money back.

6

The Skeptics

WHILE MILDRED WAS ENJOYING A GIRLS' NIGHT OUT with Sue Heedon, Ed was savoring some quality time with the neighbor's ducks and geese. While she was in the bungalow working through the instructions in *Grieving for the Man Who Left You*, he was curled up in the Winnebago with *One Hundred Years of Solitude*. And while she was spending her evenings writing in her journal, he was spending his twilight hours seated at his classic Royal typewriter, composing *The Memoirs of Edward B. Budwieser, Part I.*

10/18

This whole experience has made me stop and think. I've had to ask myself, What do I really want out of life? Do I really want to retire to the West Coast of Mexico and sit under the palm trees and play Canasta with the hired help and take long evening walks with several close friends and look out over the blue Pacific and finish my memoirs?

I've had to answer, Yes, I do.

But it doesn't look like it's going to happen. It looks like Mildred and I will be spending our golden years in Kirkland. She's going to continue living in the house, and I'm going to continue living in the driveway. She's going to continue working as a dental hygienist, and I'm going to continue delivering pizza to the multitudes.

I can honestly say, however, that my basic philosophy hasn't changed. I've always been one to council (sp?) others that when the chips are down they should Look on the Bright Side. Now that my own hour of suffering has come, I find myself in the position of having to council (sp?) myself with the same wisdom. And I'm not just referring to the possibility that Cyrus might come through with a job for me out in California! I'm referring to something much more fundamental. I'm referring to the deepest philosophical beliefs a man can have.

I've come to the conclusion that the wise men of the East were right all along. Life doesn't end with the grave. You keep coming back. You spend a lifetime in one body, which gradually becomes decrepit, and you finally get tired of its limitations and decide it's time to move on to something more befitting the beauty of your poetic soul. I'm not sure about the exact details of this move. I never learned Hindu—one of my weaknesses as a scholar. But I'm becoming convinced that my Real Self has been around before and that it will be around again. At least if there's any justice in the world.

It stands to reason. (1) If you look on the bright side, and (2) if you know they're going to give you a funeral somewhere down the road, then it's clear that (3) you're going to get another chance, sooner or later. And if you're going to get another chance, who's to say (4) you weren't getting another chance when they recycled the Real You this time around? It all makes perfectly good sense. The surprising thing is that more people haven't caught on.

I've even figured out who I was in my former life. I was Shakespeare. How else can I explain the fact that I'm the only person I know who has a genuine appreciation of the Classics? And who is the most Classical author of all time? The Bard! Q.E.D.

It's not that there's nobody else who likes the Classics. It's that I'm the only one I know who really understands them. Liking them is one thing, understanding them is another. For instance, a former colleague of mine liked them, too, and I once thought she understood them, but now I'm not so sure.

I'm learning to look at my present life as merely a brief interlude between being Shakespeare and being somebody else. I don't know who'll eventually replace "Edward B. Budwieser." I don't have a crystal ball. (Did "William Shakespeare" know he'd come back as a high school English teacher in Kirkland, Kansas? There's no textual evidence showing he [I] did, and I certainly don't remember making plans along those lines.) All I know is, whoever that somebody is who'll replace "Ed B.," he'll be somebody with an equally poetic soul, somebody equally able to "burst joy's grape against his palate fine."

I'm also learning to live with another fact: I am the last of the so-called "dead white males."

§

Dr. Digby didn't believe in reincarnation.

Ed learned this while he was laid out in the dentist's chair, his jaw riddled with novocaine. It was the morning after he discovered his prior existence as Shakespeare, and he was eager to share this information with someone.

He knew better, of course, than to suddenly announce his secret identity as the former Bard of Avon. So he eased into the topic gradually. He started by asking Digby what he thought about the journey of the soul from one body to the next.

"You mean incarnation?" grunted Digby, blowing on his long silver needle as if it were a smoking pistol.

"I mean *re*incarnation."

"To tell the truth," said Digby, putting the needle back on the tray, "I haven't given the subject a whole lot of thought."

"You spend a lifetime in one body," Ed explained, "but it gradually gets old and decrepit. So you finally get tired of its metaphysical limitations and—"

"Metaphysical limitations, huh?" drawled Digby. "I'm afraid you're getting too abstract for me. Just give me a for-instance."

"For instance, its present spouse."

"Good," joked Digby. "That's something I can grab on to."

"Anyway, you decide it's time to move on to something more in tune with the beauty of your poetic soul—"

"Like recycling a beer can, huh? First it holds Coors, then Schlitz, then Bud—"

"So you die, and after a while you come back in another body."

Digby pointed out the window at a blazing red skirt crossing the street. "Speaking of another body," he chuckled. "I don't know about you, but I'm one of those people who look on the bright side."

"That's exactly my point," Ed insisted. His voice rose with irritation. "If you look on the bright side, and if you figure they're going to dig you a grave somewhere down the line, then it's pretty clear they've got to give you another chance, sooner or later." But he was beginning to see that the fact that Shakespeare was alive and well and living in Kirkland, Kansas would be wasted on this stubby-fingered schmoe. How could a dentist who had recently advised him that Ascension Airlines was a takeoff candidate that could be stolen at 10.62—how could such an idiot even begin to appreciate such an incredible revelation? . . . What had Shakespeare, or someone, said about casting your pearls before swine?

"A risk-free investment, is it?" Digby was now over by the door catching up on the latest rebound of the Dow.

Ed could feel his jaw going deader and deader. "And if you're going to get another chance," he continued, "who's to say you weren't getting another chance when they recycled the Real You this time around?"

He heard Digby behind him, gargling. He thought he smelled Chivas Regal.

"It stands to reason," he went on. "I'm just surprised more people haven't figured it out."

Digby came over and pinched his cheek to check the effects of the novocaine. "What's it say about all this stuff in the Bible?"

Digby was not just a dentist. He also doubled as a Baptist Sunday School teacher. He was always wanting to know whether this or that Budwieser theory was based on the Scriptures or just on the vain speculations of men. This was the least of Ed's worries. The important question to him was, how did his philosophical thoughts square with his deepest and finest goals and aspirations?

He had to admit to Digby that reincarnation was not a Biblical teaching. Not *per se*. "But," he quickly added, "I think of Christ as an exceptionally broad-minded person. In fact, according to some scholars, one of his basic teachings was, 'if it feels good, do it.'"

"I'd never heard that before, to be honest."

"It's not a well-known fact. Very few laymen are aware of that basic teaching. I'd say three to four percent at the most."

"What about Babdists?"

Why couldn't they pronounce the name of their own religion? he wondered. "Among Baptists," he estimated, "the figure would be somewhat lower."

Now Digby was whistling an aimless tune. "How's the jaw? Getting a little numb, is it?"

"This also applies to philosophy. 'If it sounds good, it's probably true.'"

"You're getting a little deep for yours truly," admitted Digby, shaking his head. "That's the difference between you and me," he added. "You're a thinker. I'm more of a doer."

Before he could agree with this observation, in part, and take issue with it, in part, Digby had several powerful fingers inside his mouth, stretching it to the maximum and erecting something like a small oil rig around the broken tooth.

"Yes sir," Digby muttered, testing the rigging. "That's the difference between Ed Budwieser and Dr. Digby. The professor just *thinks* about what life might have to offer, in terms of, etcetera etcetera. Dr. Digby, on the other hand, gets out there and *grabs* for—"

Before Digby could finish this thought, Mildred popped into the cubicle to help him make the bad tooth foodworthy.

For the next hour, Ed Budwieser's Number 3 was to become the object of widespread attention. He took a deep breath, opened wide, stared at the Pelton & Crane searchlight bearing down on the locus of action, and began to count the objects that were finding their way into his mouth:

—4 latex gloves,
—20 fingers,
—1 drill,
—1 mirror,
—1 miniature oil rig,
—2 pieces of latex,
—200+ fragments of tooth and filling,
—2 ounces of blood,
—1 hose,
—1/2 gallon of water,
—1 vacuum cleaner.

Late that night, back in the Winnebago after delivering pizza, he recorded his thought for the day:

10/19

Another argument for reincarnation.

If my mouth can hold over 233 1/2 items, who's to say my body can't hold the magnificent, poetic soul of William Shakespeare?

§

The following Friday evening Ed encountered five more skeptics.

The Deuces were gathered around the Ecclebury's kitchen table when he made this discovery. They were eating taco chips and pretzels and drinking decaf and lite beer and celebrating his sixtieth birthday. Between exchanges of poker chips, they were discussing what had gone wrong with the Jiggers marriage, at the same time trying not to be insensitive about another marriage, which wasn't roaming the West in quest of ecstasy but was right there at opposite ends of that very same table.

After Ed had cashed in his unaccustomed pile of chips and everyone had profusely congratulated him on his unaccustomed winnings and he had refilled his mug for the third time, he sensed that the mood was finally ripe for proclaiming the good news about his past life as Shakespeare.

He began by changing the subject from winnings in this life to winnings in the next.

It turned out that Mark Ecclebury was an expert on the subject. He had once seen a mind-expanding documentary on the NDE, "The Near-Death Experience," so he was able to predict confidently that you go down a long shining tube just as death sets in. "And when you get to the end of that tube," he prophesied, "you come across a scene that's right out of a Matisse."

"Does it have to be a Matisse?" asked Ann Leben. "Couldn't it be a Gauguin or a Renoir?"

"It'll be a Matisse, all right. Specifically, *Joie de Vivre*."

"'The Joy of Life,'" translated Ann for the benefit of Karen Ecclebury and Mildred.

"*Oui*," replied Mark.

"'Yes,'" translated Ann.

Karen took the conversation out of the hands of the French intellectuals and steered it back to the question of the afterlife. "You know what *I* think?" she said.

Everyone insisted on knowing what Karen thought.

"I think you achieve morality through your grandchildren."

The kitchen exploded with laughter.

"*Im*morality, I think she means," said Mark, winking at Ann. Ed caught this wink. He didn't know if anybody else did.

"Let's try mor*tal*ity," said Gary Leben.

"How about *im*mortality?" asked Ann.

"No," protested Mildred, "she's got it right. Wait'll you have grandchildren."

"That's just my opinion," explained Karen.

Gary saved Karen from further embarrassment by offering his own humble opinion. "It seems to me," he said, and he waited until everyone was breathless with anticipation of his answer, "that when you die, you die."

"That's easy for a big life insurance man to say," said Mark.

"How much do you think he makes a year?" asked Ann.

"*Beaucoup,*" guessed Mark.

"How much *beaucoup*?"

"*Beaucoup beaucoup*."

Karen kept the party from turning into another French lesson by raising the question of whether anybody wanted some more decaf.

Mildred did. Everyone else wanted more beer. Karen got up to play hostess, and Ann turned the conversation back to the subject of the afterlife. "Well in *my* humble opinion," she said, "it's all a great mystery."

"You've been watching too many soaps," said Mark.

"*Merci, mon ami*," replied Ann. She playfully kicked at Mark under the table and hit Ed's shin.

Dora had once kicked him under the table. They'd been engaging in witty repartee, just like Ann and Mark were doing now—more like Beatrice and Benedick, actually—and she'd kicked him playfully. . . . Beatrice and Benedick . . . that had to have been one of his most brilliant masterstrokes, if he did say so himself. Beatrice: named, if he remembered correctly, for Dante's mysterious lady and poetic muse. Benedick: meaning—

Mildred broke in to say she didn't just *think*, she *knew* that you pick up a resurrection body the minute you cross the finish line.

"Automatically?" asked Gary.

"Only if you believe. Otherwise, you're just going to rot in the grave."

Mark drained his mug. Out of the side of his mouth he wanted to know how anybody could actually believe that crap. Ed's thought exactly.

Karen came back from the kitchen and repeated her opinion that you gain morality, or whatever, through later generations. This led to a discussion on the topic of grandchildren. Pictures were suddenly being plucked out of purses and wallets and passed around. Comparisons of extraordinary feats of intellectual maturity were being made. Prognostications of fabulous careers were being ventured. It was discovered that among those assembled in that modest kitchen were the proud grandparents of a future Harvard professor, a future CEO of a Fortune 500 corporation, and two future presidents of the United States.

After nominating his grandson for a future Nobel Prize in Literature, Ed excused himself and headed for the bathroom.

He stood before the commode and unzipped. Should he trust his aim? On three, four, five beers? Better not. He unbuckled and sat down and emptied his holding tank. Over on his left, dangling from a peg, was a brassiere. He inspected the thing, out of curiosity. Size 40C. With his index finger he explored the beams and girders and stress points. A marvel of construction. Like the one Howard Hughes built for Marilyn. Marilyn? No. Jane. Jane Russell. He caressed the empty cups and thought of Betsy.

He hated lite beer, especially when it was only 3.2 percent alcohol. Karen probably bought it at the supermarket, which could sell only 3.2. Stupid Kansas law. Another thing he hated was birthday parties, especially sixtieth, and especially his own. These were the two things he hated most about life at this point, 3.2 beer and sixtieth birthdays.

He stood up. He buckled. He zipped. Then he went over to the basin and washed. He leaned over and looke.d at himself in the mirror. Sixty. Getting greyer and greyer. Dead white male? He slapped cold water on his face. It brought him back to life. Ready to go back and reveal his true identity to an astounded public.

They were still talking about grandchildren.

"Getting back to the question," he broke in. "The obvious answer is reincarnation."

"Sure," said Ann.

"Sleeping in that old Winnebago must be getting to you," said Mark.

"How many beers have you had?" said Mildred.

"Four," said Karen. "What's reincarnation?"

"Obvious? Why obvious?" said Gary.

"Just stop and think about it," he went on. He was warming up to the subject. He gave them his well-considered theory about looking on the bright side. "If you have the intelligence to look on the bright side," he said, "you're practically forced to the conclusion that you'll get another shot at it. Sooner or later."

"Who were you in your previous life?" Ann wanted to know. "Lord Byron?"

Everyone laughed. Everyone was drunk. Everyone except Karen and Mildred.

He wiped some froth off his lips with the back of his hand. Lord Byron indeed. Ann always underestimated him, the pretentious bitch. "No," he said, "I was Shakespeare."

Everyone groaned.

"For crying out loud, Edward!" scolded Ann. "We don't even know if Shakespeare was Shakespeare."

Mark explained to Karen and Mildred that Ann was referring to a theory going around that Shakespeare wasn't the author of his own plays, someone else was. Karen and Mildred nodded their heads and said "Oh."

Suddenly he stood up and pounded his mug on the table. "Whoever it was who wrote the plays of Shakespeare," he proclaimed, "I was that person!" He surprised himself with his own passion about this issue.

"How do you know it was even the *same* person who wrote all the plays formerly attributed to Shakespeare? They could've been written by a committee."

"Or by the members of a poker club."

He hadn't considered this possibility. But it didn't bother him. When he was on a roll with a good theory, there was no objection that could stand up to it. "I was whoever wrote *Romeo and Juliet,*" he insisted. He stood up and pounded on the table. "That's all I'm sure about, *Romeo and Juliet.*" He stopped pounding and sat down to reflect. "Of course I could've written *A Midsummer Night's Dream* and *Hamlet*, and I probably did. But all I seem to remember is *Romeo and Juliet.*"

Mark, or someone, said something to the effect that he could see Ed as the author of *The Comedy of Errors* or *Much Ado about Nothing,* but not *Romeo and Juliet.*

"Maybe you were just a stagehand in Shakespeare's time," Mildred suggested. "In fact, maybe you were just a member of the audience. Think hard. Maybe that's what you remember, being in the audience at the very first performance of *Romeo and Juliet.*"

He thought hard. He couldn't remember.

Ann turned to Mark. "Behind every successful man," she said with another wink, "there's a woman."

Mark winked right back. "Behind every man who was destined for greatness but got sidetracked, there's also a woman."

He was catching all the winks. Were they making it on the sly, Ann and Mark? Well . . . they deserved each other.

"Maybe he was that lady poet, what's her name? Angie Dickinson?" The voice seemed to be Karen's. Also, the thought.

Mark put his hands over his eyes. Ann turned to Karen and explained that there were no longer any lady poets, that they were now called *woman* poets, that Angie Dickinson was an actress, that last he heard she was still living, that Emily Dickinson was the poet she was thinking of, that she was dead, that the two were probably not related, even though their last names were spelled the same, and that the Bard of Kirkland was about as close to being the Belle of Amherst as he was to being the Bard of Avon.

He caught it all, every last word. "The Bard of Kirkland." He liked that.

Gary Leben suddenly reminded everyone that they only went around once in life. Mark headed for the fridge and came back with another round. Karen grabbed the six-pack away from him and ushered it right back to where it came from.

Several male groans.

Next thing he knew Gary was on the floor in a pool of used beer. Karen was down there playing nurse. Ann was crying. Mark had his arm around her, and there was a fair amount of nuzzling being performed. "We're going home," Mildred was saying.

She drove him home in what seemed to be a long, unpleasant silence.

Then it was morning. But he had total recall of the situation. The whole conversation ran through his mind, like his brain was a tape recorder. Which had to be proof of . . . something. A magical power, maybe, from a past life as a yogi. Or maybe it was just pure genius?

He eased himself out of bed and guided himself over to his desk and carefully settled himself down at the controls of his typewriter and pecked out a set of sentences:

10/22

In the last analysis, there are basically six views of life after death.

1. Proponents of the NDE maintain that at the moment of death you go down a long shining tube until you reach a Matisse-like garden scene. (A problem: what if you're not French?)

2. Many Christians maintain that death is followed by resurrection. (What's the evidence? And what if you belong to a religion that hasn't had a chance to study the Bible?)

3. Others insist that you achieve immortality through posterity. (How about singles, like Cyrus? Are they condemned to perpetual death?)

4. There are always those, of course—bankers, insurance agents, lawyers, etc.—who maintain that death is the last hurrah. (Is this view the perogative (sp?) of the wealthy?)

5. Some "cultural sophisticates" say it's all a great mystery. (It would be, too, except for #6.)

6. Reincarnation. (The Hindu/Budwieser theory.)

Idea: a blockbuster novel with the title, Six Characters in Search of an Afterlife, which would prove E. B.'s prior existence as Shakespeare by citing personal experience, memories of the Avon countryside and the London theatre scene, offering a stunning interpretation of Hamlet's soliloquy, etc.

But before beginning his novel, Ed stretched out on the bunk to plan it.

§

He had just finished the last sentence of his profound and moving novel, a book that would make the critics sit up and take notice, that the critics would hail as "a rare treat, a masterpiece in both style and substance," that would eventually cast him in marble, when he was awakened by a knock at the door.

He sat up. He pounded his head with the heel of his palm. Then there was another knock. He got up, stretched, and went over and peeked out the window.

It was Charisse. All the way from Kansas City. She had Shaun on her hip.

"Megan's in the house," she was apologizing.

He fumbled for the doorknob. He'd forgotten that Charisse was coming today.

"She's being educated by Mildred in the ways of Dr. Spock," she seemed to be saying.

The teachings of Dr. Spock. . . . Why believe in the teachings of Dr. Spock when you have the teachings of a genius in your very midst?

He was finally able to open the door.

"Dad? You all right?"

He was all right. It was the world that needed sympathy.

"I'm, like, worried about you, Dad."

"How's my grandson?" he finally yawned, plucking Shaun from the arms of his mother. "How's Buster?"

"They used to call *me* Buster," he went on. "Buster Budwieser. I was all boy."

The three of them sat down on two frayed lawn chairs for a visit in the October sunshine. Buster Junior sat on the lap of Buster Senior.

Charisse lit a Virginia Slim.

He hated it when women smoked.

She blew a smoke ring. "What's this I hear about you being, like, Shakespeare?"

"It's just an idea. But I happen to think it explains a lot."

"Like, for instance?"

How, he wondered, had *like* become an all-purpose part of speech? "For instance, it explains why I have so much sympathy for the Classics."

"Still on that classics kick, huh?" She blew a stream of smoke from the side of her mouth. "How long's this been going on?"

He scratched his stubble and considered this question for a moment. "Since the spring of 1594."

"Oh God!"

He ignored the mother and turned to the son. "Has your mommy read you *Julius Caesar*?" he asked, poking the child in the tummy to try to make him laugh. "Did you know your very own grandpa wrote it?"

"We're into reincarnation, are we?" said Charisse, and she sent up another smoke ring. "Sounds like a merry-go-round to me."

"I've been reading that book you and Cyrus bought me on the subject."

"Oh Dad. That was a hundred years ago!"

It was ten years ago. Exactly. A gift for his fiftieth birthday. "Halfway through life," Cyrus had written on the title page, and Charisse had inserted the word *this* between *through* and *life*. Halfway through *this* life: Charisse had known something he didn't, something he had just discovered for himself.

"Did you know your grandpa is exactly sixty years old today?" he whispered in his grandson's ear. "A hundred and twelve, if you count the time he spent as Shakespeare."

His grandson looked at him with a frown.

He bounced little Shaun on his knee. "All the wise men of the East believed in reincarnation," he assured the boy.

"What about the wise *women* of the East?" asked Charisse. "What did *they* think about the subject?"

He informed her that nobody knew, because all the books on reincarnation were written by men. Then he gave Shaun another bounce. "Are you going to write a book on reincarnation when you get big?" He stopped to think for a moment. Then he whispered, "Maybe you already have."

Charisse persisted. "Why do you suppose all the holy books were written by men?"

"The male animal is more receptive to divine inspiration."

"How can that be?" Charisse wanted to know. "God's a woman. Even little Shaun knows that, don't you, Shaun?" She leaned over and chucked little Shaun under the chin. "The other day I asked him, is God a man or a woman, and he said, clear as a bell, 'God a woma, he a woma.' What'd I tell you, he's a regular genius."

"And what would you expect? The kid's grandpa is William Shakespeare!"

Charisse groaned, snuffed out her Virginia Slim on the driveway, stood up, and took Shaun from him.

"Listen, Bill," she said, "I gotta go."

He hated it when people called their parents by their Christian names. That was the problem with the younger generations. Absolutely no respect.

"Gotta get back to K. C.," she went on. "Gotta date tonight with a real neat guy."

"Does he have a name?"

"Kevin—no, Evan. Evan Something, starts with a B. A real crazy hombre. Reminds me a lot of you, Dad. Except he's got this fantastic body."

Then she walked toward the house, clutching her son tightly. Halfway there, she turned around. "By the way," she called, "happy birthday."

"Thanks." He waved at little Shaun, who stared at him.

"Your present's in the mail," she called. "A subscription to *Time*."

"Look forward to it," he called back.

"Six months," she called, and she and her son disappeared into the house.

He climbed back into the Winnebago, sat down at the typewriter, inserted a new sheet of paper, and prepared to favor posterity with his latest meditation:

10/22

Metaphor for reincarnation: merry-go-round.

§

On Sunday Ed found another person who didn't believe in reincarnation. Rev. Gilltrip, down at church.

Ed and Mildred had been going to the same Sunday School class for forty years, ever since they moved to Kirkland. They'd spent many memorable Sunday mornings discussing such topics as whether the U. S. should get out of Vietnam, whether God was the Ground of Being or the projection of man's deepest needs or dead or just in hibernation, what percentage of their sons and daughters were on drugs, whether the great bull market would last forever, whether Dustin Hoffman was better in *Midnight Cowboy* or in *Tootsie,* what kinds of persons they were, left hemisphere or right hemisphere, and why the Church had become irrelevant in the modern world. But when Rev. Horace Gilltrip had come out of retirement to replace young Tad Heedon, the subject of discussion rapidly switched from contemporary issues to the teachings of the prophets and the apostles. Rev. Gilltrip informed the class that what they needed was to get away from the secular humanist syndrome and discipline their minds by discussing the basic truths of Christianity.

And so the morning after Ed's conversation with his skeptical daughter, Rev. Gilltrip was "picking the minds of the Faithful," as he put it, on the Faithful's understanding of basic Christian convictions. It was the perfect setting, Ed thought, for introducing the topic of reincarnation.

So he did.

"Ah," said Rev. Gilltrip, pointing his index finger at God and smiling slightly. "You mean *in*carnation. That's a central Christian doctrine."

"No," he corrected the Reverend, "I mean *re*incarnation, and I've always been under the impression it's not necessarily a Christian doctrine."

The Reverend paused. "And you want to discuss it in *this* class?"

"Well, yes. That was the general idea."

If they'd have had a vote on the subject, he was sure his suggestion would have carried the day. But Rev. Gilltrip was not a proponent of holding votes in Sunday School, even if the students were mature adults of voting age. As far as the Reverend was concerned, they were all there for one reason and one reason only, and the preferences of the class were not taken into consideration. So the class spent the rest of the Sunday School hour comparing the teachings of Jeremiah and Paul. Ed, however, spent the time trying to think of an argument for making reincarnation a central Christian doctrine.

He stared at the picture of Jesus that graced the classroom and wondered: Who had Jesus been in a previous life? . . . David, perhaps? There seemed to be textual evidence. But on the other hand, there was nothing of the political wheeler-dealer about Jesus. . . . Moses? Both had been mountain climbers, both had been on good terms with God, assuming for a moment that there even *was* a God. But then of course Jesus had been quite critical of Moses on a number of points—murder, lust, etc. . . . Maybe one of the Greeks? Socrates? Both of them were great teachers. But he couldn't imagine Jesus at a banquet. At a wedding, maybe, preaching a sermon on kindness and blessing the bread and fish and then going out for more wine. But at a banquet, engaging a group of handsome young men in a spirited discussion on the nature of the Beautiful? . . . No, in his previous life Jesus had probably been somebody no one has ever heard of. Some Tibetan mystic, living in total seclusion. Some illiterate Amazonian shaman. Some Pawnee Indian, wasting his wisdom on the Kansas plains. Some Eskimo poet, leaving his well-wrought words on perishable shards of ice.

Well, then, who had Jesus reincarnated *into*? . . . St. Francis? Same free-and-easy lifestyle, same interest in birds. But Jesus also had an interest in women, a weakness the good saint didn't seem to share. . . . Napoleon, maybe? Both were leaders of men, both rode a horse—actually, in the case of Jesus, an ass. But of course Jesus hated war. . . . Shakespeare? Both were tops in their chosen field, and both sported beards. But Jesus as the master of English prose? He looked up at the picture of Jesus again, and compared it with the pictures of the Bard. Similarities, certainly. He imagined Jesus visiting a barbershop. "Cold enough for you today, milord?" "It is a nipping and an eager air." "Should we do something about this beard, good milord?" "Off the sides, sirrah; take it all off." "Leave a moustache, milord?" "Faith, and that ye shall, if it but please thee." "If I may make so bold, milord, thou'dst look good in a Vandyke." "And so shall it be, i' faith. Methinks I shall sit for another portrait on the morr—"

Rev. Gilltrip was asking him a question. About. . . ?

He smiled and said he'd have to think about it.

"Does anyone else have the time?" asked Gilltrip.

After Sunday School, Rev. Gilltrip came up to Ed and pursued the subject of reincarnation. He pointed out that when in Rome, one does as the Romans. "When we have a discussion in a Christian church," he said, planting his finger firmly on Ed's chest, "we ought to keep it within the bounds of basic Christian doctrine."

Ed couldn't disagree. He was holding his hand over his mouth, discreetly hiding the beer breath.

"Would you like to read an excellent book on the subject?" the good man asked.

He frankly wasn't excited about the prospect of reading another book on the subject of reincarnation. But Mildred and Charisse had brought him up to be gracious about accepting other people's suggestions, so he turned his head to the side and muttered yes, he'd be pleased to have the opportunity to read whatever Rev. Gilltrip deemed suitable on the subject.

What Gilltrip deemed suitable was a book with the title, *The Christian View of Life after Death.* Suspecting that there would be a quiz on its contents the next Sunday, Ed sat up half the following Saturday night in bed digesting it, washing it down with a bottle of Christian Brothers.

It was a shocking book! There was a whole chapter on the subject of reincarnation. It said the Hindus who believe in reincarnation don't necessarily look forward to the recycling process. In fact, they try to live so they don't *have* to come back. If they come back, they consider themselves failures. They try to live so that they die with a guarantee that they won't come back. When they get to retirement age, they sit in the woods and eat nuts and berries and stare into space. They would easily qualify for the Sierra Club, except that when they get out into Nature, they make a point of not enjoying it.

A shocking book, yes, but also a disappointing book. If it happened to be accurate, it would mean he'd have to sit down and sort out his priorities all over again. He was getting tired of sorting out priorities. It made him question his most cherished beliefs, including Look on the Bright Side and Time is the Great Healer.

After he finished that chapter, "Misconceptions about Reincarnation," he took a late-night walk around the neighborhood to purify his mind. When he got back he had another drink, sat down at the typewriter, and added his thought for the day.

10/29

Can one imagine Shakespeare questioning his most cherished beliefs at the age of sixty?

I think not.

First of all, he'd have to tear up Romeo and Juliet and start all over again, and last of all, he'd already be dead.

7

As Mature Adults

IT WAS LATE HALLOWEEN NIGHT in the darkened Blossum kitchen. Mildred was sitting at the table, wearing a winter coat over her bathrobe. Her face, which was lit up by the happy jack-o-lantern in front of her, was covered with a mud pack. Her hair was in curlers. Thelma was closing the back door after a stray trick-or-treater. She was costumed in a witch's hat, cape, and mask. A white mop served as a makeshift wig.

"That's the last kid *I* want to see till hell freezes over," said Thelma as she flipped off the porch light.

"They seem to be getting—"

"I know exactly what you mean, Sweetie," interrupted Thelma as she set the candy bowl on the counter. "But you was starting to tell me something?"

"I was starting to say, it just seems like the youth of today are getting worse and worse. In terms of their manners."

Thelma came over to the table and sat down. "If you ask me, it's their *morals* that takes the cake." She paused and looked at the two masks before her, Mildred's mud pack and the Greek comic jack-o-lantern. "But you didn't come clear across the alley to talk about today's morals. You was starting to tell me something important."

"I was?"

"About something which happened at work today? Something involving Dr. Digby?"

"Oh. . . ."

Thelma got up from the table, retrieved the bowl, and placed it on the table between Mildred and the jack-o'-lantern. "Could I tempt you with a candy bar?"

"Thanks," said Mildred, "but I'm really not hungry."

Thelma sat down again, unwrapped a miniature bar for herself, and leaned forward eagerly. "I won't breathe a word of it," she promised. "To *any*body."

Should she or shouldn't she? Thelma Blossum was her best friend, they shared many secrets, mostly about her Ed and Thelma's Lee Roy, who had passed away five years ago, but then on the other hand some of *her* secrets had ended up in other parts of Kirkland and had gotten back to Ed, who had traced them all the way back to Thelma, for example Ed's secret about not being able to. . . .

"Cross your heart and hope to die?" she finally asked.

Thelma put the Snickers in her mouth, then crossed her heart. "You know Thelma Blossum," she said, chewing noisily. "Quiet as a mouse."

"Well. . . ."

"Oh, is *this* what's bothering you?" said Thelma, pointing to her costume. "We'll fix *that,*" and she took off her witch's mask and hat and mop and the cape, revealing a faded nightgown. "There. Is that better?"

"That's *much* better."

"Well?" said Thelma, pulling her chair closer.

"Well . . . this is the story, not to be repeated to *any*body."

"To *any*body," repeated Thelma, undressing another Snickers.

"Here's how it started."

"I'm listening," said Thelma, finishing off the bar in a single bite.

"I must've been looking pretty down-in-the-mouth today, because Dr. Digby said 'Maybe we should get together for lunch some time, Mildred, to talk about, you know, the Ed problem.'"

"I bet he wasn't referring to Ed's bad breath, neither."

"You're right on that one, Thelma. He's always kidding around with me, Doctor is, saying 'You're looking pretty down-in-the-mouth today, Mildred,' even when I'm in a good mood, which I wasn't today, which explains the lunch offer."

"I always did say he's got him a sense of humor," said Thelma, going for a Milky Way.

"That's not all he has," said Mildred. "Anyway," she went on, "I said 'Oh Dr. Digby! Lunch! I don't really know if we should.' He said 'We're mature adults, you've got a problem that bears looking into, we could talk about it, just you and I, as mature adults.' I said 'Well, I don't know what Ed would say about that,' he said 'Ed is the problem, right?' I said 'Either Ed or the Winnebago,' and he said 'Who was the one who bought that old Winnebago?' I saw his point right away. I said 'I guess maybe you're right, Dr. Digby, Ed is probably the problem,' he said 'As mature adults, right,' I said 'Right, as mature adults, nothing more,' and I emphasized the *nothing more*. He said 'don't worry, I'll pay, it's the least I can do after all these years, what's it been, twenty-five?'"

"Oh, it's got to be at least that," said Thelma. "Must be twenty-eight, twenty-nine."

"That's exactly what I told him, I said 'It's been thirty years this month,' so we went over to the McDonald's right across the street from the office, us two mature adults did, right after I helped him give old Mr. Schutz a new gold tooth."

"Another gold tooth!" exclaimed Thelma, trying out a fun-sized Mars. "That's the fourth one, ain't it?"

"The fifth!"

"Five? I'm counting four."

"You're probably forgetting the Number 7. Anyway, as we were crossing the street, I said 'Mr. Schutz seemed quite pleased with his new gold tooth.' Dr. Digby said 'Wait'll he gets the bill, then we'll see how pleased he is.' I said 'What's the price of gold these days, anyhow?' I was just being pleasant, making conversation, I wasn't really that curious to know. He said 'We aren't coming all the way over here to talk about the price of gold per ounce, now are we, we're coming here to talk about the Ed problem, is he still spending his, ah, sleeping hours camped out in that Winnebago?' "

"Makes you wonder why he wants to know," said Thelma in a skeptical tone.

"It does, doesn't it. But to get on with the story, Dr. Digby didn't wait for an answer. We were already inside McDonald's, and he was busy looking at the menu. 'Two quarter pounders,' he told the pert little counter girl, 'with chocolate shakes and fries.' I said 'And I'll have a regular hamburger, with a glass of water.' 'No no,' he said, 'one of those quarter pounders I ordered is for you.' I said 'Dr. Digby! I couldn't eat that much! You know I usually just pack a peanut-butter-and-jelly sandwich, what are you trying to do to me, fill me out?' He just laughed. He said 'Pardon me, I forgot, that's how you keep your cute little figure, right?' "

"He didn't!" said Thelma.

"He did! Then the counter girl tapped her pencil and said 'I'm confused, exactly what did you order, we don't carry peanut-butter-and-jelly sandwiches.' He said 'Forget the peanut butter, forget the jelly, forget the sandwich, make it two quarter pounders for me, with a chocolate shake and fries—' "

"Which reminds me," said Thelma, and she jumped up from the table, "hows about a cup of coffee and a piece of rhubarb pie?"

"That'd be just what the doctor ordered," said Mildred, recovering her appetite. "Anyway, as I was starting to say, he said 'Make it two quarter pounders for me, with a chocolate shake and fries, and one regular hamburger, with water, for this beautiful young lady, chuckle chuckle, with the cute little, fantastic figure.' I said 'Dr. Digby!' and he said 'Why don't you just call me Dan?' "

"Dan!" exclaimed Thelma, almost spilling the pie and coffee.

"Dan," repeated Mildred, helping herself. "Anyway, when we sat down to eat, I bowed my head for grace. I had a hard time keeping my mind on a proper thank-you, though, because Dr. Digby kept looking at me. Then he made a remark about my teeth. At first I thought this is kind of strange, but then I remembered, that's his specialty, after all, teeth. He said 'Has anybody ever told you you have *fas*cinating teeth, Mildred, ah, Millie,' and I said 'Oh Dr. Digby!' and must've turned bright red."

"I'd of done the same thing myself," said Thelma sympathetically.

"They aren't exactly buck, the teeth aren't, they're just unusual, but he said they were *fas*cinating. I should've caught on right then and there, but I thought, Dr. Digby's a dentist, after all, and he knows a fascinating set of teeth when he sees them, and he was just trying to make conversation anyway. He's very good at making conversation, under ordinary circumstances, but talking to his assistant maybe doesn't qualify as an ordinary circumstance, because I'm not necessarily a big golfer and don't know the first thing about mutual funds versus discount brokers and the price of gold in London."

"You and me both, Sweetie," said Thelma. "You and me both."

"'*Fas*cinating teeth,' he repeated, so I repeated my line, which was 'Dr. Digby!' 'Dan,' he said, 'just call me Dan, please, we're mature adults, after all, so we can forego the formalities, can't we?' 'Okay Dan,' I said, 'How's Carole?' I was thinking, if it's going to be Dan, it's going to be Dan and Carole."

"Good thinking," said Thelma.

"He said 'Ah, Carole and I don't seem to be getting along too well these days, that time of life for her, etcetera etcetera.' Then he caught himself and said 'Not that there's anything wrong with a few biological changes, it's all part of growing . . . older.' 'More mature,' I pointed out. 'Yes,' he said, 'more mature, more . . . adult.'"

"I can see exactly where this is leading," warned Thelma.

"Just you wait. So he said 'Speaking of Carole, I'm always struck by how well you maintain your youthful, ah, appearance.' He was about to say *figure*, I could tell, but he said *appearance* instead. I didn't say anything, because at that particular time my fascinating teeth were busy biting off a piece of McDonald's regular hamburger, so I wasn't in a position to keep up the conversation about my skinny figure in comparison with his third wife Carole's more mature figure. Which was a good thing, because if we got around to the business of doing comparisons, we'd probably have to bring up the subject of Dr. Digby's *very* mature figure."

"Hmmm," mused Thelma. "I coulda sworn Carole was his *second* wife."

"Third. Myrna was his first, Ginny his second, remember?"

"I plumb forgot about Ginny," admitted Thelma.

"So has he," said Mildred, and they both laughed. "But to get on with the story. 'I just can't see,' said Dr. Digby, 'why a guy like Ed would want to keep away from someone with your, ah, youthful appearance.' I didn't know what to say to this. All sorts of comparisons popped into my mind, like I wonder why a smart young gal like Carole would want to live with . . . but I work for the man, after all, he pays my check, and the least a person can do is be polite even in her thoughts to the man who pays her check and who is also paying for her hamburger and water. So I didn't say anything, hoping for a change of subject."

"I think you did the right thing, not saying anything," said Thelma.

"Anyway, Dr. Digby said 'I just can't see it, why would a guy like Ed prefer sleeping in a Winnebago to sleeping—' and I said 'Dr. Digby!' as a warning, loud enough for the whole lunch crowd to hear."

"I hope he got the point," said Thelma.

"I think he did, because then he whispered, 'Remember, we're mature adults, and we came here to discuss the, ah, Ed problem, which is also the Mildred problem, if I'm not mistaken.' I said 'Right, we're mature adults, let's *keep* it at that,' and I meant it."

"More pie?" said Thelma.

They both helped themselves to more rhubarb pie.

"Then he said 'I hope I didn't offend you, I didn't mean . . .' and I apologized for blowing it way out of proportion, I said 'Of course you didn't, you're concerned about my problem,' and he said 'I'm just trying to be supportive.' I said 'Of course you are, and I'm grateful for it, don't ever think I'm not.' He said 'I thought you might need somebody to talk to about it,' and I said 'Well, all I can say is, I'm grateful.' 'Tell me,' he said, 'and this is strictly off the record, has Ed ever been . . . have you ever suspected him of having an, ah—' 'Dr. Digby!' I said, and he said 'Shhh, I didn't mean. . . .' 'Of course you didn't,' I said, 'you're just being supportive.' But I was beginning to have my doubts about that."

"Well I should think you was!" said Thelma.

"Oh, I was, all right. 'Okay, then, back to the question,' he said, 'have you ever, you know, suspected him of, well . . .' and he left the question dangling."

"That in itself should of told you something," said Thelma.

"It certainly did. I thought to myself, it seems to me this question has come up before. It's a question Thelma Blossum always shows an interest in, I thought to myself, and when Thelma Blossum shows an interest in a question it tends to become a major subject of conversation, and I mean no disrespect."

"I didn't take it that way, Sweetie," said Thelma.

"Good. Anyway, the theory, you'll remember, was that Ed and Dora Jiggers were an item, and you were always making suggestions about what's sauce for the gander is sauce for the goose, and what about Dave Jiggers, didn't I find him bedworthy? That was your word, *bedworthy*, I myself wouldn't have put it that way. Well of course when Dora ran off with Rev. Heedon, Dave left Kirkland for the beaches and beds of California—or was it Colorado?—so your theory of how old Dave and Mildred would hit it off under the covers never got to the testing stage."

"I bet you sometimes wish it had," said Thelma. She was looking for a reaction.

"That's beside the point," Mildred insisted, blushing. "Anyway, so the question of if I had ever suspected my husband of, etcetera, had come up before, but it had come up as a result of your natural curiosity, and this was an entirely different situation. It wasn't a matter of somebody's natural curiosity, it was a matter of an employer being supportive of his faithful employee, so I didn't know what to say, so I took another bite of my hamburger."

"Nobody can fault you for that," said Thelma.

"'I don't mean to be pushy,' he said, and I swallowed quickly and said 'Oh no, I quite understand, Dr. Digby,' and he said 'Dan; just call me Dan, please, I'd appreciate it if you'd call me by my Christian name, and I'll call you Millie, that is, if you don't mind.' Well, Dr. Digby's a fine Christian gentleman, so I said to myself why not, that *is* his name, Dan, and after all these years. . . ."

"I can already see how this is coming out," prophesied Thelma.

"It just might surprise you. Anyway, he said 'I don't mean to be pushy, but we do have a problem here, let's talk about it, let's take the bull by the horns.' 'Yes,' I agreed, 'the bull by the horns,' and I finished my Golden Arches hamburger."

"I wonder what he meant by that, *bull by the horns*," mused Thelma. "I just wonder."

"You won't have to wait long to find out," said Mildred. "'Maybe that's the root of Ed's problem,' Dr. Digby said. 'Maybe the reason he's still sleeping out in that Winnebago has nothing to do with you per se, maybe he's . . .' and he didn't finish his sentence again. 'Maybe he's *what*?' I said. 'Maybe,' he said, 'he's seeking consolation from, ah, another source.' 'No,' I said without thinking, 'he doesn't pray as much as he used to,' and I was thinking back to the early days when Ed still believed in a Higher Being. 'That's not exactly what I meant,' said Dr.

Digby, 'I was referring to another *human* source.' I said '*human* source?' and he said 'specifically, another *female* source.'"

"Now is where it gets interesting," predicted Thelma.

"Just you wait. Anyway, I just said 'Oh no, I'm sure that's not the problem.' 'Oh?' he said. A short sentence, but this time he completed it. 'Oh?'"

"Oh?" wondered Thelma.

"Oh? is a question it's awfully hard to answer, and I didn't know quite what to say, so I started in on the glass of water. He just sat there, looking at me, half smiling, like he enjoyed the way I drank my water, just like he enjoyed watching me flash my fascinating teeth."

"You've got to admit they're unusual," said Thelma.

"Ed's always maintained it's in the genes. But to get on with the story, I didn't know what to say, so I said 'This is really *excellent* water, you ought to try it sometime.' 'I'm sure it is,' he said, 'but we didn't come all the way across the street to talk about the water.' 'Right,' I agreed, 'we came to talk about the Ed problem,' and he said, 'Which is also the Mildred problem, let's keep that in mind,' and I said 'I'm not quite sure what you mean.' That's what I said, but I was beginning to get the lay of the land."

"Smart girl," observed Thelma wisely.

"Then he looked at me for a long time and said 'Have you yourself, ah, ever considered . . . another source of consolation?' This time I knew he was referring to a *human* source . . . specifically *male.* And I remembered that the question of another source had come up before. From several conversations with you, to be specific, and in the exact same words. I wasn't thinking of Dave Jiggers, because he'd already left for Colorado by the time you mentioned the possibility of another source. I was thinking of Gary Leben. You had noticed that Mark and Ann were an item because of the French conversations. Actually, you didn't know it for a fact because you don't even know them, but as you always say you don't have to be a mathematician to put two and two together, and you suggested that Gary had a healthy salary and might need some consoling and so did I, so why didn't I put two and two together and solve two birds with one stone?"

"That's what I said, all right," said Thelma. "I remember it like it was yesterday."

"It was, practically," Mildred pointed out. "So when Dr. Digby asked me if I'd ever considered, etcetera etcetera, I said 'Well . . . yes.' I figured I had to be truthful, I owed it to him for being so supportive, if that's what he was being, and besides, he had paid for my hamburger. He said 'Ah. Ah, ah, ah.' I quickly said 'But I only con*sid*ered it, and it had nothing to do with his healthy salary,' and he said 'His? healthy salary?' so I had to tell him about Gary Leben and his need for consolation. I emphasized the part about only con*sid*ering it. I didn't think he was going to fire me if it had got beyond the considering stage, I just didn't want him to get the wrong idea about me, I could see it would be dangerous, and also, it was true, and I figured I owed it to my boss to tell him the truth."

"I'll say this much," said Thelma, "you was brought up right."

"Thank you, Thelma, so were you. But Dr. Digby pursued the subject, he said 'And what about Mr. Leben, did *he* want you to get beyond the considering stage?' I said 'Dr. Digby,' he said 'Dan, if you please,' I said 'Dr. Digby, the subject never even came up between the two of us.' I was getting indignant. He said 'You mean it was just an idea in your pretty little head?' and I said 'That's right, just an idea in my head, mine, and Thelma Blossum's.'"

"Let's give credit where credit is due," said Thelma Blossum.

"I always do," Mildred pointed out. "'Well, well, well,' said Dr. Digby. I didn't know how to respond to a whole row of wells, I was also feeling a little uncomfortable with Dr. Digby looking at me, first at the teeth, then at the youthful appearance, but I had already finished the water, so I started up with the napkin. I tore little pieces off the napkin and rolled them into little balls and arranged them in little rows on the orange tray . . . or maybe it was yellow. Was it brown? . . ."

She paused and thought back to the color scheme.

"Anyway," she went on, "the point is I'd finished my hamburger and downed my glass of water and was out of fresh things to do, also fresh things to say, besides, I'd already said too much about my . . . plans for Gary and myself, actually, not exactly plans but . . . thoughts . . . considerations."

"That's all they was, Sweetie, just thoughts," said Thelma.

"'Well, well, well,' said Dr. Digby, 'who'd have thought that the fascinating, attractive Ms. Budwieser would harbor such salacious thoughts in her pretty little head?' I didn't know what to say to *this* comment, either, except maybe to say sometimes I surprise even myself, which I didn't say, although it was getting to be true. I knew what *salacious* means, from working crosswords, that wasn't the problem, the problem was the way he said it, like he was actually *pleased* his dental assistant would be out on the loose, like a common criminal, harboring salacious thoughts for all those years. I didn't know what to say, so I started to rearrange the little pills of napkins, changing them from orange tree rows to the rows of graves they have in pictures of the Arlington Cemetery in our nation's capital."

"I don't mean to be picky," said Thelma, "but ain't it across the river from our nation's capital?"

"You're probably right. Anyway, he must not have liked the thought of graves, because the next thing was, he reached across the table and captured my small dental-assistant hands in his huge dentist paws. He said 'Let's not avoid the subject, shall we, what'd I tell you, the Ed problem is really the Mildred problem, when you scratch deep enough.' "

"You've got to admit he's got a point," said Thelma with a hint of sternness.

"Maybe so, maybe not, it doesn't really matter. Anyway, I thought to myself, so that's what he calls it, scratching deep. It used to be being supportive, now it's scratching deep. But I didn't say anything on either side of this issue, I figured it was his move, and besides, I have to confess I was getting to be kind of curious to see what was next on the menu."

"I have to admit I'm kind of curious myself," said Thelma.

"What was next on the menu happened below, under the table. His knee banged against my knees, first the left knee then the right, and it was clear that there wasn't room down there for all those knees in the same spot, so I moved my two knees apart. This was to make room for a much larger knee. In between the two original knees, in fact, which was a mistake. I like to admit my mistakes, I guess it was the way I was brought up."

"So was I, Sweetie," said Thelma. "So was I."

" 'Millie,' said Dr. Digby."

"Now's where it gets shameful. I just bet."

"Another mistake I had made was to forget to take my watch in for repairs, which meant I wasn't wearing it, which meant I couldn't point out to Dr. Digby that it was time for him to finish his fries so we could get back to the business at hand, which was Mrs. Bowager's root canal. This wasn't my mistake, though, it was Ed's, for buying the watch at a garage sale for our anniversary, not actually at the *exact* time of our anniversary, a week later, after I had reminded him that he had forgotten a very important milestone. Watches aren't the kind of thing you buy at garage sales, pant suits are, one of which I happened to be wearing at that particular time, which turned out to be no mistake, more like a stroke of luck, because of the huge dentist paws that suddenly showed up under the table."

"I could see it coming," said Thelma.

"'Millie,' he said."

"Watch out, he's getting familiar!"

"'Dr. Digby!' I said. It didn't matter that I said this quite loudly, because the lunch crowd had pretty much cleared out of there by that time. The only people left were a kid with pimples who was sweeping up gum wrappers and the counter girl who had pointed out that McDonald's didn't serve peanut-butter-and-jelly sandwiches and was now fascinated with the movement of the clock, and probably the cook in the back, and they were all too young to have lots of dental work done."

"That's one of the advantages of youth," reflected Thelma, age seventy.

"Millie,' said Dr. Digby, I've been meaning to say this for a long time. . . .' But I was losing my curiosity about what was next on the menu, I figured if he hadn't said it for a long time he could hold it for another long time, whatever it was—and I had a good idea about that—"

"So do I," said Thelma.

"Anyway, so I cut him short, I quickly stood up and scraped the little Arlington napkin pills into my hand and poured them into the plastic glass and went over to the waste bin and crammed all the leftover junk into it and high-tailed it back across the street to prep Mrs. Bowager for her root canal."

"That was close," said Thelma, breathing a sigh of disappointment. "More coffee?"

She poured herself more coffee.

"There's more," said Mildred, covering her cup.

"I was wondering if there wasn't," said Thelma, sitting up straight. "Then what happened?"

"Well . . . Dr. Digby was a little late getting back, which meant I was the one who had to be the good conversationalist and keep Mrs. Bowager's mind off the coming pain."

"You do that *so* well."

"Thank you, Thelma," she blushed.

"I mean it."

"Anyway," she continued, "he didn't come and he didn't come. Finally Mrs. Bowager looked out the window and said 'That's him, isn't it, that's Dr. Digby,' and sure enough, that was him, coming out of the liquor store across the street, catty-corner from McDonald's, carrying a sack."

"It's exactly what I was afraid of," said Thelma.

"'I hope . . .' said Mrs. Bowager, but I said 'Oh no, Mrs. Bowager, he's a good Christian and very responsible.' 'I realize that,' she said, 'that's why I trust myself to his care, but . . .' and I quickly came up with the thought that he's probably just buying some wine for Communion next Sunday, he's an elder or deacon or something like that, whatever it is his denomination has in the way of spiritual leadership. 'Maybe so,' she said. Maybe not, I thought, because what was on my mind was the fact that Dr. Digby and his lovely wife Carole are Baptists, which means for Communion they use grape juice, which isn't sold in liquor stores. But I didn't say anything to Mrs. Bowager about this, because she's an Episcopalian and belongs to the

Normandie Country Club and I didn't want to get into the subject of religious preference, it's not good business."

"There's times when you're better off just keeping quiet," observed Thelma.

"Anyway, Dr. Digby was late for the scheduled root canal, because he had to stop in the cubbyhole at the end of the hall to wash his hands and put on the rubber gloves he wears to keep the AIDS epidemic under control. While we were waiting, Mrs. Bowager said 'What's taking him so long?' Then she quickly said 'Tell me, Mrs. Budwieser, and this is strictly between the two of us, how painful are root canals, anyway?' I said 'He has to stop and wash his hands, and it isn't going to hurt.' "

"Not much, it ain't," said Thelma.

"Not much it ain't is right, that's exactly what *I* was thinking."

"They say great minds think alike," observed Thelma.

"Ain't that the truth," agreed Mildred. "Anyway, I went over to the cubbyhole to see what was taking so long, but he wasn't there. So then I went over to the TV room door, where Dr. Digby keeps up on the market averages between customers, and knocked. 'Who's there?' he said. 'Mildred,' I said, 'Millie.' He said 'I'm, ah, sorry about the little missed communication.' I said 'Those things happen between adults, are you all right?' He said 'One moment, one moment please,' and I opened the door a teensy crack and looked in, just in time to see him put the half-empty bottle into the little portable refrigerator, right next to the peanut-butter-and-jelly sandwich I should've had for lunch."

"So *that's* where he keeps the stuff," said Thelma.

" 'Berightthere, berightthere, berightthere,' he said."

"I just bet he'll be right there," said Thelma skeptically.

"Then you bet right, because next thing you know he was in there checking out the customer's mouth. 'Number 2,' I pointed out to him. 'Right,' he said, 'Number 2.' 'Is this going to hurt?'

said Mrs. Bowager. 'Just a little,' he said, 'not much.' '*How* much?' she said. 'It might cause just a little pain for a few days, that's all,' he said. 'Maybe I can come back later,' she said, 'when you're feeling better.' 'I'm feeling fine,' he said, 'finefinefine.' 'You're looking at the Number 13,' I said, 'you want the Number 2.' 'Number 2,' he said, 'gotcha.' 'It'd be no problem,' she said, 'really, I could come back later.'"

"Makes you wonder what's her all-fired hurry," said Thelma.

"'Open up,' he said, and she did and he stuck the needle in her mouth and slowly pulled the trigger. 'Number 2, shouldn't it be,' I said, and he said 'Right, Number 2, that's what I hit, right?' 'Wrong,' I said, 'you hit the Number 13.' 'Oops,' he said, 'sorry, let's try that again,' which he did, making another direct hit. 'I could come back later,' she said when he stood back to admire his work, 'really, it'd be no problem.' 'No no,' he said, 'everything's finefinefine, we'll have this little gem fixed up in no time, it won't hurt a bit, tomorrow you'll wake up with a brand spanking new gold tooth.' 'Gold tooth?!' said Mrs. Bowager, 'I thought I was in here for a root canal!'"

They laughed heartily.

"Ain't that rich!" said Thelma.

"And you haven't heard the half of it. Then he said 'If you're thinking about the cost, don't worry, I'll pay, it's the least I could do, after all these years.'"

There was another bout of laughter.

"'Dr. Digby!' I said, 'I think she's right about this being a root canal, we did the gold tooth this morning, Mr. Schutz, remember?' 'Right,' he said, 'Old Man Schutz, gold tooth, very pleased with it, wasn't he,' which was Mrs. Bowager's cue to spit blood into the bowl and excuse herself in the direction of the hairdresser."

"The hairdresser!" said Thelma, wiping tears from her eyes. "It's exactly what I was about to guess."

Mildred paused. "Say, don't you have to use the bathroom? Drain off some of that coffee?"

"Keep going, Sweetie. You know how well I hold my water."

"Well. . . . After Mrs. Bowager left, I went up to the front office and told Sue to reschedule Mrs. B and cancel all the appointments for the rest of the day. Then she could have the afternoon off, I told her, go shopping or something. She said 'Is something the matter, he was acting kind of strange?' I said 'He'll be all right, all he needs is a little consolation.' She said 'Can you handle that?' and I said 'As sure as my name is Mildred Budwieser.'"

"You didn't!" said Thelma.

"I have to admit I did," said Mildred proudly. "Well, Dr. Digby was laid out in the dentist's chair when I got back to him. 'Oh,' he said, 'what did I say, what did I say?' I said 'It's not necessarily what you *said*, it's what you *did*, you numbed her up good on both sides and tried to give her a free gold tooth.' 'Mildred,' he said, 'Millie . . . Millie.' I said 'Would you like a glass of water?' 'No,' he said, 'not . . . just . . . now.' I said 'Should I call Carole?' 'No no,' he said. I said 'Oh, what *am* I going to do with you, Dr. Digby?' He said 'You're going . . . to give me . . . a nice . . . long . . . backrub.'"

"Why am I not surprised?" said Thelma.

There was a long pause.

"Where do you keep the cold cream?" asked Mildred, suddenly guilt-stricken.

"In the top cupboard drawer, same as always."

Mildred got up and retrieved a jar of cold cream from the drawer and went over to the sink and began to wipe the mud pack off her face.

"Well, I work for the man, after all, and he was in pain, and he also had a lot on his mind, which he had started to tell me back at McDonald's. I know I shouldn't have regained my natural curiosity about what was on his mind, but I did, which is only natural, you have to admit."

"And I do, I do," said Thelma, showing concern and curiosity, half and half.

"I'm not saying I was attracted to the man—," said Mildred with her back to Thelma.

"Of course not," said Thelma.

"I'm saying sometimes when you get a chance to . . . be with a real man, not just somebody you have to be a reality principle for, somebody who lives with thoughts and fantasies, howsoever innocent and harmless . . . when you get a chance to grab the gusto, well. . . ."

"You know, I couldn't agree more," said Thelma, with mental reservations.

She hurried on. "Plus the fact that, when you've worked for somebody for all those thirty or whatever years and they offer to be supportive and buy you lunch and then they tell you they find you more attractive than their rather nice-looking wife, in fact *much* more attractive. . ."

She went over to the stove and put a tea kettle on and turned the burner on HIGH.

". . . well, you just naturally feel you maybe owe them something."

"When you put it that way," said Thelma, "I'd have to say I'd of done the same thing myself."

The tears began to flow down Mildred's face. "Not everything, of course, just a little consolation. . . . I could identify, too, that had a lot to do with it."

Thelma got up and put an arm around her distraught friend. "There, there, Sweetie," she said soothingly. "It's only natural."

"There's a big difference, of course, between having a youngish wife who's going through the big change and having an oldish husband who decides to move out to the Winnebago . . . actually, not a *big* difference, but a difference, you understand?"

"Oh, I see your point, I really do," said Thelma to her sobbing friend.

"The point is just that both the man whose wife is going through the change and the woman whose husband leaves her for a Winnebago . . . both of them deserve a little consolation, wouldn't you say?"

"I certainly would, Sweetie," said Thelma, "I certainly would."

Mildred stopped to compose herself.

"Anyway, that's what happened, the sharing of secrets and the backrub and etcetera etcetera, or maybe I should just say the secrets and the innocent old-fashioned backrub. . . ." She turned on the tap and washed her hands in the sink compulsively. "It really didn't get much farther than that—"

"Oh, I believe you," said Thelma. "And don't worry, I won't tell *any*body."

"And that's also *why* it happened, and I'm not a bit ashamed or anything, in fact if I had it to do all over again, I'd . . . I'd probably. . . ."

"You'd probably. . . ?"

Mildred walked over to the telephone and took the receiver off the hook and let it dangle.

"Well . . . to tell the truth, I don't know what exactly I'd do that was different . . . except. . . ."

"Except?" said Thelma, leaning forward.

"Except . . . maybe call Carole."

8

Thanksgiving

BUT DURING THE GREATER PART OF NOVEMBER, Carole Digby was to receive no call from Mildred Budwieser.

This does not mean that Mildred never reached for the phone. She did—many times. In fact, she actually dialed the Digby number on several occasions, during the periods she knew Doctor would be at church practicing with the Angelic Voices or at the meeting of his stockpicker club, the Raging Bulls. Once, she even stayed on the line long enough to hear Carole's three-syllable "Hel-lo-o," but then she reconsidered and quickly hung up and went into the bathroom and stood before the cracked mirror and rehearsed her speech just one more time.

Finally, on the Sunday before Thanksgiving, she had the speech polished and ready and spelled out in capital letters on a piece of scratch paper.

She skipped church that morning so she'd have plenty of time to make sure her lipstick wasn't too daring and her slip wasn't showing and she was doing the Christian thing. Then she waited till the football game was on and Dr. Digby would be glued to the set cheering for the Chiefs, who were on the verge of true greatness, in Doctor's opinion with a strong second from Ed. The Chiefs had been on the verge of true greatness for ten years, but this year was different, because they had drafted well and were only a quarter backer and a stiff end away from being right up there with the Broncos, who they were playing that day, and with the Forty Niners, who had beat them last week because of the disparity in the passing game, in Doctor's opinion but not Ed's.

First she looked up the Digby number to see if it had changed since yesterday.

Then she made herself a cup of strong coffee.

Then she dialed a wrong number.

Following this she looked up the Digby number again to see where she had gone wrong.

This time she dialed the right number. Doctor answered.

She hung up.

Then she had an idea. She went over and turned on the TV and sure enough, it was halftime and there were ads on the subject of getting rich by being bullish on America and then they were talking about the disparity in the passing game.

She waited till the game started again and the Chiefs fumbled the kickoff. Then she rechecked the Digby number, went into the bathroom to drain the decaf and check to see that the slip wasn't showing and ask herself if she was doing the right thing, the Christian thing, and came back and propped up the piece of scratch paper in front of her and picked up the receiver and jabbed at the redial button.

"Hel-lo-o," said Carole's attractive voice.

"WE'VE GOT TO TALK," she read into the phone.

"To who am I speaking?"

"THIS IS MILDRED BUDWIESER," she read. "I BEFORE E EXCEPT AFTER C."

"Mildred? Are you all right?"

"I THINK THERE ARE SOME THINGS YOU OUGHT TO KNOW," she read.

"What? Hold it a sec. Can you turn that damn thing down?" said Carole. She wasn't swearing at Mildred. She was swearing at a Chiefs fan.

"That's better," said Carole, referring to the noise level.

Mildred wasn't so sure about it being better. But she didn't say anything. It wasn't in her script.

"Now," said Carole, "what were you saying?"

Her eyes ranged down the page of her handwritten notes, looking for a sentence that would fit the situation.

"YOUR HUSBAND, MY BOSS, DR. DIGBY, TOOK ME OUT FOR A HAMBURGER." This sentence didn't fit the situation.

"WE TALKED ABOUT THE ED PROBLEM, WHICH TURNED OUT TO BE THE ~~MILDRED~~ ~~MILLIE~~ MILDRED PROBLEM ." This didn't fit, either.

"NOTHING, I REPEAT NOTHING, WAS SAID THAT WOULD REFLECT NEGATIVELY ON YOU, CAROLE." Neither did this.

"It was just an innocent peck on the cheek," she finally blurted out. This sentence was not in the script, and it didn't go to the root of the matter. It also wasn't completely accurate. But it seemed to fit the situation.

There was a long silence.

Carole was probably looking down the page of her own notes, she thought. That would explain the silence.

There was laughter in Carole's notes. Then, "Oh my God . . . oh my God."

More silence.

"Are you there?" asked Carole. "Mildred, are you there?"

"Y—yes."

“Is that what you called to tell me? It was just . . .” and Carole hushed it down to a whisper to keep it out of earshot of the Chiefs fan, “. . . it was just an innocent kiss?”

“It’s *one* of the things I had in my notes,” she said, getting bolder.

“Has Dan been . . . oh my God . . . is he up to his old . . . oh, *God*,” said the Baptist elder’s or deacon’s third wife, who was having a hard time finishing her sentences.

If Carole was having a hard time finishing her sentences, Mildred was having a hard time starting hers. This left Carole with the floor to herself.

“Listen, Honey,” said Carole, and she laughed again, “don’t take it so serious. You didn’t upset the balance of the universe.”

This was nice to know. She herself wouldn’t have put it that way, because she had never taken the night course in creative writing out at the University, though it was still nice to know that she, Mildred Budwieser, hadn’t upset the balance of the universe.

But she spent the next two days and nights trying to figure out who had.

§

The morning before Thanksgiving, Ed Budwieser woke up with a splitting headache. He’d had a rough night. Unable to find exactly the right word to begin Part II of his memoirs, he had gone to bed early. At one o’clock he got up and poured himself a glass of Liebfraumilch and waited for the flash of inspiration. At two o’clock he got up and poured himself another, just to help the Muse along. At three he got up to drain off the first two glasses and replace them with a like amount, still hoping it might prime the poetic pump. At four he got up again and decided to finish off the bottle.

Now he yawned and stretched and pounded his head with his fists. He looked out the window. What he saw was a grey November sky. Not a good day for the pizza business. So he climbed out of bed, put on his robe, sneaked into Mildred's house (forgetting it was already ten o'clock and she'd be at work), called his supervisor, and left a message on her answering machine. Then he returned to the Winnebago and climbed back into his bunk and tried to silence the anvil chorus that had taken up residence in his skull.

Late that afternoon he was awakened by the sound of the VW pulling into the driveway alongside the Winnebago. After giving his situation a great deal of thought, he got up, dressed, went outside and checked the antifreeze and windshield wipers, kicked the tires, came in and checked the refrigerator for food and drink, inspected his road maps, reached into his closet and retrieved his Ulysses costume—a pair of bell-bottoms and a Greek fisherman's cap—, put it on, and then embarked on a long and difficult journey.

He steered his ship in a westerly direction. But he was not setting sail for San Francisco and Cyrus. The object of his quest was none other than the former Dora Jiggers, now Dora Heedon (or so it was thought). She'd be somewhere out on the West Coast.

He had decided during his rough night that the rumor about Dora and Rev. Tad Heedon had been just that—a mere rumor. Hadn't Dave Jiggers once told Karen Ecclebury, who had told Mildred, that Dora had told him that all the loose talk about her so-called "affair" with Rev. Heedon was nothing but a false, malicious rumor, that she and Rev. Heedon were just good friends who happened to be in the habit of having coffee together two or three times a week, that the relationship was purely and solely Platonic, *absolutely* nothing more? And if Dora Jiggers said it was nothing more than a false, malicious rumor, you could take it to the bank, it had to be just that, a false, malicious rumor. . . .

He maneuvered his way through the middle of town, avoiding the main arteries and the rush-hour traffic.

He couldn't see how Dora, at forty-nine, would run off with a man half her age, give or take a few years. Hadn't she once hinted to him that she preferred older men? They'd been talking about Shakespeare's plays, he remembered. He'd been singing the praises of *Hamlet,* and she replied that she was beginning to prefer *King Lear*. He knew she wasn't referring to her husband Dave, either, because later in that same conversation she alluded to Dave in disparaging terms. What were the words she used? "That old fart"? No, the age difference alone was all the evidence he needed to disprove the totally preposterous theory that his Dora had run off with young Tad Heedon. . . .

The digital sign on the Kirkland State Bank building spelled out S-N-O-W W-A-R-N-I-N-G-S. But nobody ever paid attention to that sign. It was always wrong. Local DJs even had contests for the best jokes about its mistakes.

In fact, he couldn't see Dora Jiggers running off with *anyone* else, let alone a preacher who was half her age. He knew her well, very well indeed, and he just couldn't see it. After all, they'd been colleagues for, what was it? twenty-six years? Not just colleagues, either. Close friends. In fact *intimate* friends, with the same tastes, the same aspirations for Sunset High, the same appreciation for Hank Constant, the same delight in the Classics. . . .

He passed the Westside Shopping Mall.

He thought of the time Dora had come and sat down with him in the faculty lounge. And it wasn't just to talk about the curriculum. She had wanted to ask his opinion on an important matter—she probably wanted to know whether she should stick with Dave, or whether, if she left her husband, there would be someone else waiting for her . . . someone mature but not too old . . . someone wise but witty . . . someone with a masculine baritone voice and a deep love of the Romantics. But just then Gary came in and interrupted them and wanted to know if they'd seen today's "Doonesbury," so she never got to reveal to him what was on her mind. But he had a strong, undefined sense of what it was. . . .

He passed the sign bidding farewell to those leaving friendly Kirkland, "an All-American City," and inviting them to come back soon.

He remembered the time he had offered to drive her home. She accepted, and as they were driving along he managed to steer the conversation in the direction of the epidemic of divorces among the faculty at Sunset High. She sighed, as if she were trying to tell him something, and remained silent the rest of the trip. He stared straight ahead, equally silent, but through the corner of his eye he saw her glance up at him with what could only be interpreted as longing. And when they arrived at the Jiggers residence, what did she do? Instead of inviting him in to steal a few intimate moments before Dave got home, she quickly jumped out of the car. Afraid of her own passion, that's what she was. She walked quickly to the front door, but then turned around and waved goodbye to him—a hesitant move, but one filled with secret yearnings. . . .

He drove past the last gas station on the way out of town.

Dora Jiggers and Rev. Heedon? Run off together? They had to be kidding! You could take it from someone who knew, Dora had had chances before, and with a lot better than the callow Rev. Tad Heedon! And soon she'd have another chance. In two days he'd pull in to an isolated gas station somewhere in the middle of the Mojave Desert, would fill up at the single pump, would stride boldly yet cavalierly up to the cash register and indifferently plunk his credit card down on the counter, would glance at the attractive blonde standing next to him, languidly inspecting the turquoise jewelry; she'd glance up at him, and then, with surprise and joy in her glistening eyes, whisper his name. . . .

Five miles out from the last gas station, the Winnebago sputtered to a stop.

The one thing he'd forgotten to check was the gas gauge.

§

After the affair with her boss, which couldn't really be categorized as an affair, no matter what Thelma Blossum might have thought, it was more like a . . . a Christian act of charity, that's all it amounted to, and he wasn't just a boss, he was a . . . a friend in need. . . . After her Christian act of charity to a friend in need, that's exactly what it was, nothing more, it hadn't upset the balance of the universe, Mildred had gotten in the habit of taking walks in the evening. Not around the Kirklande Centre, with Thelma. Around the block, alone.

But as the weather grew colder, she had shortened her evening walks. Instead of going all the way around the block, she just walked around the Winnebago. She'd get into her white nightgown, the gift Ed had remembered to buy for their silver anniversary, and go outside and enjoy the moon, which was getting fuller and fuller, like it was ready to have a child. She circled the Winnebago, which usually had lights on but no sign of Ed, who was in his bunk bed reading books written by the wise men of the East who listed eight steps to putting the hurt behind you. Then she sat on one of the outdoor folding chairs and wondered why Ed always made everything so complicated, why he had to read books recommending eight *hard* steps when she herself could find books in the Barnes & Noble Relationships section that recommended four *easy* steps.

But he was an intellectual, that was his problem, that was *exactly* his problem. He was like Rev. Heedon, *Mr.* Heedon, in that respect. They tried to read too much into things. And see where it got them? What it got them was Budwieser's Folly and the loss of a nice young wife like Sue!

Then she'd go inside and climb into her own bed and close her eyes and pray to God, thanking Him that *she* wasn't responsible for upsetting the balance of the universe and asking Him to have pity on the poor intellectuals who were. But she couldn't sleep. She kept worrying about the balance of the universe being upset, and about Mabel, and about what was happening in her own life, all the changes, and about whether they traced back to Ed and the fact that she was trying to be his reality principle, which was her own theory, or to the so-called affair with her boss, which went against the way she had been brought up but was caused by her horoscope that day, which was Thelma's theory, or maybe even to the genes and the blood line, which is what Ed would say.

But on Thanksgiving Eve, when she came out of the front door of the Budwieser bungalow, wearing the white nightgown with her hair loose and ready to be blown by the wind that was bringing an early snow, and carrying an apple pie, one of Ed's favorite recipes, which flew in the face of Dr. Marliss Windell's advice about good riddance, the Winnebago was gone.

She walked around it anyway. Where it had been. Then she sat on one of the folding chairs in the falling and blowing snow and ate a piece of the pie.

It was so good she offered one to Ed.

§

Truckers hate snowbirds.

He'd forgotten that. He'd read an article on the life of the snowbird the last time he was in Dr. Wunder's office. But that was five years ago, back in the days when he hadn't even known what a snowbird was, and over a five-year time span you tend to forget such sentences as "Truckers and snowbirds are natural enemies" and "Truckers will stop and help stranded motorists, but not if they are driving RVs."

But now he remembered those sentences. He remembered them as the trucks came grinding along the road, ignoring the thumb with which he signaled them to stop to help a fellow traveler in his hour of need. He remembered them as he trudged the half-mile through the blowing snow to the mailbox he could just now dimly see at the top of the hill. He remembered them as his natural enemies the truckers roared past him, downshifting and coming too close and splashing cold dirty slush on his Ulysses bell-bottoms.

He'd also forgotten how fortunate he had always been to have Mildred along. She was a real trooper, and he thought of the times she drove back to the last service station to get help while he stood guard over the paralyzed Winnebago. And she did it without much complaining. The one thing he didn't appreciate about Dora, he now realized, was the bitching. Nothing seemed to suit her exactly. There was always something wrong with this, that, or the other thing. Not Mildred. That was one area in which she excelled. She had her drawbacks, of course, don't we all, but complaining wasn't one of them. She was a real sport. . . .

He finally got to the mailbox. It was covered with snow. He brushed off the snow and saw a name: J_sus _ernandez. He opened the box and reached inside and pulled something out. Nothing but a piece of cheap jewelry. A crucifix. Exactly what he needed, he thought with annoyance. He put the thing back in its snow-covered tomb and closed the tomb and looked around. Where was the nearby farmhouse he was expecting to find? All he could see was a long country lane leading through the falling and blowing snow to a distant clump of trees, probably hiding the living quarters of J_sus _ernandez and family.

He left the snow-covered mailbox and started walking up the lane toward the farmhouse.

J_sus _ernandez. When he got there, should he address him as "Señor *Fer*nandez" or "Señor *Her*nandez"? Maybe avoid the issue and simply call him "Jesus"? No, that sounded too sacrilegious. Why did they insist on naming half their sons "Jesus"? Pronounced "Hay-zoo," of course, to cover up the sacrilege. . . . Just last Easter, he'd played Jesus in the choir's pageant. That was Rev. Heedon's idea, but it met with popular approval among the Deuces. He wasn't wild about the thought, but Dora said, "You've played every other major character, why not give it a go as J.C.?" So he gave it a go as J.C., against his better judgment, and they strapped him on a home-made cross for twenty minutes, dressed in nothing but his boxer shorts and the white terry-cloth robe Mildred had bought at a garage sale. He felt like a fool up there, groaning and uttering one of the Seven Last Words every two minutes and forty-some seconds, right on Rev. Heedon's schedule. The worst part of it, though, was forgetting his line—he was about to speak the fourth of the Last Words when Mrs. Krzynzky's granddaughter ran out of the sanctuary screaming "Mister Stranger Danger!" No, playing Jesus certainly wasn't his favorite way to spend an Easter Sunday morning. Especially considering the fact that they'd just finished depositing Hank Constant in a plain old pine box six feet under, according to good old Hank's express wishes. . . .

He came to the end of the lane and found himself standing before the J_sus _ernandez farmhouse. It was a typical old Kansas farmstead, surrounded by agricultural implements of a bygone era: a rusty hay rake, a rusty hay mower, a rusty iron-wheeled Case tractor, and pieces of rusty equipment he couldn't identify. The house was apparently designed by the same architect who had conceived the cracker box. It had a sagging porch, it had narrow broken windows, its lightning rods were in sad repair. It looked as if it hadn't been painted since the Depression.

It was also deserted.

But this did not deter him. He mounted the front porch and broke down the door and went in and looked around. On the kitchen wall he found an ancient telephone. Good. He'd call 9-1-1. He lifted the antique earpiece from its cradle and turned the crank on the dusty box and put the piece to his ear.

No answer. Just a dead line. Damn!

He investigated the kitchen cupboards and drawers and found nothing but an old Sears and Roebuck Christmas catalogue, with half the pages missing. He paused and gazed out the broken window at the snowstorm. All he could see were the swirling gusts of white stuff. Nothing else. It was like he was at the edge of the world: he knew there was something out there beyond what he could see, but he had no idea what it could be.

Then a flock of wild geese caught his eye; they were waddling across the back yard. They kept turning their heads this way and that, as if they were looking for something or somebody. Looking for J_sus, probably. Or the _ernandez kids. They reminded him of children, the geese did. Always needed somebody to take care of them. Feed them. Or play games with them. Maybe tell them stories. Read them the Classics. Or take them home to their mamas and papas. That's what Mildred would say. The woman loved birds.

But he couldn't stay here and worry about the education of geese. He'd freeze to death. He'd just have to continue his long journey, going back to the highway and flagging a truck and making friends with a natural enemy.

He braced himself against the elements and went outside. The geese turned and waddled toward him. An attack? He quickly made a snowball and threw it at them. They honked indignantly and scattered.

Trudging along the country lane, he could now remember that line from the Seven Last Words of Christ: "My God, my God, why hast Thou forsaken me?" They seemed to have more meaning now, those Last Words, as he was fighting his way through this Antarctic blizzard. "Today thou shalt be with me in Paradise." Another Last Word, the second one. What Jesus had said to one of the thieves. Gary Leben played the thief. His—Ed's—idea: insurance salesman as thief. Paradise? That would be the West Coast. Gary Leben? With him? In California? Oh, hell. . . .

He finally got back to the J_sus _ernandez mailbox. It was open. He looked inside.

Nothing. Nichts. Nil. Zilch. Zero. Zip. Empty. The crucifix had disappeared.

He wearily sat down beside the empty box to rest, bundling himself up in his thin red coat and curling up on the ground and shutting his eyes, waiting for inspiration.

"It is finished," he was still able to think.

Jesus. Another dead white male. . . .

§

It was Thanksgiving Eve. She was in her dining room, alone. She was dressed in her Sunday best and was wearing an Easter bonnet. She was setting the table and talking to Thelma Blossum, her best friend, who was not there.

"You know," she said, starting with the plates, "we haven't had a really enjoyable Thanksgiving in a long time. Back in Baggs, we used to have one good Thanksgiving after another. We had lots to be thankful for. America. Freedom. Family. Baggs was in some respects a very stifling town, but you had to hand it to those folks, they knew what Thanksgiving was all about."

She went into the kitchen and came back with eight glasses.

"There's no use dwelling on the past, though. I'd like to go back to Baggs for one last Thanksgiving, I really would, but I guess it's just not going to happen. I was talking to Sue Heedon the other day about Thanksgiving, and how we used to celebrate it back in Baggs, and she agreed with me."

She did the knives. Blades facing in. But don't cut yourself. That was the rule for remembering which way the blades faced.

"'Those were the days,' Sue said. 'You can't go home again,' she said. 'That's true,' I said, 'you can't go home again.' I told her Mom passed away five years ago, and Dad's in an old folks home recovering from one of his strokes, so it just wouldn't be the same. My twin sister wouldn't be able to make it either, I'm afraid. It'd be a mistake to let Mabel out, she'd be a danger to herself. That's a secret, but I told her anyway."

Next came the spoons and forks.

"Ed and I have a lot to be thankful for. When you stop to think about it, we still have America, freedom, and family. If Ed would just come in from the Winnebago, things would be about perfect, just like back in Baggs. As a matter of fact, I think that's what I'll suggest. It'd be just what the doctor ordered."

Now, where would everybody sit? That was always the toughest part.

"I'll put Charisse and the kids on this side of the table. I'll suggest she bring along that nice young man she's been telling me about, I believe his name is Wesley Something, or maybe it's Something Wesley. She's left-handed, so she can sit on the far corner next to Ed. I'll put Wesley next to me, and I'll put the children in between them. I just hope Wesley's right-handed, like me. I'll have to remember to ask Charisse if he's right-handed. If he's not, maybe she could suggest another young man with family values, one who's right-handed."

She paused for further thought.

"I'll reserve that side of the table for Cyrus and his new wife. I'll put Cyrus next to Ed, even though they're both left-handed. Let's see. . . . I'll put his new wife next to me . . . no, that wouldn't work, she'll be right-handed. You should never seat a right-handed person at the left of a left-handed person. It's not normal. . . . On the other hand, maybe Cyrus has changed, maybe he's learned to eat right-handed. It'd certainly solve a lot of problems."

The doorbell rang.

"I guess I'll have to ask Ed to give the prayer. You're always taking a big chance when you have Ed give the prayer, because he never fails to use the occasion to complain about something or other. But he's the man of the house, and it's the duty of the man of the house to give the Thanksgiving prayer. I know what I'll do . . . I'll have him write it out beforehand and I'll edit it for him. That way we'll keep the complaints to a minimum, which will keep it short."

The doorbell rang again. She paused, then kept talking.

"It'll be nice to get to know Wesley and Cyrus's new wife. Felicia. That'll be her name. No—Felicia is Debbie's daughter. I'd forgotten about her. She'll be Monique. What a lovely name. Anyway, I can tell them all about growing up in western Kansas. I just hope Ed doesn't spoil it all by talking about poetry and reincarnation. That would be just like him, spoiling a perfectly good conversation by bringing up the subjects of his self-imposed exile and his past life as Shakespeare. Maybe I can have him promise to keep his ideas to himself. If that doesn't work, I'll just have Charisse and Cyrus help me keep the subject of conversation on an even keel. I'll suggest they tell stories from the Budwieser family tradition. Like the Christmas Charisse told Cyrus there wasn't really a Santa Claus, it was just their dad, and there wasn't really a Tooth Fairy, either, it was just their dear old mom, and Cyrus lit up like a Christmas tree and said, 'Okay, now, who's the Easter Bunny around here?' "

She stopped to smile at this memory.

"And if that doesn't work, we can always talk about the grandchildren."

Again, the doorbell. She continued to ignore it.

"After dinner, we can sit around and eat popcorn and watch 'Wheel of Fortune.' Charisse doesn't think it's the greatest idea in the world to have the kids watch the Wheel, but Ed and I think it's good for them. Ed thinks of it as an educational device, because it helps them know the difference between vowels and consonants. I think of it as teaching good shopping habits, because in the bonus round you notice the difference between frivolous stuff like Winnebagos and good old American cash."

By this time the ringing was non-stop. She finally went to the door and answered it. She put her hands to her face, horrified, and backed away from the real Thelma.

"You all right, Sweetie?" asked Thelma, coming inside.

"Is that you, Thelma?" she asked.

"Is something the matter?"

She began to cry. "Help," she said.

"Who . . . who should I call?"

"Get Ed," she said, "he'll know what to do."

"He's not out there," said Thelma. "The Winnebago's gone. That's why I came over, to find out the true story."

"Ed. . . ," she said.

"Should I call Rev. Gilltrip?"

"No," she insisted, "somebody like Rev. Gilltrip is to be called only in extreme situations. I am not an extreme situation."

"That leaves Dr. Digby."

"I hesitate to call . . . him," she broke down.

"We're about out of options," said Thelma. "What about . . . Dr. Rex?"

"Dr. Who?" she sniffled.

"Dr. Rex. You know, Mabel's doctor."

"Mabel's doctor?"

"Your sister Mabel's doctor." Thelma was talking into her ear. "Your twin sister Mabel." She was talking to her like she was an old lady. "The one who's a danger to herself." This was being said very loudly.

"Oh. . . ," she whispered, wiping her eyes. "Yes. . . ."

§

The day after Thanksgiving, one of the headlines on Page C5 of the *Kirkland Bugle* reported:

Motorist Rescues
Retired Teacher
from Blizzard

But the good Samaritan mentioned in the story was not identified, the Winnebago was mistaken for a delivery truck, and the reporter did not know the rule of I before E except after C. Nor was she aware of the importance of the "Mr. Edgar Budweiser, a longtime Kirkland resident," who had been rescued from the blizzard. She did not know that he was the leader of the local crusade for educational reform, that he was on an arduous pilgrimage, and that in a previous existence he had been the greatest writer of all time.

She did not know the true story. . . .

He heard the flashing lights and saw the siren. They reminded him of . . . no, they weren't like anything he'd ever seen or heard before.

"It's all a big mystery," said Ann.

Not so, my pretentious friend.

"I'd like to buy a vowel, Pat. I'd like to buy an A."

"We'll give you more than one A. We'll give you *three* A's."

"I'd like to solve the puzzle."

"Already?"

"AUTHOR OF FINNEGANS WAKE."

"I'm absolutely amazed. How did you *do* it?"

"Elementary, my dear Sajak."

"For an extra $500, to whom does that refer?"

"James Joyce, 1882-1941; Irish writer, noted for his mastery of the English language, major architect of the modern idiom; educated in Dublin, he repaired to the Continent in 1902, living there in self-imposed exile, returning only briefly to his homeland; author also of *Dubliners*, a collection of short stories that made a vital, some would say incomparable, contribution to that genre; of *A Portrait of the Artist as a Young Man*, a semi-autobiographical novel about his early years among the Jesuits; of *Chamber Music*, a collection of what must candidly be acknowledged as minor poems; of *Exiles*, an Ibsenesque play (seldom if ever performed) with scatological themes; of the redoubtable *Ulysses*, universally acknowledged as the greatest novel of the twentieth century; and of *Finnegans Wake*, the most obscure book since the *I Ching.*"

"Wow! You don't belong *here*, you belong on 'Jeopardy'!"

The straps were too tight.

He complained with an indication of his index finger.

They loosened them.

He calmly lit a cigarette and stared coldly into her guilty eyes. She stood there pleading with him—him, the man they called Buster. He abruptly flicked his smoldering Benson & Hedges into the raging river, turned brusquely, and nonchalantly walked away as she, the former Ms. Jiggers, wept bitterly and gnashed her teeth.

The ambulance door slammed shut.

"When you die, you die," said the wealthy life insurance agent.

Wrong again, Leben.

"I'd like to thank my late grandfather, the undiscovered genius, virtuoso, and Renaissance man Eduard Budwieser, who taught me all I know about life, and letters, and the vast potential of the human spirit. I believe I can say without fear of contradiction that had it not been for that great man's presence in my life, and the genetic potential he bore, I would not be standing before you here today, accepting this, the most illustrious and esteemed of all trophies, the Nobel Prize for Literature."

Sirens again. Also, lights.

A face.

"Would you happen to be the one who put a Help Wanted ad in my box?"

"Our manners, Ms. Mode. Let's remember our manners."

"*Sir*, would you happen to be the one who put a Help Wanted ad in my box?"

"That's better. I may very well have been that person. To which Help Wanted ad are you referring, young lady?"

"'Live-in care for elderly Christian woman. Room and board + $200 per mo. References.'"

"Ah, yes. I did indeed. It sounded like something quite in line with your aptitude."

"But I can also—"

"Will that be all?"

"One more thing, kind sir—"

"Yes? But be quick about it. I'm meeting the Secretary of Education in five minutes."

"I was just wondering if you'd be so kind as to consent to act as a reference?"

"Why yes, my dear young lady, I'd be happy to."

"Thank you very much, Sir."

"My pleasure."

He was on a long journey, a journey that would take him across many treacherous passes and turbulent torrents and perilous deserts, a journey that was fraught with danger, a journey at the end of which he could say. . . .

"Who's the stiff?"

"Oh, just some drunk they found in a ditch."

"Dead, is he?"

"I'd say he's got a little life left in 'im."

she was thinking about the person who always said that Mabel's condition traced all the way back to the bad genes. This was Ed.

"Where is he?" she finally got up the courage to ask. "Why doesn't he come visit me?"

"He?"

"Ed. My husband."

"Would you like to, hmp hmp hmp, explore your feelings about him?"

This sounded like a question, but it was really an order. She didn't say anything, just to see what would happen.

"How do you feel about your husband?" he repeated.

She didn't say anything again. She was thinking maybe it was a trap.

"Affection? . . . Love? . . . Anger? . . . Hostility, perhaps?"

Oh. It wasn't a trap after all. It was a multiple-choice exam. "Anger?" she guessed.

He smiled at her.

She'd gotten the correct answer! She smiled right back at him.

"Anything else?" he asked.

She was about to say Love? but then she decided to play it safe. She was already one for one, and she didn't want to ruin her record. So she shook her head No.

He patted her hand. "We're making progress," he said, smiling again. Then he looked at his watch and got up and started to leave.

"What about Ed?" she reminded him.

"Ed?"

"My husband."

"Oh. Ed."

"Where is he?"

9

The Noble Truth of the Cause of Pain

"WHY AM I HERE?" she asked him for the dozenth time.

"Don't worry," he kept saying.

"Things will turn out fine," he kept saying.

"Get lots of rest," he kept saying.

But how did he expect her to get lots of rest when he wouldn't tell her why she was there?

"Think of me as your friend."

He said this over and over. It was his favorite sentence.

She finally asked him, maybe a little sharply, "Aren't I paying you for this?"

He cleared his throat, hmp hmp hmp. "Yes you are," he said. "You, and the insurance company."

She thought about this. She, and the insurance company. Who had paid for that insurance, anyway? *She* had. Not directly, maybe, but it was part of the benefits package Dr. Digby offered.

So, putting two and two together, she was paying for *all* of it. Which meant: if Dr. Rex was her friend, and she was paying him for it, then what it amounted to was Hire-a-Friend. Which was exactly what she told him.

"Hmp hmp hmp," he said. "Would you like to talk about it?"

"I thought the best things in life were supposed to be free," she went on. "Isn't that what the Bible says?"

"Is the, hmp hmp hmp, fee a problem?"

And what was she supposed to say? She had been brought up right. You never discussed the fee, you didn't let people know that the fee was *always* a problem.

"Do you have a first name?" she wondered. "If you're going to be my hired friend, I want to know your first name."

"Hmp hmp hmp, Dr. Rex will do just fine."

"Is that what your wife calls you? Dr. Rex?"

He hmpped his throat and stood up and went over and looked out the window.

Had she said something wrong? Maybe he didn't have a wife. Or maybe he had a wife but was separated from her. That was probably it, they were married but separated. So she began to think of him as Edward. Ed for short. Like her husband.

"The bars. . . ," she said one day. She was referring to the bars on the windows. They were ruining her view of the trees and garden.

"They're there for your own, hmp hmp, protection," he said. "Do they bother you?"

Of course they bothered her. But she didn't let on. She told him they made her think of Mabel.

"Hmp hmp hmp," said Dr. Rex, and there was a long silence. The mention of Mabel probably made him think of his wife, and

"Your husband is, hmp hmp hmp, getting a little rest of his own." He had his back to her when he said this, and he was looking at his watch again.

"Why, what's the problem?"

"Hmp hmp hmp, just a minor temporary setback, hmp hmp hmp, he'll be up and about in no time, no time at all."

She didn't believe it. All the throat-clearing plus not being able to face her plus the repeating of "no time, no time at all"—these were all dead give-aways.

"Is that its real name? Loony Manor?" She already knew the answer. She was just being a good conversationalist.

"Hmp hmp, it's Lune*berger* Manor, if you please."

"What a lovely name," she said. This was a lie. The name *Luneberger* made her think of hamburger, and *hamburger* was not a lovely name. But they said the way to get him on your side was to humor him. That way he'd recommend you get out early.

Then she stopped to think: why did she want to get out early if Ed was getting some rest of his own?

"Why am I here?" she kept asking him.

"Let's talk about it, shall we," he usually said. He didn't ask it, he said it. That's exactly what Ed would notice. Ed used to point out when people made errors in grammar.

But other times Doctor would say, "You're the expert," and then smile mysteriously. Which sounded like an invitation for her to ask him about *his* problems. But it really wasn't. The smile just proved that what he was saying was, he didn't know the answer either.

"I'm your friend," he kept saying.

This was getting on her nerves.

She finally thought to ask, "Are you Mabel's friend, too?"

"Hmp hmp hmp, why, of course."

She didn't say anything. Instead, she got up from her seat and went over to the window and looked out through the bars at the bare trees and the snow on the ground. It was her way of saying if Dr. Ed was Mabel's friend, why was Mabel still cooped up in Loony Manor, why wasn't she getting any better? And if both she and Mabel were still cooped up, why were they paying him? Why weren't they getting their money's worth?

It was something she'd been worrying about for days.

§

"I don't know why they put me here," she said to Thelma.

They were sitting across a table from each other in the visitor's room. It was early in spring, and Dr. Rex had said she was now well enough to have visitors. The first person she called with this news was Thelma, who came right over for the chance to be Visitor Number One.

"There, there, Sweetie," Thelma said soothingly. "I'm sure it's related to your . . . you know. . . ."

"My. . . ?"

"Your. . . ." Thelma tried to finish the sentence with her hands. *Affair* was the word she was looking for.

"Oh," she said, "I feel *so* guilty."

"But it wasn't your fault," Thelma quickly consoled her. "Your horoscope for that day predicted it. 'A tall handsome man will come into your life.' That's what it predicted, and that's exactly what happened. Which means you can't be held personally responsible."

"Then why do I *feel* guilty?"

"It's not guilt," explained Thelma, "it's stress."

She thought about this for a minute. Yes, she *had* been under a lot of stress lately.

Thelma reached into her purse. She pulled out a pencil and notebook, and then she pulled out a yellowed old newspaper clipping. "Would you like to see exactly how much stress?" She looked closely at the clipping. "There's ninety-one points for—"

"Points?"

"Anxiety points," explained Thelma. "It's the scientific way of measuring your stress level. They give you ninety-one points for a divorce, plus—"

"But I'm not divorced. I'm only separated."

"It's practically the same thing, Sweetie, but if you want to be picky we can cut it down to eighty points. That would be fair, wouldn't it, eighty points? You also get sixty-eight points for retirement, plus—"

"Wait a minute," she said. "Retirement? I'm not retired."

"Look at it this way," said her best friend. "Do you think Dr. Digby is gonna take you back? If and when you get out of here?"

"Well, I hadn't really thought about—"

"Tell you what," interrupted Thelma. "If it makes you feel better, we'll cut those retirement points in half, which comes to thirty-four points, just for worrying about it." Thelma was writing all the figures down. "And if your spouse stops working, you get fifty-eight points."

She got up from her chair, walked around the table, and stood behind Thelma. She was starting to get interested in the subject of anxiety points.

"And if this was Christmas we'd give you fifty-six points, but since it's only St. Patrick's Day and it's not even here yet, we'll just make it twenty-five. And of course they put you in here on Thanksgiving, which is also a holiday, so we'll give you another twenty-five. Isn't that fair, twenty-five points in honor of the Pilgrims?"

"I was kind of hoping for thirty."

"Don't worry, we can make it up on the next category, which is sex difficulties, on account of the sleeping arrangements. We'll let you have the full fifty-three points on—"

"Is that all?" she broke in. "Just fifty-three points? It seems like at least a hundred." She leaned over, adjusted her bifocals, and looked at Thelma's calculations.

"Sorry, Sweetie, we gotta go by the book. The full fifty-three points, even though it's really Ed's fault."

"I thought it was mostly the horoscope's fault?"

"That don't get Ed off the hook," said Thelma. "Plus you get forty-five points on account of Dr. Digby, they've got a category here called 'trouble with the boss'."

"So what's my final score?"

"Let's not get in a hurry, Sweetie, there's another fifty-six points for change in health of a family member—. . . ." And right away you could tell, there was an awareness of a mistake having been made.

"Change in health?" she said. "*Which* family member?"

"Oh no," said Thelma, putting her hand to her mouth. "I wasn't supposed to say."

She returned to her own side of the table and confronted Thelma. "*Which* family member?"

"I was sworn to secrecy."

"Ed?"

"My lips are sealed."

"It's Ed, isn't it?"

"You didn't hear it from Thelma," said Thelma.

"He's sick, isn't he?"

"Now don't worry yourself, Sweetie. Them miracle drugs is working just fine."

"Oh no," she said, putting her face in her hands.

"Look at it this way, Sweetie," Thelma consoled her. "You get fifty-six points for him being sick. Which gives you a grand total of, let's see, four plus eight plus five plus five plus three plus five plus six, which comes to thirty-six, put down six and carry three, plus eight plus three, mmm, mmm, mmm, mmm, mmm, mmm, coming to a grand total of three hundred and seventy-six points."

"Is that above average?"

"It's over the top," reported Thelma. "It'd be the same thing as . . . well, let's just say if you was married to three and a half spouses and they all up and died at the same time."

"Ed," she said, mostly to herself. "I should've figured it out."

"There there, Sweetie, how could you possibly of known?"

"Still, I feel so guilty."

Thelma checked her clipping carefully. "Hmmm," she said, shaking her head. "There's no mention of guilt."

§

"Why am I here?" she asked Rev. Gilltrip.

She thought maybe he'd have an answer to this question, because just a minute ago he had an answer to why Dr. Rex couldn't answer the question. The answer being, because Dr. Rex was missing the dimension of the Transcendent.

Rev. Gilltrip leaned forward and looked her directly in the eye. "Have you done something . . . bad?"

She looked him directly in the hands.

"Are we hiding something, Mildred?" he asked softly.

She coughed.

"Some . . . secret?"

Who had been telling on her? She got out a handkerchief and blew her nose.

"Some . . . sin, maybe?"

That darned Thelma!

"Would you like to make a confession?" he said with a kind voice.

She'd never confide in Thelma again. In fact, when she got out, she'd get even. She'd tell everybody Thelma's oldest and deepest secret, about Lee Roy's sex difficulties.

"It'll be just between the two of us."

She cleared her throat.

"Confession is good for the soul."

She'd heard that idea before. Was it really true?

He smiled at her in a non-threatening way.

She broke down and started to tell Rev. Gilltrip about her . . . her. . . .

"Is *affair* the word you want?" asked Rev. Gilltrip gently.

"I was looking for the word *dalliance*," she said between sniffles.

He frowned. He probably didn't believe she knew such a sophisticated word.

"I know that word from crosswords," she explained.

"Would you want to tell me about your . . . dalliance?" He kept staring at her, like he was reading between the lines. So she told him the whole story, from beginning to end. Except that she left out the part about what happened after she finished giving Dr. Digby the backrub.

He just sat back and listened. He did it in a kindly fashion. It was almost like he actually *approved* of a person having a dalliance. Or maybe he just enjoyed the story.

"Is that all?" he said after she had finished.

She peeked up at him. He was smiling. He was on her side!

"How's Ed coming?" she got up the nerve to ask.

"Ed?" he said. He was probably wanting to hear more about the dalliance.

"Ed, yes," she said. "How's he coming? Nobody seems to know."

"He's . . . resting comfortably."

Then he took her hands between his paws and squeezed them. Almost like the way Dr. Digby had done. Except that Rev. Gilltrip didn't suggest they should call each other by their Christian names. Or make a comment about her fascinating teeth. Plus, his hands weren't as big. They were more like Thelma's, soft and old, with veins showing through, and liver spots.

He suddenly stood up.

"Oh, you're not leaving me now, are you, Reverend?" she said. She meant it, too. She wanted him to stay and explain the words *resting comfortably*.

"I have to go now," he said nervously. "There are others in my flock."

"Others? flock?" What did that make *her*?

But he didn't answer. He was already gone.

She went to the bathroom and tried to pee, but nothing came.

As she was sitting there, she decided she'd go directly to the source for more information. She'd ask God about Ed. Not right there, of course.

She went to her room and tried to pray, but nothing came.

She was sure this failure had nothing to do with sin—she had already confessed her secret to the good Reverend, and hadn't he recommended that confession was good for the soul? Besides, she couldn't remember dalliance being categorized as a sin.

No, the failure was probably stress-related.

§

She told Dr. Rex about Dr. Mrs. Marliss Windell, Ph.D., and about journaling.

He smiled and asked her if that had been helpful.

She smiled and nodded and said yes, oh yes, it had been very helpful.

It hadn't really been that helpful. It had also brought back some painful memories. But talking to Dr. Rex was getting to be frustrating, because she never knew where he wanted her to take the conversation. This was why she had come up with the idea of going back to journaling, thinking maybe he'd leave her alone to write instead of always pestering her by making her guess what he was driving at. Besides, she was getting tired of sitting around and visiting with the other patients.

They were all weird, the other patients. Or just plain crazy. What stuck out in her mind was the conversation she had at supper with a former jockey named Zero, who leaned over to her and said did she want to know what happened to Champ's wife, pointing to Champ, a former boxer; he killed her, he said, that's what happened to her. How? she wanted to know. Hatchet, he said, very very gory; right through the skull, he added, giving a demonstration on himself with his table knife.

Dr. Rex went along with her journaling suggestion. He had them give her an old typewriter and a supply of paper.

Next afternoon she wrote:

Good Friday

Dear Journal,

Carole Digby came by to see me this morning. She just happened to be in the neighborhood, she said, and she suddenly had the idea, why not go see dear old Mildred, find out how she's coming?

Dear old Mildred suggested a walk in the garden. That's exactly what she was going to suggest, Carole said, a nice Spring morning like this shouldn't be wasted indoors. Also, she whispered, less prying ears out there.

We walked along the garden path and talked about the hyacinths and the hollyhocks, how well they were doing as compared to last year. We talked about recipes for apple pie. She puts in less cinnamon than I, that's because Dr. Digby has an ulcer which reacts negatively to too much cinnamon, and with the amount of pie he eats it can be a cause for concern. Another difference is, our recipes for crusts. She uses her mother's old recipe, but I use Betty Crocker's recipe, because of the extra flakiness, which is always a big hit when I serve it to the Deuces.

We got to the end of the path and talked about the new zoo, which is right across from Luneberger Manor, in fact you can see it through the trees. Isn't it nice, she said, and I agreed, except that in my opinion it's a waste of taxpayers' money. That's not what I told her, though, I just said my favorite animal was the elephant. Hers was the tiger, it reminded her of Robert Redford, but elephants reminded her of fat men. We both laughed, thinking of our husbands in comparison to Robert Redford. Then we sat down on the bench and went through the list of animals and gave them grades on a scale of 1 to 10. We both ranked giraffes high. Nines. Ostriches were sixes: nice eggs and interesting to watch when they walk, but lacking in a sense of reality. Peacocks were overrated, we agreed, threes or fours at the most. Monkeys and baboons were twos: cute, but they had bad habits and pink behinds, plus absolutely no sense of shame. Cows were zeroes. We were both of one mind on the subject of having cows in a zoo in the middle of Kansas. Just what's the point? I said, and she agreed, she threw up her lovely hands and said what's the point? What's the news about Ed? I said, but she wasn't through with the ranking of animals. She hated crows, she said, didn't I hate crows? Yes, I said, now what about Ed, they never talk about him, they always change the subject when his name is brought up. Kangaroos! she said. Did you know they're the same as wallabees? Practically the same, anyway, did you happen to know that? No I didn't, I said, and speaking of Ed, how's he, but she didn't let me finish my sentence, she put her face in her hands and broke down in tears and said we're getting a divorce.

So that explains it, I thought to myself, that's why she came all the way out to visit me. It had nothing to do with dear old Mildred and how she's doing, it had to do with the breakup of a marriage. His third. Her second, that's not counting the annulment.

She told me all about it, starting with her getting suspicious when Sue Heedon started driving around in a brand new BMW. How does a woman of her background and tastes suddenly develop a fondness for expensive German cars? is how she put it to herself. And how does a woman in her financial situation suddenly come up with the wherewithal to afford one? Number one, she's divorcing a man who's not going to be good for one red cent of alimony, being an ex-minister living God knows where, and number two, her only visible means of support is a teensy-weensy dental receptionist wage, and she put her thumb and finger apart about the width of her cigarette to show the size of the salary. So she confronted the good doctor, Carole did, and asked him those exact same questions. She said explain! He said we've got to talk.

That's the short version. The long version must have taken over an hour and yielded five gallons of tears and finally arrived at the conclusion that all men are basically alike, who needs them? I agreed, except that I pointed out some of the differences in men, such as that Ed always liked to dress up in costumes, which Dr. Digby never did. No, she said, Dan liked to dress down, and we both laughed. Also, I pointed out, the only way Ed ever cheated on me was in his mind, while Dr. Digby really cheated on her. Yes, she said, that he did, and if Dan had just stuck to what was in his imagination, and she let the sentence dangle. I finished it for her, in my mind. If he'd just stuck to what was in his imagination, maybe I wouldn't be here. Maybe that's what she was thinking and was too polite to say.

Then we got around to comparing ourselves. One difference is our age, except that I was surprised that Carole is fifty-four, even though she doesn't look a day over forty. Which is what I told her, meaning it as a compliment, but she said look again, and she pointed out the fact of two face lifts and the wonders of modern chemistry, referring to the color of her hair, which is auburn. Another difference is how we dress. We both wear pants, except that I wear pant suits and she has a preference for harem pants, which is what she was wearing today. I wouldn't have guessed what they were, but that's what she told me: these are harem pants, she said. I said I thought harem pants were out of style, but she winked and said harem pants are never out of style.

Difference number three is grandchildren. Carole doesn't have grandchildren, in fact she told me she's never even had children because she had a hard time getting pregnant, and when she was finally successful there was that first divorce, so she opted for termination. I guess I'd have to say it was a good thing, although I'm basically pro-life. When there's a divorce it's always better if there's no children involved. Plus the fact that Carole pointed out that if you believe in reincarnation it's okay to have a termination, which is her word for abortion. She explained that if you send them back to where they came from, the little tads will simply get another chance to be born, they'll just get recycled into another mother, who'll probably be more loving anyway. Stop to think about it, she said, it makes perfectly good sense. Which it does, if those happen to be your beliefs.

This got us off on the subject of reincarnation. Carole said she visited a psychic, and he told her she used to be the top dancing girl in Buddha's harem! That explains why she used to put up with Dr. Digby's sexual shenanigans, she said, she had figured if she could handle being in Buddha's harem in the 5th century B.C. she could handle being in Dr. Digby's now. It also explains the harem pants, she said, and besides, men found them very attractive, wink wink. The problem was, she went on, Dr. Digby now wanted a divorce, which was going to leave her without the wherewithal to live the way she had grown accustomed to, because she'd have to split the alimony with the two other exes. She said there weren't enough rotten teeth in the whole city of Kirkland to keep Dr. Digby's exes fed and clothed and housed and running around in expensive German cars.

Then all of a sudden she said she'd been going on and on about herself, I should tell her about myself. I'd like to know why I'm here, I said, do you have any idea? She thought for a minute and then said she was sure it could be explained in terms of my past life. I told her I didn't think I had a past life, all I could recall was being dear old Mildred. She said of course I couldn't recall, I needed her psychic to help me explore the vast resources of my memory. Those were her exact same words, "vast resources of your memory." Then I wanted to know if seeing a psychic would cause any psychic pain. She said not to speak of, just a teensy little trauma due to the shock of recognition of seeing your past life running before you like a television program without the ads, but the trauma was worth it because of the wisdom and self-understanding you gain. I said no thanks, I don't believe in reincarnation, I believe in the resurrection of the body, being a Christian. To each his or her own, she said, and then she dove into her purse and came up with a fancy checkbook and wrote down her new telephone number on the back and said that if I changed my mind about consulting her psychic I should give her a ring. Then she thanked me very much, she was sure I could identify, that's why she'd come all the way out to see me, and then she hugged me and went back to her new apartment.

But she forgot to tell me about Ed, and of course I didn't think it'd be polite to keep asking. She had other things on her mind than somebody else's sick husband.

Mildred B.

§

Why was she there?

This question kept her awake most of that night.

Dr. Rex didn't seem to know the answer. That was because he was missing the dimension of the Transcendent. Whatever that meant. . . . Maybe Thelma was right, the reason she was in Loony Manor was on account of her way-above-average stress level? But of course she couldn't be held responsible, because it was the horoscope that made the tall handsome man come into her life. . . . But how could that be? Hadn't Dr. Digby already been in her life? And was he really as handsome as all that? Better looking than Ed, maybe, but not even in the same ball park as Robert Redford, in terms of good looks. Besides, what about her guilt feelings? If she couldn't be held responsible, why did she feel so bad about it? . . . No, that couldn't be it. She couldn't argue with the high stress level, she was sure it was a new world record. It was the horoscope part, the part about not being guilty, that didn't make any sense. . . . Rev. Gilltrip was right, then. She was there as a punishment for her sin. Which meant she was guilty. Even though she had done exactly what Rev. Heedon recommended in terms of doing what felt good. Which of course was absolutely no excuse. . . .

She imagined herself at the Last Judgment, hoping to pick up a new resurrection body. She was standing in line with all the other big sinners, listening to God hand out His verdicts.

"Let's see," He said to a shaggy-headed artist, "aren't you the guy who spent the taxpayers' money painting pictures of My Son swimming in pee?"

"Uh. . . ."

"And what do you have to say for yourself?"

"It felt good, so I did it."

"Didn't you stop to think maybe it was sacrilegious?"

"It depends on your personal point of view."

"What about MY personal point of view, was that ever taken into consideration?"

"I thought You might appreciate it. It's creative art and You're a creative artist, and besides, it all depends on how you interpret it."

"And how do *you* interpret it?"

"Swimming in pee is a symbol, it stands for something else."

"For what, may I ask?"

"Uh . . . for walking on water."

"Guilty!"

"Oh please, please."

"Next."

The man ahead of her was somebody who'd had an alternative lifestyle.

"Explain that," He said.

"It felt good, so I did it."

"Didn't you ever read the Bible? My Holy Word?"

"It's nothing but a bunch of myths and fairy tales. Besides, it was written in the olden days, so it's irrelevant."

"Here it is, Romans something, 'Thou shalt not have vile affections,' which means exactly what it says."

"I can't help it, it's genetic, ten percent of the population was born that way."

"So what it comes down to is, you blame Me."

"That's one way to look at it."

"Guilty!"

"Oh please, please, I admit it wasn't Your fault, it was a matter of choice."

"Too late. Next."

It was her turn.

He looked sternly down on her. "Let's see," He said with a big frown, "what does this big A stand for, in the record?"

"Big A?"

"There's an big A here in your personal file. What does it stand for?"

"Uh . . . probably . . . adultery."

"Adultery, huh? How do you explain *that*?"

"It felt good, so I did it."

"What about the Ten Commandments?"

"What about the Eleventh?"

"I don't remember giving out eleven commandments."

"It's in there someplace, just look it up."

"Who do you think you're talking to, anyway? I'm the Person who wrote them."

"I guess you're right."

"You *guess* I'm right! Didn't you ever listen in church?"

"Well . . . I had other things on my mind."

"Such as?"

". . . The roast in the oven?"

"The roast in the oven!"

"If the sermon gets too long, the roast'll burn."

"You're more worried about a burnt roast than about burning in hell?"

"Not burning the roast is listed as one of the ten recommended ways to keep your husband happy."

"Recommended! By who?"

"By *Good Housekeeping.*"

"*Good Housekeeping!* What about the Bible?"

"It's Your Holy Word, of course."

"Well I should think so!"

"But it's a little weak in one area."

"Weak in one area?"

"It doesn't say anything about keeping your husband happy."

"Guilty!"

"Oh please, please, I'll behave better next time."

"There'll be no next time. Next."

But maybe that was going too far. Maybe that was being way too judgmental. Because if she promised to behave better next time, shouldn't God give her another chance? Isn't that what the Bible emphasized, the Almighty being a God of mercy? And how could a God of mercy send her to hell without giving her a second chance? No, that's not why she was there. It wasn't the sin, it had to be something else.

Well, then. Carole Digby must be right. The reason she was cooped up in that institution had to do with something in her past life. She couldn't remember what it was, but Carole had pointed out that of course she couldn't remember, she needed a psychic to help her.

But if she'd already had a past life, that meant there was reincarnation. And Rev. Gilltrip had pointed out to Ed that reincarnation was not a Christian doctrine. So if she was a Christian, then how could she have been reincarnated? No, it just didn't square with her fundamental beliefs, this idea that she'd had a past life. . . . On the other hand, Ed had been brought up as a Christian, and he believed in reincarnation. She just wished he was there right then, Ed was, and they could talk about reincarnation and whether or not it fit into Christian beliefs, and he could explain that it was all right to learn about your past life from a psychic, if the fee was reasonable. But of course he wasn't there, in fact she didn't know where in God's creation he was, nobody seemed to want to discuss the subject, which probably meant. . . .

What it all came down to was, she was on her own. Dr. Rex was right on one point. She was the only expert on her own life.

Early next morning, she gave Carole Digby a ring.

§

Good Saturday

Dear Journal,

I just got through talking to Carole.

She has a plan.

(1) Tonight she's going to bake a cake with a file in it. (2) Then she's going to bring it to me tomorrow, which is Easter Sunday, when everybody's busy having their families visiting and lying to them about how good they look. (3) I'm going to eat the cake, except for the file. (4) Then I'm going to cut off the bars with the file and escape through the window using my bedsheets for a rope.

That's her plan, in four easy steps.

Now, if I can only remember them!

M. B.

10

Signs of the End

HE WAS ON HIS BACK. They were attaching apparatus to him. Running tubes up his nose. Thrusting needles into the veins of his arms. Invading the privacy of his person.

A breast leaned over him. It brushed up against his rib cage with its soft white roundness.

He divided the distance between his eyes and his toes and waited, hoping for a sign of life.

Nothing. Just a vague urge. Memories of happier times.

"Something . . . wrong?" he was able to murmur.

"Shhh," she whispered.

"Don't worry," she whispered.

"Relax," she said gently. "Get lots of rest."

"What. . . ?"

"Just a little accident," she said soothingly.

"How . . . Why. . . ?"

"A little bit too much wine."

The room was floating in a cloud of white. There was a white ceiling. White walls. White paraphernalia hanging here, there. White sheets, white pillow. White nurses in white costumes, white shoes, white stockings. A white curtain. And now a white doctor. Grey hair, grey beard, but a white face and white frock.

In this strange new world, white was clearly the color of choice.

Doctor separated his eyelids with well-manicured fingers and shone a dazzling white light into his eyes. First the right one, then the left.

"Hmmm," said Doctor.

Meaning what? Lucid? Extraordinary?

A thought fluttered through the white clouds and landed at the tip of his mind. Maybe he should follow the lead of Einstein? Donate his brain for medical research? He could envision an article in *Scientific American*: "Genius: Scientific versus Literary."

Gary suddenly appeared in this new white life. Gary Leben. The Ace of Spades. His friend, author of the opinion, "When you die, you die," was sitting on a chair at the foot of his bed. Smiling. Being cheerful. Asking when they were going to let him out of this godforsaken place. Also, asking whether he recalled this or that role he'd played in some distant past. Hamlet? King Lear? Julius Caesar? Romeo? Chichikov?

Yes. . . . Yes. . . . Yes. . . . Of course. . . . Who was Chichikov?

"Remember? The Russian guy? The scam artist? Went around buying dead souls?"

"Oh." He thought about the question of dead souls for a while. Then he shook his head. "You lose track of time," he apologized.

"It's the drugs," Gary explained.

The drugs. He hadn't thought of it in that way. He'd thought it was because a new Ed Budwieser was taking shape, right before his very eyes. That's how he'd been explaining all these . . . changes. The loss of a sense of time. The feeling of being disconnected from ordinary things. The strange way the world was looking at him. Like the time he showed up in Sunday School dressed as . . . oh yes.

"The Ghost of Christmas Past," he murmured. "I remember playing that."

"We'll have you up and playing Christmas Future in no time," predicted Gary, slapping him playfully on the leg. Then he winked. "That is, if we can pull you away from the nurses."

"Right," he sighed.

Gary was getting up to leave.

"Oh, by the way," said his friend with a stiff laugh, "Ann sends her greetings. 'Tell old Ed to hang in there,' she says."

"Right."

Gary was edging toward the door.

"We're gonna beat this, old buddy," he heard his friend say from a distance. "I just *know* it."

"Right."

"With those miracle drugs. . . ."

Then Gary left, taking the rest of the sentence with him.

Karen was there. Karen Ecclebury. Mark's wife, the staunch believer in immortality—or whatever—through grandchildren, was perched on the guest chair, clasping her purse tightly to her bosom, preparing to perform her and Mark's Christian duty.

"Has Mildred been to see me?" he asked. It seemed like a good question to get the ball rolling. Logical, too. He couldn't recall having seen Mildred's among the many faces.

"You're separated, remember?"

"Right. . . . I need to talk to her." To settle the question of who's to blame for this or that particular, etc.

"Well, actually, she's been pretty busy lately."

"Busy? . . . Oh yeah. Teeth."

"Actually, not teeth so much as. . . ."

"Sure. I understand. Mabel's going downhill, right?"

"Well, actually . . . right. Mildred *has* been spending a lot of time in Loony Manor. Now that you mention it."

"Oh."

"Actually, that's why she hasn't been in to see you."

"I see."

"She's been pretty busy lately."

"Sure. It's not teeth-related, though."

"No, it's more . . . Mabel-related."

"Yeah."

"She's been spending a lot of time in Loony Manor."

"Right."

"A *lot* of time."

"You mentioned that."

"Plus the fact that you're separated, and everything. . . ."

He reached over and spit a substantial amount of lung-related unpleasantness into the bedside container. "Actually," he tried to joke, "that was blown out of proportion by the media."

Karen got up to leave.

"Oh, by the way," she said. "Mark sends his greetings. 'Tell old Ed to hang in there,' he says."

"Right. Say hi to Mildred."

But Karen didn't say anything on one side or the other of this issue. She was already gone.

The Eccleburys's Christian duty had been accomplished.

He was alone with his thoughts.

His thoughts gravitated to the question of blame.

He didn't blame Dr. Wunder. He remembered a conversation he'd had with the good doctor. He'd said if the drugs didn't work, he wouldn't go the malpractice route. He said it wasn't clear how that would benefit him. Doctor was doing the best he could, he pointed out, it was just that he was too far gone before they rescued him from the Antarctic wastes.

Dr. Wunder had agreed.

He also didn't blame Mildred. It wasn't her fault she didn't warn him about being low on gas. It's very difficult to warn a person about running on Empty when you're prohibited from entering a Winnebago to check the gauge. Yes. Mildred was completely blame-free in this matter.

Another person who was completely blame-free in this matter was himself. How could he be held responsible for not noticing that the gas gauge was on Empty? The gauge was poorly lit, on account of the dashboard light being dead. No sir. He couldn't blame himself. It'd make no sense.

He began to worry. He was running out of candidates to blame.

Nurse came in to fluff his pillow. Nurse Comfort. She brushed up against him with her 38C holster.

He noticed a sign of life. A stirring downstairs. Definitely. About 5.2 on the Budwieser scale.

"Did I wake you?" she whispered.

"That's okay," he whispered back.

"Can I get you something?"

"Maybe a little Liebfraumilch?"

§

The miracle drugs didn't seem to be working.

He asked Dr. Wunder to make a comment on this fact.

"Hmmm," was Dr. Wunder's comment. He had his back to Ed and was reading a newspaper. It looked like the *Wall Street Journal*.

"Why aren't the drugs working?" he repeated, with a little more force.

"Hmmm," added Dr. Wunder.

"Well, what are the odds on their working?" he asked, this time somewhat irately. He didn't mean to be pushy, he knew he was merely a patient, but he thought of this as a relatively important question. Even more important than the other question that had been occupying his mind, about the crack on the ceiling and why it kept spreading.

"MalMed Pharmaceuticals," mused Dr. Wunder. "Closed yesterday at 47.28. Up 1.79."

"WHAT ARE THE ODDS ON THEIR WORKING?"

Dr. Wunder finally looked up. "Their?" he said. "Odds?" But his back was still to the audience. He was staring out the window through his Coke-bottle glasses and scratching his chin.

"The drugs," Ed said irritably. He wasn't being himself. He wasn't being a good patient. He was being *im*patient. "What are the odds on the drugs working? In percentages. Or, in dollars and cents."

"In your situation," said Dr. Wunder, and he stopped to reflect, "I'd say it's about . . . oh . . . twenty-five percent."

Twenty-five percent!

"That's up nine percent in the last year," Doctor pointed out.

"That means . . . there's about a seventy-five percent chance they *won't* work." He could still do the lower forms of math.

"Hmmm," said the good doctor.

Then he left. Probably to call his broker.

Maybe if it were fifty percent? Maybe then the miracle drugs would be working. Or seventy-five. Or even ninety-five. If the odds were ninety-five percent or above, he was sure they'd be doing the trick. . . . Maybe not exactly *sure,* but he'd sure as hell feel a lot better about his chances.

§

He was feeling good! No pain. A clear mind. Exceptionally canny. Optimistic about the future. Ed at his best; the classical Ed.

Then Rev. Gilltrip came by to celebrate Good Friday.

The first thing the Reverend wanted to know was, why had Ed neglected to fill out the religious preference space on his admittance form?

This was a big thing with Rev. Gilltrip. He said the clergy always found it helpful when patients indicated their religious preference. He said Ed would find it helpful, too. It'd keep the priests and rabbis out of his hair.

At first Ed pretended he thought Rev. Gilltrip said priests and rab*bits*. So he asked him how rabbits got into the picture. But the Reverend just corrected his minor error. Then Rev. Gilltrip became curious and wanted to know how Ed got rab*bits* out of rab*bis*. So Ed told him. He said he was a magician in his past life.

Rev. Gilltrip frowned.

Then he made a joke about keeping priests and rabbis out of his hair. He mentioned his lack of hair, which would make it difficult for spiritual leaders to climb aboard in the first place.

Rev. Gilltrip did not find this amusing.

He tried to explain. He said the Reverend had said that if he filled out a religious preference form, he'd keep the priests and rabbits out of his hair, and he had replied—

Again, Rev. Gilltrip interrupted, he'd like to stress the importance of taking just a very small moment of one's precious time, and our time becomes more and more precious, doesn't it, as we get older, ah yes, and face the inevitable. . . .

He didn't hear the rest of the sermon. He was thinking about the fact that the good Reverend was in his professional mood. Probably because he thought his parishioner was at the limits. Preachers tend to think that way, he thought. They tend to be worst-case scenario persons. Rev. Heedon being the exception.

Rev. Gilltrip kept pressing the point about the importance of having a religious preference. Ordinarily Ed would have made a few stinging rebuttals to this point, but he'd noticed that being camped out in the prone position has a tendency to take the fighting spirit out of you. The drugs were no big help, either. So he did the wise thing. He agreed with the Reverend. He didn't do it wholeheartedly, though, he just said hmmm. His voice said hmmm, but his mind took the fifth.

After they disposed of the topic of religious preference, he wanted to chit-chat, but Rev. Gilltrip wanted to talk business. He tried to get the Reverend onto the subject of the Chiefs' chances that fall, but the good man's time card was not marked for pleasure, it was marked for business. Since his business was theology, theology it was.

Rev. Gilltrip's first point was that Ed was not in good shape.

He said hmmm.

The second point was that he must be feeling guilty about Mildred, because of the separation and everything, and what was he prepared to do about it? He knew the Reverend wasn't suggesting he climb right up out of bed and go home for a friendly session with Mildred, either. He knew the man was recommending the act of prayer.

This time Rev. Gilltrip would not accept hmmm for an answer. He wanted Ed to make an English sentence, with a subject and a predicate. A sentence on the topic of theology, and very existential.

His mind raced to and fro, thinking of all the theological sentences he had memorized back in the days of his youth. *Repent and be saved,* was one such sentence. *Woe is me,* was another.

He finally came up with a brand-new sentence: "I blame God."

This was a regular English sentence, with a subject and a predicate, it was on the general topic of theology, and it qualified on the point of being existential. But he had a sense it wasn't what the good reverend was looking for.

"I thought you didn't believe in God," said Rev. Gilltrip. "I was under the impression, and correct me if I'm wrong, that you believed in the Eastern concept of reincarnation."

"I *used* to believe in reincarnation," he quipped, "but I've come full circle. Now I believe in God again."

"I'm so very glad to hear that," Rev. Gilltrip said, missing the subtle humor. "Would you mind telling me what made you change your mind?"

"If there's no God, there's no one to blame."

He thought he remembered that one of the things they taught preachers in seminary was the art of theological debate. They had whole courses of study on how to prove that you're wrong and they're right. But Rev. Gilltrip must have skipped class that day to go to a Saints game, because he didn't have a rebuttal to Ed's argument in his entire arsenal. All he could say was, "Ah. That's certainly an interesting proof for God's existence."

Finally the Reverend recovered his wits and began paging though his Bible. He came up with an appropriate passage: "'Who shall deliver me from this body of death?'"

This was a very good question. But Ed had already given the topic some thought, and he wasn't in the mood to pursue it with his opponent. Frankly, he was just a little tired. Maybe it was from all those drugs, maybe it was from sorting out his priorities, maybe it was from being put at a competitive disadvantage. He really didn't know why. The point was, he was tired. So he thanked Rev. Gilltrip very much for taking an interest in his welfare and pressed the button for the nurse.

Rev. Gilltrip was not finished with him, however.

Did he have a favorite hymn?

Did he have a favorite Bible verse?

Would he like a little prayer said over him?

These were the Reverend's questions.

No.

No.

Well, okay, but keep it short.

These were his answers.

After Rev. Gilltrip got through recommending him to God, with certain reservations, and had gone on to harvest other fields, Nurse Comfort finally showed up. He asked her about the hospital's policy on the behavior of the clergy toward the patient. She said she'd have to ask her supe, but as far as she knew, there was no such policy.

He had a suggestion.

He proposed that the hospital adopt a new policy. The clergy should be required to keep the conversation bright, smile a lot, and lie, if they have to.

§

How did they do it?

How did those flies keep from falling off the ceiling?

Was it a miracle, or could it be explained in scientific terms?

He asked the man on the other side of the curtain for his thoughts on this phenomenon.

The man didn't say anything.

"Out in western Kansas, where I grew up, the flies were omnipresent. . . . Not omni*potent.* Omni*present.*"

The man apparently didn't know Latin.

"Flies would gather at the slaughter of a beef, for instance."

The man moaned.

"Have you ever slid down the wet stomach of a dead cow in your uncle's slaughterhouse? A *Schlachthof,* as the Germans call them?"

The man didn't know German, either.

"'Don't ever let your mother catch you doing that,' my uncle said."

The man had no interest in the Budwieser family.

"Did you realize that flies undergo metamorphosis?"

Still no answer. Just a soft moan. The man probably hadn't taken Biology 101.

He gave up trying to educate the man and dozed off.

Nurse came into the room. She fluffed his pillow, then went over to the other side of the curtain. A few minutes later she left the room.

Pretty soon she was back. She was followed by two blue-and-white-clad men, pushing a gurney.

There was movement over there. Also, low voices.

He thought: this is not good.

Several minutes later a sheet-covered figure was wheeled out of the room on the gurney, propelled by the blue-and-white-clad monks.

A great sadness spread through the room. Sadness, and terror.

§

He'd been doing a lot of thinking since Rev. Gilltrip left. He'd been reconsidering his position on having a religious preference. The Reverend probably had a point there, about keeping the priests and rabbis out of his figurative hair. Maybe he should request an interview with the nurse and have her run over to Records and have them assign him a religious preference?

On second thought, maybe he should just let things stand. If he let things stand, maybe the priests and rabbis would flock to his side. Maybe one of them could cut him a better deal.

With a Protestant minister, you have only two choices. You either make it all the way home, or you head south. This was an advantage. It simplified things. On the other hand, it cut the odds down to fifty percent. That was the point at which gambling became dangerous. It wouldn't be so bad if you only had ten percent invested, but in that particular situation you were forced into being fully invested. It was winner-take-all.

A priest could offer you three choices, the third being a chance to work your way home gradually. It would just be an extension of life. He'd like that. So far, he'd have to say he'd been favorably impressed with life. On a scale of one to ten, he'd give it about a ten. That was from the perspective of the hospital bed. From the perspective of the bunk bed in the Winnebago, he'd have to rank it somewhat lower.

He didn't know about a rabbi. Would a rabbi promise you another way home, or would he just say so long, it's been good to know you? He should have paid more attention the day they covered that particular topic in Comparative Religion. If he remembered correctly, it would depend on whether the rabbi was Orthodox or Conservative or Reformed. And of course in these latter days, when women have become rabbis, things have gotten even more complicated.

The minute women come into the picture, things always get more complicated.

So, he decided, he'd just let things stand with regard to the religious preference flap. He'd welcome a visit from a priest or a rabbi. Why not? He believed in a free market. In fact, maybe he should buzz the nurse and have her put a sign on his door:

Soul for Sale

Inquire Within

No Reasonable Offer Rejected

That would be the American way.

A thought he'd recently been turning over in his mind was that for most of his life he'd been flirting with error. He'd always been one to say, Time is the Great Healer. He still believed that was true, on a short term basis. But he was beginning to have doubts about the long term.

Short term he was a bull, but long term he was definitely bearish.

Another saying for which he'd always been known was, Look on the Bright Side. Stretched out on that hospital bed, he'd had to reconsider that saying. He'd come to the conclusion that it was still true, but that it had a limited application. It works very well when you're up and about, he thought, but the minute they horizontalize you and put tubes in your nose and expose you to the clergy, it loses its charm.

One thing that happens to you when you're in a hospital bed is that your memory starts to work overtime.

He asked Nurse Comfort about this. He said, "Is it unusual for patients in my . . . situation to remember insignificant details of their past?"

"Not at all," she said. "Studies have shown that it happens in approximately ninety-three percent of all cases."

"That's good information to have," he said.

She smiled.

"Was it federally funded, the study?" he wondered.

"Of course."

"Ah," he said. "My tax dollars at work."

She smiled again and applied the business end of her stethoscope to his chest. She seemed pleased with what she heard. . . . Maybe *pleased with* wasn't the phrase he wanted. Maybe the phrase was *resigned to.*

"Forty-five percent of those surveyed reported memories extending back from zero to five years," she went on. "Twenty-one percent, from five years and one day to ten years. The rest could remember anywhere from ten years and one day to . . . well, one woman had a vivid recollection of an event that occurred ninety-seven years ago to the day."

"Amazing," he said. "What was it—the event?"

"I believe it was a conversion experience."

He groaned.

She put a thermometer in his mouth. He closed his eyes.

"Are you remembering some insignificant detail from *your* past, Mr. Budwieser?"

He was indeed. The insignificant detail that kept popping up on his screen was the big discussion the Deuces had had last summer on the question of the afterlife. . . . Mark Ecclebury kept insisting that you go down a long shining tube right after you die, and you end up right in the middle of a Matisse painting . . . but Karen kept claiming that you continue to live through your grandchildren. . . . Gary Leben kept laughing and saying that when you die, you die . . . and Ann kept saying that there's no way to know, it's all a big mystery. . . . Mildred came forth with the conventional idea that you pick up a resurrection body when you cross the finish line—at least if you had the sense to believe . . . but he kept maintaining that the Eastern concept of reincarnation explained everything. . . .

He wondered what Nurse Comfort would think about this topic. He thought of asking her about the afterlife-related beliefs of other patients. It would be nice to know what the studies had shown about the question. He was curious to know the statistical breakdown. But he was running out of the ability to make audible sentences.

She seemed to be writing something on his chart.

He'd never put much stock in the theory of resurrection. That was for soft-minded people, like Mildred. . . . And he couldn't put any stock in Karen's theory about immortality through later generations. Megan would probably end up like Mildred, and what kind of immortality was that? . . . As far as Gary's theory was concerned, the guy could afford to say that when you die, you die—he had a cushy job with a major life insurance company and money in the bank. . . . And Ann's theory? What was the French word for *bullshit*? . . . That left Mark's theory about the long shining tube and the Budwieser theory of reincarnation. . . . But Mark never knew as much as he claimed to. So. . . .

Was it his imagination, or was Nurse Comfort closing his eyelids?

What was Nietzsche's classical line? "That was life? Well, then, once again!"

He'd be back!

The only question was, as whom?

Interlude

11

Breaking the Rules

"IS YOUR HUSBAND STILL LIVING?"

This was a hard question. She didn't know about Ed, whether or not he was still living. And as Carole pointed out after they escaped from Luneberger Manor yesterday afternoon, they couldn't call the hospitals to find out, because they were in hiding from the authorities. She remembered what Dr. Rex had said, that Ed had had a minor temporary setback, and then Thelma told her they were giving him miracle drugs. Which were what Jesus used to give sick people who believed in Him. Besides, Rev. Gilltrip had said Ed was resting comfortably, and preachers were supposed to never lie, they had taken courses at cemetery, which was Ed's word for *seminary*, where they learned how not to, and besides, it was in their contract. . . . Except that she also remembered what Thelma used to say, "Sweetie, preachers are the biggest liars of all," and just yesterday morning, which was Easter, the Reverend had come by for a few quiet moments and they went for a walk in the garden, the two of them, and she asked him about Ed and all he said was "Ah yes, Ed. . . ." and she pressed the point and asked him right out if she'd ever see him again, and he hesitated and said "Ah, yes . . . perhaps . . . ," and she accused him, she said "You mean in Heaven, don't you?" but then he didn't answer, he just reached over and patted her hand, like she was a little girl. Meaning Ed was dead.

"Is your husband still living?" repeated Dr. Buller.

"Probably," she said, squirming in her chair.

"Probably!?" Meaning, what kind of an answer is *that*?

What she'd meant was, Probably, if there's an afterlife. Which she was pretty sure about, because she believed in the resurrection of the dead and life everlasting for true Christian believers who hadn't opted for cremation, and now she was beginning to believe in reincarnation, too, which was why she was sitting there in Dr. Buller's office, to find out about her past life. So there was a good chance of life after death, even for Ed, with either resurrection or reincarnation to rely on. Or maybe both.

"I mean 'Probably, if there's an afterlife'," she explained. Then she stopped to think: why was she bothering to explain? And why was he asking her all those questions about her name and her maiden name and her social security number and whether or not her husband was still living? He was a psychic, which meant he already knew the answers!

"Probably." He smiled as he made a big check mark on the form he was filling out. He was thinking she had a sense of humor. Which she did, she just wasn't using it at that particular moment.

Dr. Buller looked exactly like a psychic, except he didn't wear a scarf around his head and he didn't have gold jangling jewelry and he wasn't wearing a long silk dress. Plus the fact that he wasn't a woman. But he was dark-complected and he had a gold earring in a pierced ear, which were dead give-aways, even though he was trying to disguise his true identity by sitting behind a regular businessman's desk. And on the desk there was another clue, a picture of a beautiful young dark-complected woman, who was probably Cleopatra in a previous existence but was now his wife.

"Address?" asked Dr. Buller.

"What?"

She was stalling, thinking of what to say. Should she give him her old address, where she and Ed had lived for most of their marriage? No, because he'd send mail there, and the police would be able to track her down. What about her new address? No, she didn't know it, there was no necessity to, because she wasn't planning to get any mail, being a fugitive from the mental health system, as Carole put it. Maybe she should give him the address of Luneberger Manor? No, because number one she didn't remember it and number two she didn't know whether or not Carole had told him she had escaped from a mental institution. Which wasn't even true, she hadn't actually *escaped*, because the original plan hadn't panned out, the one involving the cake and file and climbing out the window and letting herself down on bed sheets. Carole had tried to bake a cake with a file in it, but the cake fell all three times she tried it, so Carole came to Luneberger Manor yesterday and instead handed her a package and whispered for her to go to her room and put on the disguise and then come out nonchalantly and they'd just casually walk right out of there. Which she did, she went to her room and put on one of Carole's wigs and some dark sunglasses, which she wore on her forehead, like Carole always did, and a pair of Carole's harem pants, which didn't fit, being too big in the hips and waist so that they required a safety pin, and then she and Carole just strolled through the front door like they were sisters at a garage sale and were leaving because they hadn't found exactly what they were looking for, at a reasonable price. And nobody knew the difference, they had pulled it off so well.

"Where do you live?" asked Dr. Buller.

"Oh," she said. All of a sudden she had the sense he was testing her, he already knew the answer but was checking her mental health situation and she'd better be careful how she phrased it. "I'm living with Carole," is what she finally decided to say. Which was true. At least temporarily, until Dr. Buller discovered which of her past lives was the reason why they'd put her in Loony Manor in the first place. Then . . . well, she'd just go across that bridge when she came to it.

"Carole?" he asked.

"Carole," she repeated loudly. Was he deaf, or something? . . . A deaf psychic? No, she couldn't imagine such a thing.

"Carole," he said out loud to himself. "Carole Carole Carole."

He was probably going through the list of all the Caroles he knew, trying to remember which one had a friend she had sent over, named Molly Wise, which was the pen name Carole had given her as part of the disguise. It took a minute, because it was a long list, it included a lot of the non-Caroles he knew who had been Caroles in a previous existence.

"C-A-R-O-L-E," she spelled out. She was helping him trim down the possibilities, by cutting out the Carols who spelled their name without the extra E.

He looked at her with a question mark in his eyes.

"Spelled with an extra E," she explained, in case he'd missed the point. Which he hadn't, of course, being a psychic.

"I heard you," he said. "I'm just wondering who the hell *Carole* is."

"Carole Digby," she explained. She didn't realize psychics swore.

"Carole Digby," he said slowly, scratching his temple and shaking his head.

"Dr. Digby's third wife," she explained, attempting to jiggle his memory.

He smiled. "And would you mind telling me who Dr. Digby is?"

Was he trying to embarrass her? Or did he really not know? If he was trying to get her to blush, he wasn't being very nice, and if he didn't already know, he wasn't much of a psychic. Either way, she was beginning to lose her faith in psychics.

"He's my boss," she explained. Which was the truth. At least it used to be the truth. Or part of the truth.

He kept scratching his temple and smiling. "And who the hell," he said, "are *you*?"

"What?"

"You're pulling my leg," he said.

"No I'm not. I'm Mildred Budwieser," she said, forgetting she was in disguise.

He kept smiling. Then she happened to look down on his desktop and notice the sign, with his name on it. But it didn't say:

DR. B. S. BULLER
Psychic

It said:

CHUCK BALLESTEROS
Certified Financial Planner

Was Dr. Buller using a disguise, too? Carole hadn't said anything about that. Why wasn't he—Mr. Ballesteros, or whoever he was—why wasn't he getting to the point of why she was there, which was to find out about her past life? Why didn't he know who Carole was? And how could somebody named Chuck be a psychic?

Then it dawned on her. She had come to the wrong place! This office was on *North* Polk. The real Dr. Buller's address was probably on *South* Polk.

Mr. Ballesteros kept scratching his temple, but his smile was spreading itself into an awful grin. "Mildred Budwieser," he repeated slowly. "And where do *you* fit into the world, Ms. Budwieser?"

She didn't really want to tell Mr. Ballesteros where she fit into the world. He wouldn't understand. She knew she'd better say something, though, or he'd call the police. The problem was, if she told him the truth, they'd take her back and lock her up and throw away the key. . . . But on the other hand, she had been brought up never to lie.

"I am a graduate," she finally said, "of Luneberger Manor."

§

"He knew everything about me!" she said the minute she burst into their apartment. This was after the session with Dr. Buller. The *real* Dr. Buller.

"What'd I tell you?" said Carole. She was holding a gin tonic and beaming with happiness.

"He knew about me working crosswords, and about Cyrus and Charisse and Felicity and little Shaun and Megan, and about my friend Thelma, and about the dalliance . . ."—she was going to say "with Dr. Digby," but then she stopped to think that her new roommate was still *Mrs.* Digby and it wouldn't be polite to mention his name until the divorce became final, so she quickly went on, ". . . and about Rev. Heedon and Dora and the Deuces and the whole fruitbasket-upset epidemic, including Ann and Mark getting ready to take their French conversations under the covers, if they haven't already—and he thinks they might have, he said he wouldn't put it past them. And he even knew about Rabbi Scheinblum, who was moving to Seattle!"

Carole kept beaming and being happy. "What about Ed?" she asked.

"Oh, I found out all sorts of things about Ed. Including why he used to hide the Mogen David and dirty magazines and dark glasses and cigarette holder behind the bathtub."

"He did?"

"He did," she said proudly.

Carole sat down at the dining-room table. "Why was that?"

She sat down across from Carole. "It had something to do with his fantasies and worrying about being a dead white male."

"What?" said Carole, leaning forward. "I don't understand."

She had to confess it was kind of hard to explain.

"I should think it would be."

"Well . . . it made sense when Dr. Buller was talking about it."

"I'm sure it did."

"Oh, it did."

"And what did he say about your past life?"

"He said that in my last life I was . . . tum de dum . . . Mrs. Archie Bunker!"

"Edith Bunker? Oh, no. You're smarter than Edith Bunker!"

"Thank you," she said, blushing. This was the best compliment she'd had in a long time.

"A *lot* smarter."

"That's probably because of my schooling," she said, trying not to sound too proud. "Schools in Kansas are lots better than schools in New York."

"Maybe that's it."

"I'm sure it is."

"And is that why they kept you cooped up in Luneberger Manor? Your being Edith Bunker?"

"Oh no. He said it was because in my next-to-last existence I was Ophelia."

"The Ophelia complex!" exclaimed Carole. "I should've known."

"Who was Ophelia?" she wanted to know. She'd been planning to look it up in the dictionary, but she figured Carole might already know about Ophelia, so why not ask her?

"Ophelia was Hamlet's wife."

"Oh," she said, and nodded. She didn't have to ask who Hamlet was. She knew all about Hamlet, from spending most of her present life with Ed. Hamlet was Shakespeare's youngest son.

"Hamlet drove Ophelia crazy. Not crazy, but. . . ." Carole was waving the gin tonic around, trying to find a word that would be more sensitive to her feelings. "What about Ed?" said Carole suddenly, forgetting about a replacement for the word *crazy*.

"He mentioned something about Ed being somebody called False Stiff."

"You mean Falstaff?"

"That's probably it. False Staff. He said Ed had a lot of False Staff in him."

"He was probably referring to their similar builds," guessed Carole.

"Why, was False Staff fat?"

Carole laughed. "Does the pope wear a white dress?"

She was surprised Carole didn't know about the pope wearing a white dress. "Just in public," she said. Of course when the pope went to bed, he probably wore pajamas and had fantasies, just like other men.

Carole kept laughing. "So who else did Ed used to be?"

"Walter Mitty."

"Walter Mitty? Who the hell is Walter Mitty?"

"A submarine commander and a millionaire banker and a world-famous surgeon, among other things."

"Are you sure?" Carole looked like she didn't believe it.

"That's what Dr. Buller said."

Carole shrugged her shoulders. Like she couldn't figure it out, either. "What else did he say?"

"He also said he didn't charge a fee."

Carole laughed. "Of course not."

"He said he was doing it for his own enjoyment."

"Hmmm," said Carole.

"Is something wrong with that?"

"I'm just thinking."

"About what?"

"Oh . . . nothing."

While Carole was thinking about nothing, she thought about Dr. Buller—the real Dr. Buller. He hadn't looked at all like a psychic. He wasn't dressed like a psychic, and he wasn't dark-complected, like Mr. Ballesteros, plus he wasn't wearing a gold earring. He was disguised in faded blue jeans and a tee shirt, and he was a white male. Ordinary-looking, not handsome and not ugly. Kind of tall, maybe the age of sixty or so, losing some hair to the male baldness pattern but making up for it by not having shaved for two or three days.

His office hadn't been what she had imagined, either. It wasn't dark, it wasn't decorated with little plastic stars and planets, and it didn't have a crystal ball sitting on the table, glowing in the dark and with spirits mysteriously rising out of it, ready to obey his every command. It was just an ordinary office. Instead of a table there was a desk, instead of a crystal ball there was a computer screen lit up with a moving pattern of criss-crossing lines, and instead of the stars and planets there were a map of Antarctica on the wall and a bookshelf with books like *The Thurber Carnival* and *Cosmicomics* and *Lost in the Funhouse*, plus a book by Woody Allen on wildlife called *Without Feathers*.

But he was really Dr. Buller, which was the first thing she had checked on when she got to the house on South Polk, and he knew who Carole was, which was the second thing she'd checked on. In fact, he said he'd been expecting her. And he even called her Molly Wise.

"Anyway," said Carole when they were finished thinking. "What else did he say?"

"He asked me what I really wanted. And what Ed wanted. He said to think about my answer very carefully, because wishes have a way of being granted."

"What did you tell him?" Carole seemed very interested in this.

"I said I didn't have to think carefully about it, I already knew I really wanted things to go back to what they were before Ed quit his job and moved out to the Winnebago and then left town and . . . passed away."

"Passed away?"

"That's what happened to him, isn't it?"

"Let's not jump to conclusions," said Carole. "And what did you tell Dr. Buller about what Ed really wanted?"

"I said if I know Ed, what he really wants is being alive."

Carole laughed. "You didn't!"

"I did. And he said 'doing what?' and I said 'Being a good husband and father,' and he said 'Oh?' like he didn't believe it. So I had to say 'Well, not really, what he really wants is to move out to the West Coast and write his memories.' He said 'And?' meaning what else, so I had to tell him, I said 'Plus have mistresses.' Then he looked at me very closely and said 'And what does Mildred think about that?' So Mildred said 'Mildred thinks he can have all the mistresses he wants, just so they're only in his mind.' 'Why only in his mind,' he said, 'why not really?' So I said 'Mildred doesn't see how he could afford mistresses on just Social Security.'"

Carole laughed again. "You never cease to amaze me."

Mildred blushed. "Then," she said, "he started talking about a conflict between what Ed wanted and what I wanted."

Carole raised her lovely plucked eyebrows. "Conflict, huh?" she said, swishing the ice cubes around in her empty glass. "Then what did he say?"

"He didn't say anything. He slid his chair over to the computer and pressed a button and the screen magically changed, from the criss-crossing lines to something like a sheet of paper. Which he stared at."

"Oh?" Carole was starting to get really interested. "Then what?"

"He kept staring. Then he said, I predict. . . ." She was getting so excited she could hardly say the words.

"Yes?"

"He predicted Ed would be okay!"

"He did? That's what he said?"

"And that I'd see him again!"

"What else?"

"He predicted travel and adventure!"

"Travel and adventure?" Carole got up and went over to the kitchen counter.

"He's just like a fortune cookie!"

But Carole didn't say anything. She was busy making herself another gin tonic.

"He's a real psychic," Mildred called out. Unlike Mr. Ballesteros, who she didn't think she should mention, because then she'd have to explain how she'd accidentally told him her real name was Mildred Budwieser and Carole might get upset and emphasize how important it was to not blow her cover or they'd both be in deep doo-doo. Even though it was really Carole's fault, the case of mistaken identity, for not driving her to Dr. Buller's in the first place, and for making her take a taxi while she herself took off in the Mercedes to have Rafael do her toenails.

Carole came back with her drink and sat down again. "What else?"

"Oh . . . nothing."

"Nothing?"

"Uh . . . nothing." Her mind wasn't going blank, she just didn't want to tell Carole the secret.

"Nothing sounds like something," said Carole, who was staring at her like she already knew the secret. Or at least had a good idea.

"Except. . . ," she said.

"Except?"

"Except . . . we didn't have a dalliance, if that's what you're thinking."

"I'm not thinking anything. I just want to know what the hell else went on between the both of you."

"Well. . . ." Should she or shouldn't she? A secret wasn't a secret if you told somebody else, that's what Thelma used to say, she always said things like, "What they don't know won't hurt 'em," and "It's something God and the history books don't need to know." On the other hand, Carole was paying the rent—Carole, plus Dr. Digby—and maybe she owed her—Carole, not Dr. Digby—something.

"Well?"

"I told him about . . . a secret."

"A secret." Carole put down her drink.

"About my past life."

"Your past life."

"Not as Edith Bunker or Ophelia Shakespeare," she explained. "As Mildred Budwieser."

"You told him a secret about yourself." Carole was staring at her again. Right into her eyes.

"Not *a* secret," she confessed. "*The* secret."

"You told him the secret of your life." Carole was not putting question marks at the end of her sentences. Which meant she was not approving.

"Not . . . actually."

"And what the hell's that supposed to mean?"

"It means . . . I didn't tell *him*. . . . I told his tape recorder."

Carole put down her drink. "That bastard," she said. She was angry. "That goddamn bastard!"

§

"Shhh!"

Carole wouldn't have needed to whisper. They were still in the Mercedes, which ran so quiet you could hear your heart pounding.

She had been brought up on ten rules. One, that God was the only true god, which she still believed, even though now she also believed in reincarnation. Two, not to worship other gods because He was jealous of his position as Number One, which made a lot of sense. Three, not to take His name in vain, which she never did. Four, not to work on Sundays, unless of course you were a nurse, which she wasn't, so she didn't. Five, to honor her parents, which was only natural and which she did and expected the same from her children. Six, not to kill, which was the easiest one to follow, as long as you didn't keep a gun in the house, which of course she didn't. Seven, not to commit adultery, which she . . . well, at least she hadn't made a habit of it. Eight, not to steal, nine, not to bear false witness against her neighbor, which didn't include gossip as long as it was done with Christian love, and ten, not to covet. And she had a pretty good track record in those last categories, too—if the coveting hadn't gotten any further than the wishing stage, if it hadn't led to stealing, which it hadn't.

Was breaking into somebody else's house the same as stealing? Carole had said no, not if what you were planning to take was something that already belonged to you, such as a tape you had been tricked into making. This made sense, except that the tape itself belonged to Dr. Buller. She had pointed this out to Carole, and Carole had pointed out that okay, they wouldn't actually *take* the tape, they'd erase it, if that would salve her conscience. Which it would, to a degree.

"Shhh," whispered Carole.

Carole was parking the car a couple of blocks from the residence on South Polk. This was exactly according to plan, to hide the brand-new Mercedes in the driveway of a house where a party was being held and sneak nonchalantly over to the DA, which was the code name for the "Designated Area," meaning Dr. and Mrs. Buller's house. The B's, the "Bullers," were in California visiting their daughter's family, so nobody would be home and they could just break in and destroy the E, the "Evidence," and not cause any damage, and nobody would be the wiser.

Carole was dressed in her silk harem pants and Mildred was dressed in a white nightgown, which was her Ophelia costume. They were both wearing rubber kitchen gloves, to keep from making fingerprints. Nobody was supposed to recognize them, and in case anybody asked, which was highly unlikely, they were just a couple of refugees from unhappy past lives who were looking for an old friend who used to live in this neighborhood. That's what Carole was planning to say, and she herself was supposed to keep her mouth shut and pretend to be deaf and dumb and just smile and nod at everything Carole said, even if it was an exaggeration, which was Carole's word for *lie*. Except that if it was a police officer and he took them in for questioning, she was secretly planning to point out that it was all Carole's idea and that she wasn't responsible for her actions.

"Shhh," whispered Carole.

They were turning into the Buller driveway. The moon was coming out from behind the clouds, so Carole shut off the flashlight.

All of a sudden there was a dreadful cry, like a cat was being run over out in the street. They stopped in their tracks.

"Shhh," whispered Carole.

"That wasn't me," she whispered back.

"I know," whispered Carole. "That was a peacock. Buller's neighbor owns a pair of albino peacocks."

"I didn't know albino peacocks made so much noise," she whispered. She also didn't know they even *made* albino peacocks. She'd always thought a peacock was a peacock, period, except of course that some of them were boys and some were girls.

"Shhh," said Carole.

Nobody had seen them. It was past midnight and everybody was in bed fast asleep, all the mommas and the papas and the kiddies. The peacocks had noticed them, but peacocks couldn't talk, even though they reminded her of parrots, who could. What about albino peacocks, though? Could albino peacocks talk? Probably not, because they sounded like wounded cats, and who ever heard of cats talking? Except in stories. And this wasn't a story, this was real life. Even though it sounded like a story, being dressed in a disguise based on one of your past lives and having just escaped from a mental health facility, which out in western Kansas they used to call a nuthouse, and sneaking around in the moonlight with the idea of burglarizing the house of a psychic.

A psychic!

"Carole," she said, and this time she didn't whisper.

"Shhh," said Carole, who was trying some keys in the door lock.

"I just thought of something."

"Keep your voice down."

She kept her voice down to a whisper. "I just happened to remember—Dr. Buller is a psychic!"

"So?"

"That means he knows what we're doing this very instant!"

"He's in California."

"But he's a psychic."

"Psychics aren't as good at a distance," said Carole, who wasn't finding the right key.

"Aren't as good? What do you mean, aren't as good?"

"Thought waves don't travel long distances."

"Oh," she whispered. She hadn't realized that fact. She wasn't an expert on psychics and reincarnation, like Carole. She'd only had two past lives—that she *knew* of, as Carole always emphasized. Carole had had ten: (1) the unhappy stripper in Buddha's harem, (2) Jesus's friend Mary Magdalene, (3) the Wife from Bath, (4) Mistress Quickly, (5) Moll Flanders, (6) Hester Prynne, (7) Madame Bovary, (8) Grushenka, (9) Molly Bloom, and (10) a Japanese princess whose name Carole couldn't pronounce but who had been suffocated by a sumo wrestler.

"Damn it," said Carole loudly. She couldn't get the lock open.

"Maybe it's not locked?" Mildred suggested. "Maybe he forgot to lock it? Or maybe he was relying on his psychic powers to tell him when somebody was breaking in?"

"Bullshit," said Carole. "I'm going to find a brick."

While Carole was off in the back yard looking for a brick, Mildred tried the knob. It worked. The door opened. She had been right, the door wasn't even locked! Dr. Buller had either forgotten to lock it, or he was relying on his psychic powers, from a distance.

Pretty soon Carole came back with a stick she had found by the creek that ran through the back yard.

"It's open!" Mildred told Carole. She opened the door to show she wasn't lying.

"Hell," said Carole, throwing the stick away.

The plan was not to turn on any lights, which might arouse suspicion. That's why Carole had brought the flashlight along, to find their way to Dr. Buller's study, where the tape was hidden, without using the house lights.

"Shhh," whispered Carole. They were tiptoeing up the stairs.

"Why do we have to whisper?" she whispered right back. "Nobody's home, are they?"

"Listening devices," whispered Carole.

"Listening devices?"

"They always have listening devices hidden someplace."

"The Bullers? Psychics?"

"Anyone whose house is broken into."

"Oh," she said. Then she thought of something else to say. "What good is a listening device when you're in California?" she asked.

"Shhh," whispered Carole.

§

"This is Molly Wise," said her voice on the tape. "What do you want me to say?"

"Just talk about the days of yore," said Dr. Buller's voice on the tape. "I'll leave you alone so you won't be nervous."

Then there was the sound of footsteps walking away to watch "Another World."

"This is about back in western Kansas," said her voice. "At the time of Ed's and my wedding. Not right *at* the time of our wedding, a little before.

"It was on a dare, there was this rich old geezer out east of Baggs who always went to Europe for vacations, locked the gates and just took off for the museums of Europe, his mother died and left him the wherewithal to go to Europe for vacations, to visit the great places of Europe, he wasn't married, but he had the wherewithal, they say he used to sit around in his garden admiring the statues standing there in his pool, sit there in the shade holding an alcoholic beverage and staring at the statues, sit there all dolled up in a blue blazer and grey cravat with a diamond sticking into it, sit there with no place to go and stare at a couple of very naked statues.

"Ed dared me—this rich old geezer was on his European holiday at the time—he dared me one spring evening, he said I'll bet you anything you're afraid to go with me out to old Wrathbonne's estate and sneak in, we won't steal anything, we'll just admire the statues, it was our first date, one month before our high school graduation, I was all innocence but Ed had read the selected poems of Lord Byron.

"I'd always been the adventurous type, innocent but adventurous, so I said I bet I'm *not* afraid, so we took Rufus's old '36 Chevy out to the Wrathbonne estate and parked it about a quarter of a mile down the road behind some bushes and walked from there. We heard the horses in the pasture whinny, and I wanted to go back because horses always reminded me of death, but he grabbed my hand and pulled me along.

"There was nobody home, just a locked gate, so we climbed over the wall, he pushed me over first, then over he came and the moon was full and just coming over the horizon, we walked among the hyacinths and hollyhocks and I gave him the names of all the flowers and he pressed my hand to his heart so I could feel the beat and I began to love him, in an innocent kind of way.

"And he said I'll bet you anything you're afraid to wade in his pool, the one with the two statues—the statues old Wrathbonne used to admire, sitting there in his blue blazer and diamond-studded cravat and sipping a beverage. I was always adventurous, so we took off our shoes and socks and laid them carefully on the grass and wading we went, and he pressed my hand to his heart again, the beating was wilder, and he said do *you* have a heart, and I said yes, and he said let's see, and we saw, and he said take a look at those two statues, would you, and we gazed and gazed at them, a him and a her, and he said in my dreams I think of you as being like her, so I took the hint and said in *my* dreams I think of *you* as being like *him,* and that was true, it had never been true before on account of his pimples, but it became true at the very instant I said it, and I began to love him, but this time without the innocence, it was a heart-pounding kind of love, I'd never felt it before or since, standing there in old man Wrathbonne's pool by the statues, and then it was like . . . it was like Jesus climbed down from heaven and gave us each other's hands and told us everything was all right . . . and afterwards we laid there in the grass like the statues, just the way He had made us, all youth and adventure and beauty and perfection, looking up at the stars and giving them names. . . .

"Afterwards there was the storm, of course. We hadn't noticed the dark clouds, actually we'd *seen* them, we'd just figured they were part of the beauty of everything at that particular moment. Then all of a sudden the rain started coming down in tiny little drops, so we quick jumped up and got dress—. . . put everything back on and high-tailed it out of there, over the wall and down the road past the horses, who were making all those dreadful whinnies, and got back to the car just as it was beginning to rain cats and dogs. And to thunder and lightning. And then wouldn't you know, the car didn't start, we had to sit there in the front seat like two drowned rats, shivering and laughing and . . . kissing and . . . and scared. Because of the tornado, and because what if I had got. . . ?

"The tornado. I guess it was a tornado, although there was no mention of it in the paper next week. What happened was this, we were in the back seat, like I said, shivering and laughing and everything, and all of a sudden there was this huge clap of thunder and the car started spinning around, twirling like a majorette's baton. Then there were voices—one voice, actually, warning us—not that we'd done anything wrong, of course—remember, Jesus was our chaperon. Ed didn't hear it, the voice, but that's because he wasn't paying attention, he never was a good listener and this time was no exception. But *I* heard the voice, and *I* felt the car spinning around, and how else could you explain everything that happened after that?

"What happened next was that the car wouldn't start. Ed got out and walked around it and pounded on the hood, while I stayed inside and tried to start it. Then I got out and tried to push it, which was a mistake, while he sat behind the wheel and tried to steer. Nothing happened, of course. Then he had this bright idea, I should be the one to walk the mile down the road to the next farm and get help. Farmers are more sympathetic to women than men, is how he explained it. So I walked down the gravel road to the next farm and got the old farmer and his wife out of bed and told them that me and my brother were out looking for snipes in his father's car, which wouldn't start, and did he happen to know anything about old '36 Chevies? It turned out he did, he knew exactly how to put the distributor cap back on, then he made Ed look under the hood and explained to him about the importance of distributor caps, and he didn't charge anything for his knowledge, and even better, when he said goodbye he winked and said his lips were sealed.

"We were married that summer, which is the next thing that happened. At first Dad wanted a private ceremony, but I insisted on a proper church wedding and so did Mom, so he was overruled. But I got sick the day of the ceremony. Ed's dad Rufus wanted to postpone it or cancel it or something, but everybody else had a sense of what the big hurry was, so he was overruled and we had the ceremony a couple of hours later, in the afternoon.

"Then we moved to Kirkland, Dad and Mom thought it was best for all concerned, and Ed got a job waiting tables in a restaurant and started working on his degree and writing his memories. I stayed home and knitted booties, and we both joined the choir down at church and sang praises to Our Lord.

"And that's it. That's how it all started. That's how. . . . The funny thing is, we wouldn't've had to . . . what I mean is, we lost. . . . I'm not saying I'm pro-choice, I'm saying it's not a good idea for young ladies to try to push cars and go for help, that's the job of young gentlemen. Young ladies are the ones who should stay behind the wheel."

§

"And *that's* the big secret?" said Carole. She wasn't whispering now. She was speaking loudly. She was angry again.

"I'm sorry," said Mildred. "But it was really Ed's fault. Ed's, and Lord Byron's."

"And we came all the way across town to break into this damned house, we risked our lives and our freedom, not to speak of our reputations—"

"Shhh," said Mildred.

"—just because your goddamn *husband* knocked you up in a farmer's pond and you didn't want the world to know?"

"We weren't married yet," she said. Carole was missing the main point. Carole was also forgetting whose idea it was in the first place, to come all the way across town to keep the world from knowing the big secret she'd been hiding for all those years, the secret she hadn't even told Thelma Blossum.

"Shit," said Carole.

Mildred started to cry.

"Oh hell," said Carole.

Mildred kept crying.

"Actually," said Carole, putting an arm around her, "it was a very nice story."

Mildred wiped her eyes. "You really think so?"

"Very charming."

"What did you like about it?"

"Oh . . . the statues . . . the horses . . . old Wrathbonne."

"Really?"

"The whole thing reminded me of something."

"Oh?"

But Carole didn't say what the story reminded her of. Instead, she went over to the desk and sat down on the chair in front of the computer. She pressed a button. Pretty soon wonderful psychic magical things started to happen. Lots of words and numbers started to show up on the screen. "Mouse driven," were two of the words she could make out. In ordinary life mice didn't drive, but a psychic's study didn't belong to ordinary life. Then the screen said "MS-DOS Shell." Probably a secret code, or somebody's pen name in a past life. Carole typed something on the keyboard, and the screen began to do magic tricks, showing a picture of a book called *Microsoft Windows 98*, then showing two flocks of birds flying in opposite directions, then showing a lot of tiny pictures of things like file cabinets and computers and clipboards. Then Carole took hold of a little white toy and clicked it, and pretty soon there was a picture of another book called *WordPerfect*, and the screen turned white. Carole clicked the toy a few more times, and all at once there was a sheet of paper standing up straight and tall, with words typed on it.

"Let's . . . see . . . what . . . we . . . have . . . here," said Carole, leaning forward for a better look.

Mildred was standing behind Carole. She leaned forward, too, but Carole's head was too close to the screen, so it blocked out the view.

"What does it say?" she wanted to know.

Carole read:

Part I. [Completed]

1. Ed encounters Ms. Mode and learns of her secret plan. Mildred is stunned to discover Scheinblum's marital problems.

2. Gloria wins a trip to Mexico. Mildred helps Ed decipher a coded message. Ed visits Dr. Digby and receives valuable financial advice. Mildred and Thelma discuss Ed's secret desire. Mildred humiliates Ed; he responds by professing his love for Dora, who spurns his advances.

3. Ed enjoys a bout of telephone sex with Betsy. Rev. Heedon offers spiritual guidance to the multitudes as Ed fantasizes about Dora. Ed has a religious experience, buys his dream vehicle, and heads for the West Coast, only to encounter misfortune on the way. Mildred comes to his rescue. Ed uncovers useful information about Dora and Rev. Heedon. A suspicious Mildred pumps Betsy for information on Ed, then plays her trump card.

4. Ed attempts to communicate with Cyrus, begging for forgiveness and a job.

5. A heartbroken Mildred, trying to sort out her feelings for Ed, reveals important truths about the members of her doomed family.

6. Ed realizes an astounding truth about his past, only to discover that nobody will believe it.

7. Dr. Digby reveals his true feelings for Mildred, after which they enjoy an afternoon of passion.

8. Mildred confesses to Carole but insists on her own innocence. Ed heads for the West Coast. Mildred discovers that Ed is missing. Ed gets lost in a blizzard. Mildred has a breakdown. Ed is rescued by a complete stranger and is rushed to Kirkland General in a coma.

9. Dr. Rex consoles Mildred. Thelma advises Mildred of the nature of her mysterious ailment. Rev. Gilltrip discovers Mildred's secret. Carole reveals that her husband has run off with Rev. Heedon's wife. Mildred plots her escape from Luneberger Manor.

10. Ed hovers between life and death. Dr. Wunder confronts Ed with distressing news. Rev. Gilltrip visits Ed and suggests a solution to his problems. A corpse is discovered in Ed's room. Ed reflects on the afterlife as the end closes in.

Ideas for Part II.

A. Give Ed the chance to realize his literary potential. [Use first person point of view.]

B. Have Mildred—

But Carole didn't get to finish reading. All of a sudden there were car headlights flashing into the window, and the sounds of a garage door opening and gravel being crunched in the driveway.

"It's him!" whispered Carole. "It's Buller!"

"Dr. Buller!" she whispered back. She'd been right and Carole had been wrong. A psychic *always* knew what was going on, even if he was thousands of miles away in California.

"Just when things were starting to get interesting!" whispered Carole.

"What'll we do?" she asked. She was getting frantic. She'd been brought up never to steal, and here she was in Buller's house, taking something that didn't belong to her. And the worst part was, Dr. Buller knew. Dr. Buller, and God.

"Quick," whispered Carole. "Into the monitor."

"What?" She didn't know what a monitor was. All she could think of was the statue of the Minuteman, from American History, but she didn't think that was what Carole meant.

Carole pointed at the typewriter screen. "Climb into the monitor!"

She looked at the little monitor. "Is that possible?"

"Anything's possible, if you're a fictional character."

She'd never thought about it that way. But it made a lot of sense. So she made herself very small and climbed inside the monitor. This was fun! Just like the old Jiggs and Maggie comic strip, with the characters jumping in and out of the picture frames, doing all kinds of acrobatics.

The garage door was being closed.

"Hide!" Carole whispered after her. "Stay alert! Wait for further instructions."

She stuck her head out of the monitor. "What about you?" she wanted to know. "What's going to happen to you?"

The back door was being opened.

"I'll just stay here and be the story consultant."

"What's that?"

"It's somebody who recommends to Buller what he should write."

"Will he let you? Won't he call the police?"

"Don't worry about Carole. She has a way with men."

She couldn't disagree. And it was nice to have the story consultant be somebody you could trust. She wiggled herself back inside the monitor.

Now there were voices down below.

"Oh yes," said Mildred, sticking her head back out. "Give it a happy ending."

"Of course."

Somebody was coming upstairs.

"But be sure to teach Ed a lesson!" she whispered, and she totally disappeared behind the screen.

Part Two

12

The Prize

I JUST WOKE UP. I must have been sleeping for about two days. It must be . . . Sunday. That would make it . . . Easter.

They've attached a tag to my big toe. This seems to suggest they've given up on me. What's the world coming to? You take a little nap, they give up on you. I don't mind saying I've lost faith in the medical profession. No interest in quality. All they care about is high volume.

Why did I tell Dr. Wunder I'd never go the malpractice route? I spoke too soon.

They've also sealed my room. I can't begin to say how much this disturbs me. I've never been claustrophobic, but I do like to keep my doors unlocked. Out in western Kansas we always kept our doors unlocked. People would go on a two-week vacation and leave their doors unlocked and when they came back everything would be just where it belonged. The neighbors would've come in and maybe rolled and smoked a few cigarettes and listened to the grain prices on the radio, but they'd have left everything exactly as they found it.

That was before the world was redesigned to include the options of theft and murder.

The worst thing about it, though, is the jiggling. My bed keeps jiggling. This must have been what woke me up. But it's not the Magic fingers. I don't recall putting a quarter in a box. How could I have put a quarter in a box when I was asleep for a couple of days? Impossible. Besides, they take all your money when they bring you in here. So it's definitely not the Magic fingers. Probably just a low-level earthquake—say, 5.2 on the Richter Scale.

There's a knock at the door. Jeez, I hope it isn't the gurney.

What I need is a good lawyer. Somebody to argue my case. I don't know, though, with the fees those guys charge. . . . Maybe I could get someone to take my case on a contingency basis? If I did that, however, I'd have to drop a countersuit on them and claim damages. But then my lawyer would say what damages do we claim? I'd say threatened loss of life, that's what damages, and he'd say number one, we have to have more than a threat, we have to have actual damages in dollars and cents, and number two, what value can be placed on my life? I'd say what about punitive damages, plus the fact that my life is priceless? He'd say they were just doing their jobs, and is my life worth anything to anyone else?

I don't mind saying I've lost faith in the legal profession.

Oh! It's Dora Jiggers and Betsy Bandero! They're the ones who were knocking. I'd know them anywhere. Dora is attired in a tight leather outfit and spike heels. Betsy is sporting a striking negligee. They're both smiling, showing lots of personality and enthusiasm and cleavage. Just like the *Molls* cover.

This is going to turn out better than I thought. Much better.

"O my poor, dear man, what have they done to you?" they ask, and it's XXX and OOO.

"They scourged me and spat upon me and delivered me unto mine enemies," I inform them. "Other than that, I seem to be okay."

"Let's see," they say.

I sit up on the edge of the bed, full of life and ready to go.

They remove a high percentage of my clothes, starting with the white terry-cloth robe and backless hospital gown and working their way down to the boxer shorts. They weigh me and measure me and take my pulse and blood pressure and check my vision, with and without the glasses. Perfect on all counts. Then they instruct me to lie down. I oblige them.

They run the tips of their delicate, practiced fingers over certain of my more sensitive skin cells.

"We're looking for any signs of unusual growth," explains Betsy.

"You missed a spot," I point out to them.

Their probing fingers oblige me.

I say Thank you. I don't mind saying I was well-brought-up. Out in western Kansas we were always taught to say Thank you.

"Sit up," Dora tells me.

I sit up.

"Say ahhh."

Ahhh it is.

They move to the corner of the room for an extensive medical consultation. Or maybe they're just comparing notes?

A thought occurs: "This is a dream. At the sound of the buzzer, you will revert to your normal state. Your molls will vanish, and in their place will suddenly appear a pair of unkempt hags, bringing your morning bedpan."

My nimble mind formulates a pair of hypotheses. One: it is indeed a dream. Two: it is really real. I proceed to formulate the key pros and cons of Hypotheses One through Two.

I. It is a dream. Pro: it certainly has the main characteristic of a dream: it's too good to be true. Con: it's lasted longer than your typical dream: no interruptions from the mundane world. Also, they've touched me in all the right places.

II. It is really real. Pro: it seems like reality—it's being shown in technicolor. Con: when I pinch myself I feel no pain. True, I don't wake up, but the lack of pain is a cause for doubt.

My molls return to my side, and my reflections are aborted.

"Well, what's the prognosis?" I ask.

"You seem to be fine," replies Dora.

"Except that you've lost a lot of weight, and you're all white, and we can practically see right through you," adds Betsy.

"Must be the hospital food."

"No," says Dora, "what we have here is a common set of symptoms, characteristic of 98.6% of resurrection bodies."

So that's the story. A brand-new resurrection body. No wonder I'm feeling so good!

§

We leave my room and promenade down the corridor.

Dora is hanging onto my left arm, and Betsy is firmly ensconced on my right. This is just like that magazine cover: the notorious gangster and his molls, out for a casual stroll. All I need are my dark glasses and hat and a pin-striped double-breasted suit and my gold cigarette holder. It would also help if they'd look up at me adoringly. But as Mildred used to remind me, you can't have everything. Be satisfied with the hand that's dealt you.

We pass a mirror. Who is that handsome devil being adored by two molls? With dark glasses? A pin-striped double-breasted suit? And a gold cigarette holder? Oh! It's me! The new Ed Budwieser!

Who says you can't have everything? Maybe that's true about life, but this is resurrection.

I light a cigarette with a flick of my omnipotent wrist. "Where to?" I inquire.

"You get three guesses," they reply in unison.

This is too easy. "We're going to meet my disciples."

"Who do you think you are?" asks Betsy.

"Disciples?" asks Dora. "*What* disciples?"

One observation I have about resurrection is that when you're asked two questions simultaneously, you get to choose the one you wish to answer. Just like a presidential news conference.

I choose not to answer Betsy's question, Who do you think you are? Instead I opt for Dora's question, What disciples?

"My former students," I remind her. She and I used to teach high school English together. That was before she reputedly ran off with Rev. Heedon and Ms. Mode rid Sunset High of its last dead white male.

"And just what makes you think they remember you with awe and reverence?"

"I taught them about young love. Also, the parts of speech."

"My experience has been," says Betsy, putting her head on my shoulder and gazing soulfully into my eyes, "that young love is not a subject that can be taught. It's inherent."

"What about the parts of speech?"

Dora reaches up and kisses me on the lips.

"Obsolete," she says.

"They now have software programs that can check your grammar," adds Betsy.

Touché.

We pass a food cart piled high with caviar and decorated with champagne on ice. I stop to imbibe. But this small pleasure is interrupted when they remind me that I still have two guesses on the subject of our destination.

"So, are we going for a trip in the Winnebago?"

"That old thing?" replies Dora.

"Didn't it break down on your trip to the West Coast?" asks Betsy.

They have a point, but they're forgetting that the Winnebago has probably also picked up a resurrection body. I remind my two molls of this likelihood.

"This may be true," says Moll Number One, "but it needs more than a resurrection body. It needs a resurrection engine."

"Also," adds Moll Number Two, "resurrection tires."

Again, valid points.

We pass a group of smiling nurses. They wink and blow kisses at me. I raise my right hand, casually and nonchalantly, in acknowledgment.

I still have one guess on the subject of our destination.

Oh. "We're going to visit Mildred."

"Ed! I'm surprised at you!" says Dora, turning and putting her hands on her shapely hips. "'For in the resurrection, they neither marry, nor are given in marriage.'"

"It's in the Bible," says Betsy. "Matthew 22:30. Also, Mark 12:25 and Luke 20:35."

I think I'm going to like this new body!

§

The corridor is longer than I remembered. It's exactly long enough to give you time to make your three guesses, and for your molls to ridicule them.

I stop to consider my surroundings. One thing I notice is that the walls are no longer white. Alabaster, I believe it's called. Another thing, no laundry carts. Just the food carts. Good planning. A third thing, the nurses are no longer scowling. They're all smiles. This could be because they're no longer clad in white dresses and white shoes and stockings. Instead, they sport outfits from the Lands' End ladies swimwear line, plus purple spike heels and Easter bonnets.

We walk on.

Finally, we get to the end of the corridor, hang a right, and enter an auditorium.

It's "Wheel of Fortune."

My two molls escort me to the contestant podium, cover me with affectionate kisses, and take front row seats.

I immediately notice that I'm the only contestant. No coed majoring in film studies at USC. No retired Army colonel from Sedona, Arizona. No real estate agent from Denver. Just me.

This is a good sign.

The slices on the wheel itself show only prizes. No money, just prizes. Perhaps because in the resurrection they neither spend nor are given money to spend. They apparently take vacations, however. All the prizes on the wheel are vacation trips: to Tahiti, to Rio, to Katmandu, to Acapulco, to Disney World, etc. The major cathedrals on the European itinerary are well-represented, as are the pilgrimage sites of India. There's even a trip to a Secret Destination.

Pat asks me to introduce myself to the television audience. "Give us your name," he says, "tell us where you're from, and say something interesting about yourself."

"Hi, I'm Ed Budwieser," I tell everyone, ("Look directly into the camera," Pat says), "I'm from Kirkland, Kansas, I'm a retired high school teacher," ("What was the subject?" asks Pat), "I taught English, I was a role model for the youth of America," ("We need those role models," says Pat), "and I've recently become a proud great-grandfather. I'd like to say hi to all my many friends back in Kirkland, especially the Deuces, and my former wife Mildred and her sister in Luneberger Manor and my two mistresses in the audience, Dora and Betsy, and my son Cyrus in San Francisco and my daughter Charisse and my grandchildren Felicity and Shaun and my great-granddaughter Megan. Hi, Buster." I wave to the camera.

"I call Shaun 'Buster'," I explain to Vanna. "That's what they used to call me. 'Buster Budwieser.' I was all boy."

Vanna shows no surprise at this personal revelation. She is all smiles.

"Are you ready?" says Pat. "Spin the wheel."

I spin the wheel. The pointer lands on Secret Destination.

"Tell us about it, Charlie," says Pat.

Charlie tells us about it. He's all excitement. "Ascension Airlines will fly you and two guests of your choosing to a Secret Destination. There you will achieve serenity, go on national TV, become a cultural icon, and have many adventures. And finally, God will answer your most burning questions."

The audience shouts and whistles. I acknowledge their delight at my well-deserved fortune.

"Let's get going," says Pat. "It's a phrase. Say the secret woid and you win a hunned dollas."

Actually, I just made up that last sentence. Back in my early Kirkland days I was a big fan of Groucho.

Vanna is very alluring in her silver, backless evening gown. She gives a sweep of the arm to indicate the blank letters of the phrase:

_ _ _ _ _ _ _ _ _ _ _ _ _ _ _ _ _ _ _ _.

"I'll have a T," I say.

Vanna flips over three letters. The puzzle reads:

T _ _ _ _ _ T _ _ _ _ _ _ T _ _ _ _ _ _.

Everyone in the studio audience claps.

"I'll have the H," I say. I'm very confident. Not cocky, confident.

Vanna gives me two for the price of one, resulting in:

T _ _ _ _ _ T H _ _ _ _ _ T H _ _ _ _ _.

Applause again. I sense that the audience is behind me one hundred percent. I believe the word is *simpatico*.

"I'd like to buy a vowel."

"Sorry," says Pat, "but resurrection bodies have no truck with filthy lucre. All you have to do is *say* the vowel, we'll give it to you."

"What if it's not there?"

"Trust me," he says, "it will be."

He seems like an honest man, so I take his word for it. "I'll have an E."

"We'll give you more than one," says Pat. "We'll give you *five* E's."

Vanna touches five letters while the audience registers its glee. The board now reads:

T _ _ E _ _ T H E _ _ E _ T H E _ _ E _.

I can't believe my luck. "I'd like to solve the puzzle," I say triumphantly. A hush falls over the audience as Ed ("Buster") Budwieser prepares to speak. He says: "TIME IS THE GREAT HEALER."

Vanna flips over all the letters to reveal the extent of my genius. The audience explodes with applause. The two guests of my choosing rush up to me and cover me with hugs and kisses.

I wink at the camera.

The camera winks back at me.

13

Faith

"What's taking so long?" Dora keeps saying.

"Let's get this show on the road!" Betsy keeps saying.

"I never did trust Pat."

"Rilly. Vanna's the one *I* got a problem with."

"The people at 'Wheel of Fortune' were as good as their word," I remind them. "They never promised that our holiday would begin immediately after I won the prize. They guaranteed only that *if* I solved the puzzle, *then* they would fly me and two guests of my choosing to a Secret Destination, etcetera. They said nothing about 'a forty-day wait.' "

We are gathered around a computer screen. A travel agent is initiating us into the mysteries of airline scheduling. While massaging her keyboard in search of cut-rate fares and a minimum number of layovers, she speaks the language of "advance purchase," "spring special," "weekend stayover," and "no-refund policy."

My molls are not impressed with these fine points. "Let's get it over with," they keep sighing. I sense that they are anxious to board the plane, take off, order drinks, relax and enjoy an adult movie, land, be whisked away in a private limo to the hacienda, and check in, so that they can stroll along the beach with their gorgeous hunk and vie for his affections.

Though I sympathize with their anxiety, I counsel patience. "A thing I learned back in ordinary life," I tell them, "is that there's a reason for everything."

"So what's the reason for the forty-day wait?" asks Dora.

"Judging by certain recent incidents," I explain, "I am expected to spend some quality time with my disciples before we take off."

"Incidents?" says Betsy. "*What* incidents?"

"I am referring specifically to such events as my sufferings, my martyrdom, the great earthquake, awakening on the third day with a resurrection body clad in a white terry-cloth robe, and the arrival of you two ladies at my sepulcher."

"Oh?" says Dora.

§

I keep confronting a problem. My disciples can't seem to recognize me. I don't think it's the grey beard. I don't even think it's my imperially slim physique. Or the dark double-breasted suit and sunglasses. Or the new-found joy. I suspect it's the resurrection body.

The subject of resurrection never came up in English 4. It did not figure prominently in the poems of Robert Frost, nor in the short stories of Ernest Hemingway, nor even in the balcony scene in Act II of *Romeo and Juliet*. It is mentioned in the Bible, to be sure, but ever since *Abington* v. *Schempp* (1963), instructors have not been allowed to teach religion in the public schools. So through no fault of my own, my former charges were never taught the ins and outs of the resurrection body. This explains why even the best and the brightest of my old students don't recognize me. The only things they seem to notice are my traveling companions.

Take Pete Principal, for example. He was fly fishing in a Colorado stream when I caught up with him.

"Pete!" I called from the bank of the rushing river.

Pete glanced over to where my molls and I were standing. Then, as if he had no care in the world, he went back to his troutnapping.

"Pete!" cried my companions.

This time he gave us a long look, through squinted eyes.

"Is that you, Ms. Jiggers?" asked Peter, wading ashore. "Ms. Dora Jiggers, formerly an instructor of Language Arts at Sunset High School in Kirkland, Kansas?"

"The same," replied she.

"Who's your friend?" inquired Pete as he waddled up to greet us in his waders, expectorating tobacco juice left and right.

"Pete, I'd like you to meet Betsy Bandero, late of Southern California," introduced Dora. "Betsy, I'd like you to meet Peter Principal, a former student of mine. Pete won a Boy Scout badge in fly fishing."

"Gladameetcha," responded he, doffing his insect-lanced hat.

"Charmed, I'm sure," returned Betsy, extending the back of her hand and batting her eyelashes.

"Hi, Pete," said I.

"L. A.?" queried Pete, bending over to kiss Betsy's hand.

"San Diego," cooed Betsy, coquettishly cocking her head to one side.

"Hi, Pete," said I.

"Ah yes," retorted Pete. "San Diego, population 1,223,400 (2000 census)."

"It's grown since then," corrected Betsy.

"People keep having babies," explained Dora.

"Mass migration from a friendly neighbor to the south," added Betsy.

"Hi, Pete," said I.

"Who's the scarecrow?" queried Pete.

So my molls interpreted everything to Peter Principal, showing him by many infallible proofs how it was necessary for me to face the agony of white male death, to awaken to life abundant, to go on "Wheel of Fortune" and win a trip to a Secret Destination, and to round up my disciples for a pep rally and last-minute instructions before departing for a life of serenity, worldwide fame, hair-raising escapades, and high-powered theological discussion.

They neglected to mention the part about taking along "two guests of my own choosing."

I corrected them on this point.

"Oh yeah," said Betsy. "That, too."

§

Eleven former students have come to see me off. There would be an even dozen, except that one of them is reportedly in St. Jude's, where he is listed in critical condition from rope burns about the neck.

We gather at the Information Desk of the Kirkland International Airport—an appropriate setting for the last earthly words of Ed Budwieser. Besides my disciples, there is a fringe of idle curiosity seekers and, of course, the everpresent gaggle of local reporters, who rudely thrust microphones and lights and cameras into my face and subject me to an impromptu press conference.

"What's yer personal impression of Vanna is Pat really as clever and charming as he seems how's it feel to win a trip to wherever could ya tell us more about the Secret Destination are ya rested from yer forty days in the wilderness what's it like to have a resurrection body where'd ya get the silly costume how d'ya rate two broads?"

I raise my arms majestically, charismatically.

I speak into the microphone. "May I have your attention, please."

"CAN'T HEAR YOU," says a voice in the back. "SPEAK UP!"

"THE MIKE DOESN'T SEEM TO BE WORKING," says another.

It's working, all right. It's just not in sync with my remodeled organ of speech. "YOU'RE PROBABLY WONDERING WHY I CALLED YOU HERE TODAY."

A hush descends over the crowd.

"Could you modulate that just a little?" says Pete Principal.

"I will read a prepared statement, after which I'll take questions. . . . There, is that better?"

"That's fine, as far as volume is concerned," says Jim Evereddy. "Now, if you could just cut down on the melodrama, all systems would be go. Remember what you taught us: you are reading a poem, you are not giving a karate demonstration."

"Also," chimes in Johnny Evereddy, his younger brother, "you might suck in your gut before you begin. It relaxes you. Remember, this is what you taught us. 'Suck in your gut, and lock eyes with two or three significant persons in the audience.'"

I can't help thinking that my students have been well-taught.

I read my prepared statement:

"It's always difficult to say goodbye. But before I do, I'd like to thank the many persons who have been significant in my life: my mother Mary, who brought me into this world, and my father Rufus, who taught me how to make bird cages, and my grandmother, who gave me the name *Buster*, and my first wife Mildred, who got me interested in 'Wheel of Fortune,' and my children by a previous marriage, Charisse and Cyrus, who gave me the book that aroused my interest in the subject of the afterlife, and the Deuces, whose spirited disputes on the issue narrowed my options down to two," etcetera etcetera. "Last but not least, I'd like to thank a certain Higher Power, who made it possible for me to be here today with a brand-new resurrection body."

The curiosity seekers in the crowd begin to meander toward the gates to meet their loved ones.

I stay them with a word:

"Wait! I'm not through."

They turn around and gape.

"I'd also like to take this occasion to forgive several people: my first wife Mildred, who neglected to meet my every requirement, and my physician, Dr. Wunder, whose remedies failed me in my hour of need, and my dentist, Dr. Digby, who gave me questionable financial advice, as well as Ms. Mode, who subjected me to severe humiliation, and the Deuces, who always underestimated me. To all of them I say, God bless. Now, the questions."

Q. An unconfirmed rumor has it that you once didn't believe in God. What happened to make you change your mind?

A. Number one, this resurrection body, and numbers two and three, a couple of very fine ladies.

Q. Tell us something about your resurrection body, wouldja? For instance, do you have to use the bathroom?

A. Let's just say I don't get up in the middle of the night as often as I used to.

Q. What about sex? Can you have sex with, for example, your—

"Tell him it's none of his business," Dora whispers in my left ear.

"Tell him we're not that kind of girls," Betsy whispers in my right ear.

A. It's none of your business, they're not that kind of girls, and I'm not running for president.

Q. Would you accept a draft?

A. Perhaps when I return.

Q. And when will that be?

A. No man knoweth the hour, nor the day.

Q. Approximately?

A. It depends on a number of factors, including how soon things get really bad. When I do come back, however, it won't be a pretty sight.

Q. What in your opinion is the number one problem facing the American people?

A. A lack of appreciation of the Classics.

Q. To what do you attribute this lack of . . . what was that again?

A. Appreciation of the Classics.

Q. How do you spell it?

I spell it out.

Q. To what do you attribute this lack of depreciation of the classes?

A. Poor pedagogy.

Q. Poor what?

A. Let me give you an example of *good* pedagogy.

My students smile and exchange glances. They know what's coming next.

"It's a pop quiz," I say. "Ready?"

My students feign groans. The curiosity seekers head for the exits.

"Now then," I say. "'O, wild West Wind, thou breath of Autumn's being.' Who penned those celebrated lines?"

"Keats," says Andy Principal.

"Keats, hell," says Philippa Martinez. "It's Shelley, isn't it, Mr. Budweiser? 'Ode to the West Wind'. The opening line."

I hate it when women swear. I also detest it when they mispronounce my last name. But I overlook these petty faults. "Correct," I say. "Now, what were Shelley's dates?"

"1792-1882," says Andy Principal.

The media pack up their gear and head back for their stations and the "Five O'Clock News." My eleven former students can now relax, as can my two ladies.

"Now stop to think," I say. "If Shelley were born in 1792 and died in 1882, how old would that make him when he died?"

"He'd be about your age," says Jim Evereddy.

A murmur of disapproval spreads through the crowd. They do not appreciate having their role model pilloried.

"Ninety," says Andy Principal. Andy is Pete's older brother. They used to live over on East 25th, the sons of Fred and Maxine Principal. Andy was a decathlon man, and Pete was the brain in the family. Their Senior yearbook predicted Andy would compete in the Olympics and Pete would some day be a Harvard professor. Andy now drives a waste disposal truck in Oakland, and Pete is a weekend fly fisherman, specializing in Colorado streams.

But back to the subject of Shelley's age. "Ninety," says Andy Principal.

"Correct," I say, my nimble mind subtracting 1792 from 1882. "Ninety. But what is one of the main characteristics of the Romantic poets? I refer to their longevity."

"They all died young," says Philippa Martinez.

"Excellent!" I say. I always reward accurate answers with compliments. It's good pedagogical technique.

"What about Wordsworth?" says Tom Zweifel. "William Wordsworth, author of 'Lines Composed a Few Miles Above Tintern Abbey.' He lived to be eighty. Dates: 1770-1850."

I stiffen slightly. "Wordsworth was not your prototypical Romantic poet. Keats was."

"John Keats, 1795-1821," says Philippa Martinez.

"Excellent!" I say.

"What about Coleridge?" says Tom Zweifel. "He was a prototypical Romantic poet, and he lived to be sixty-two. Samuel Taylor Coleridge, 1772-1834, son of a clergyman, experimented with opium, author of 'The Rime of the Ancient Mariner,' 'Kubla Khan,' and 'Dejection: An Ode.'"

"I challenge that," I say. "Not as to the details and the use of drugs, which I cannot condone, but as to his being a prototypical Romantic poet."

"That's what you taught us," maintains Tom. "Here, I have it in my notes. See? 'Coleridge—quintessential Romantic poet'."

"Aha," I reply, elevating my right index finger. "*Quintessential*. Not *prototypical*."

Another hush descends over the crowd. I can read their thoughts: "That's our Mister Budwieser, all right. Mind like a razor!"

"So what were Shelley's correct dates?" asks Andy. "In case it's on the final."

"Percy Bysshe Shelley, 1792-1822," says Philippa Martinez.

"Excellent!" I say. "Now, where were we?"

"'Ode to the West Wind,'" says Jim Evereddy.

"Ah yes," I recall. "'O, wild West Wind, thou breath of Autumn's being—'"

"I don't mean to be critical," interrupts Tom Zweifel, "but here it is, late spring, and you're reading a poem about *autumn*, fer chrissakes. What gives?"

"Tom," I reply patiently, "there's a reason for everything."

A voice suddenly bursts over the loudspeaker: "MAY I HAVE YOUR ATTENTION PLEASE. LAST CALL, ASCENSION AIRLINES, FLIGHT 40. ALL PASSENGERS PLEASE COME TO GATE 7."

There are hurried kisses and handshakes. No time to put young Mr. Zweifel in his place by explaining the religious significance of the Shelley poem, the Biblical reference, the fulfillment of prophecy, etc. Time only for last-minute advice for life without Mr. Budwieser, M.A.:

"Do unto others."

"An eye for a tooth."

"Blessed are the C students, for they shall be elected."

"Love one another." I squeeze my molls to set an example. Again, good pedagogical technique.

"Don't forget to read your children the Classics."

Then I place my keys in Pete's capable care, adjust my dark glasses and black hat, light a costly cigarette, insert it into my gold holder, take a long drag, gather my two molls about me, fling a telling response or two over my left shoulder at Tom Zweifel, and stroll casually in the direction of Gate 7.

§

Dora is worried.

We are sitting in a small space directly behind the cockpit, and my blonde moll is showing unmistakable signs of anxiety.

"What's to keep us from suffocating?" she wonders aloud.

I patiently explain my hard-won insight, that there is a reason for everything. "I believe I can say without fear of contradiction that if it were not for my faith in this cardinal truth of existence, I would not be what I am today."

"So what's the reason for this cubbyhole?"

"It was designed for a resurrection body and a pair of beautiful ladies. And it's not a cubbyhole. It's a space-saving device."

"Is that why we're so cramped?"

"You have to sit up straight and hold in your tummy."

"Let's get back to the question of what it's designed for," says Betsy. "It looks to me like it's designed for mail." She indicates the three canvas bags on which we are sitting.

"Appearances are deceptive," I inform her. "Canvas is an environmentally-responsible product. That would explain its use within this context."

"Let's see 'bout that," she says.

She pushes Dora off her canvas bag and starts to open it.

"What?" I reprove her. "Have ye no faith?"

"I got lots of faith," says Betsy. "I just like to check it out once in a while."

The canvas bag appears to contain postcards.

Betsy takes several apparent postcards from the spacious bag and reads the addresses: "Ross Ice Shelf . . . South Pole . . . Ross Ice Shelf . . . South Pole. Notice anything significant about these places?"

"They're in Antarctica!" says Dora.

"Didn't you say we were headed for Mexico?" says Betsy.

"We are," I say confidently.

"Then how do you explain those addresses?" asks Dora.

"Computer error," I patiently explain.

Dora is still worried.

"Maybe we're on the wrong plane," she suggests. She is strumming her fingers and staring out the window.

Once again, I remind her that there is a reason for everything. I list all known instances of this fact, citing widely-accepted scientific theories as well as Scriptural texts. "I believe I can say without fear of contradiction," I conclude, "that if it were not for my faith—"

"So how do you explain the fact that we're over the ocean?" she interrupts.

I take her hand in mine and gently explain how appearance is often mistaken for reality. The metaphysical reflections of Plato figure prominently in this explanation, which is exceptionally convincing.

Betsy, however, looks out the window.

"I don't know nothing 'bout this Plato guy," she says, "but we're still over some ocean."

I smile at her naïvete.

"Look," says Betsy. "Look and see."

I look, but I don't see.

"You're looking like a man," she says. "Wipe that steam off the window."

Oh.

Well.

Looks like the Pacific Ocean.

"It *could* be interpreted as heading for Antarctica," I acknowledge. "A superior explanation, however, would be that we are indeed *now* headed deep south, but that once we dispose of these postcards we will immediately turn around and head directly for Mexico."

"It could also be interpreted as being on the wrong plane," says Betsy.

And still Dora worries.

She has gone into the cockpit to promise the pilot a pleasant surprise if he will fly us to our destination, but she remains anxious.

"What about the landing field?" she frets.

Again I explain that there is a reason for everything, adding that God will provide.

"I don't see how we can land in the snow with rubber tires," she worries.

"Remember, 'God's in his heaven, all's right with the world.'" I point out that I am living proof of this maxim.

"Maybe this plane comes equipped with snow skis."

"Then again," I point out, "maybe it doesn't."

"Why don't you *look and see* if there's any snow skis aboard?" suggests Betsy.

"They are in a secret compartment," I theorize. "That would be God's way of providing."

Betsy is not satisfied with this theory. She pushes me off my canvas bag, opens it, and inspects its contents. Exactly as I thought. There is no mail inside. No postcards, no first-class letters, no junk mail, no complimentary cereal boxes, no soap samples, no Book-of-the-Month-Club dunning notices. No snow skis, either. Just a body.

The body belongs to Pete Principal.

Peter isn't dead. He could, however, use some first aid.

Betsy quickly sizes up the situation. She throws herself down on the floor of our cubbyhole, stretches her voluptuous body over the living corpse of Peter P., gently places her hand under his dazed but handsome head, and begins to administer mouth-to-mouth resuscitation. This seems to be effective, so she proceeds to unbutton all available buttons and to loosen all restrictive clothing.

At last Peter comes to. He sighs.

She returns his sigh.

But Peter misinterprets. Thinking that *she* is now the one who requires first aid, he rolls over and stretches his muscular frame over her voluptuous body, places his hand under her raven-tressed head, resumes the mouth-to-mouth resuscitation, proceeds to unbutton all her available buttons and loosen all her restrictive clothing, removes his waders, & etc.

I bend down to point out this mistake to Peter Principal. "I think you're misinterpreting the situation."

Dora bends down and whispers in my ear: "Let's discuss the problem of the landing field."

I sit up. She and I engage in spirited but amicable debate on the problem.

Dora's theory is that Ascension Airlines equips its craft with snow skis. My theory is that God will provide.

We discuss the pros and cons of Dora's theory.

"It seems to me," I say, "that if Ascension Airlines did indeed equip its craft with snow skis, we would have noticed this important fact about the plane as we boarded it. I, for one, did not notice any snow skis attached to the landing gear. Did you?"

She points out that we were in a hurry at the time, that we were running after the aircraft as it was taxiing down the runway, that there may well have been snow skis attached to the landing gear but that it was neither the time nor the place to inspect the details of our personnel carrier. "For instance," she says, "did you catch the markings of this plane?"

"AA," I reply. "In spray-painted letters. Ascension Airlines. And I saw no snow skis."

"AA also refers to a well-known worldwide organization."

"But do they operate their own airline?" A point in favor of Ed Budwieser.

"Well," she quickly resumes, "perhaps the plane comes equipped with a mechanical device that replaces the tires with a set of snow skis, which will allow us to land on the ice fields of Antarctica without incident."

I disagree.

"It is my understanding," she says, "that your assumption is that God will provide, that this is how the problem of the landing field will be resolved. Do I understand your position correctly?"

"You do."

"Well," she says, her eyes shining with misplaced triumph, "if God will provide, why wouldn't he provide by equipping the plane with a mechanical device that would replace the tires with snow skis, just as we are descending?"

"That's not the way God works," I reply. "He doesn't use mechanical devices. He specializes in miraculous intervention."

"For instance?" she says.

"'His ways are past finding out.'"

"If His ways are past finding out, that still doesn't rule out the use of mechanical devices. Maybe miraculous intervention takes the *form* of using mechanical devices. Have you considered that possibility? It's plausible, from a theoretical point of view. Divine miracle through human means."

"Perhaps what is at stake here is a definition of miracle."

Betsy sits up. "Oh, *God!*" she interjects. She is apparently finished with the administration of first aid and is now free to get up and move about the cabin at her own pleasure. "Why don't you just ask the effing *pilot* about the problem of the damn landing field?"

I hate it when women swear. She does, however, have a point.

Dora knocks at the cockpit door. It opens, leaving the cargo department awash in the drone of the Briggs & Stratton engine. She says something to the pilot, a tall, handsome chap—a somewhat younger, less mature Ed Budwieser, except for the ponytail and pierced ear. He shakes his head. She goes over and sits on his lap. She whispers something in his ear. It probably has something to do with the problem of the landing field. He whispers something back. This continues for some time. It is a complex and difficult problem, the landing field, which explains the length of the conversation. Then she strokes his cheek. There's undoubtedly a piece of lint on it. That would explain why she is stroking his cheek. Just a piece of lint, that's all. Then she runs her fingers through his hair, bends down, and kisses him on the forehead. I'm sure it's the forehead. It couldn't be . . . no, it's probably the forehead.

These acts could be misconstrued as signs of affection. After we get to Mexico, I'll have to talk to her about this matter. We have to be careful about appearances, I'll point out to her, and she'll reply that it was only her way of thanking the young man for being helpful. Besides, she'll add coquettishly, he reminds her of a callow, less mature me. Was I jealous? she'll pout. I'll flash my mature smile and cavalierly retort—

Dora gets up from her temporary seating position, closes the cockpit door, and comes back to give us the solution to the problem of the landing field.

We listen for her words.

These are her words: "WHAT DO YOU THINK THESE PARACHUTES ARE FOR?"

"*What* parachutes?"

In answer, she opens her canvas bag and inspects its contents.

There are indeed parachutes. Three of them.

"How do they work?" I ask. This is not an idle question.

Betsy volunteers the information that she used to belong to a sky-diving club. This is good information to have, given the parameters of our particular situation. We are fortunate in having Betsy aboard, fortunate indeed.

She helps us with our parachutes, then dons one herself. Under ordinary circumstances, I would prefer to see her donned in a silver, backless evening gown, reminiscent of Vanna, but these are not ordinary circumstances. Under the present circumstances, I enjoy seeing her in a parachute.

§

Betsy is explaining the procedure. "Count to ten before pulling the ripcord."

"Does it have to be ten? Couldn't it be another number?" I'm thinking of two.

"No," she says, "it has to be ten."

"An alternative," suggests Dora, "would be to float down together, in formation, for several miles."

This suggestion leads to a heated discussion of several topics: the wind resistance factor; the weight of resurrection bodies relative to regular bodies; their ability to tolerate pain; probability; risk management; and gambling as a moral vice.

I choose this moment to make an impassioned speech. My first point is that I am an amateur in the business of sky-diving. My second point is that amateurs make poor formation flyers. I conclude with the observation that I would prefer to take a rain check on this outstanding opportunity.

They look at each other and wink and nod agreement. "Fine speech," they are thinking.

Dora returns to the cockpit. She closes the door, explaining that the reason for this has nothing to do with the desire for privacy. It has to do, she informs us, with maintaining constant air pressure.

When she returns ten minutes later, she announces that we will be jumping in thirty seconds.

The question of the order of jump is quickly broached.

"Ed, you go first," says Dora. "You're our big, strong male leader."

Betsy seconds the motion.

Peter Principal smiles his agreement.

It's three to nothing, with one abstention.

Too late to ask for a recount.

Ten, nine, eight, seven. . . .

I'm having second thoughts about the resurrection option.

Six, five, four. . . .

Maybe I should've gone for the long shining tube?

Three, two, one. . . .

Immortality through grandchildren?

14

Serenity

The textbooks are correct. Winter days in Antarctica are extremely short. The sun hardly ever rises, and when it does, it immediately drops back down.

In her anxiety over the problem of the landing field, Dora neglected to worry about the problem of inadequate lighting. She overlooked the fact that by the time we land, it will be night.

Darkness is spreading over the icy bay below me.

The sun is slowly disappearing.

I am reminded of Mildred's western Kansas wisdom. "You can't have everything," she used to say. "Be satisfied with the hand that's dealt you."

But what a hand! Two libidinous, pulchritudinous molls. Extreme privacy. Large blocks of uninterrupted time. One could hardly ask for more.

What did Charlie say? "You will achieve serenity."

Serenity? Is that the word we want? Serenity . . . serenity. Synonym, *repose*. Infinitive, *to lie down*. How did I have Hamlet put it? “And by a sleep to say we end the heart-ache and the thousand natural shocks that flesh is heir to: ’tis a consummation devoutly to be wish’d.” Excellent, well-put, if I do say so. Full of double meanings. Consummation—and with both of them! Serenity indeed.

At last! The West Coast of Antarctica!

Exactly as I imagined it. Majestic landscape. Pristine snow. Wild, jagged rocks. Plenty of fresh cold water. Penguins, with the mien of butlers, to serve us fish on slabs of pure ice. Dora and Betsy in fire-red parkas, underneath which. . . .

But I anticipate. Dora and Betsy have not yet landed. Or, if they have, they are nowhere to be seen. Not at night.

No sense in looking for them now. I’ll wait till morning.

My parachute, properly deployed, will make a nice warm tent.

What are those damned penguins doing on my parachute?

Well . . . it *would* have made a nice warm tent.

Ah yes. The West Coast of Antarctica.

A thought occurs. Does Antarctica even have a West Coast? Does it have an East Coast? Or only lots and lots of North Coast?

Why did they not they discuss this question in fourth-grade Geography?

A mental note: write my senators and representative. Subject: curriculum reform.

Dawn is breaking. I have but minutes to locate my two wondrous ladies.

Up and about, you resurrected hunk, you.

I scan the horizon.

They are nowhere to be seen. . . .

Perhaps there was a problem with the parachute straps. . . .

Perhaps the wind currents have wafted them to another shore, where they now repose, yearning for my presence. . . .

Perhaps the engine of that frail craft has sputtered to a stop, leaving them to plummet into the vast ocean and thence to the depths beneath. . . .

Perhaps. . . .

Why are the penguins gazing into the empyrean?

It appears that somebody is falling out of the sky.

Dora!

Where, then, is Betsy?

Peter Principal!

Well . . . one moll is better than none.

But it is not Dora. Dora is a tall, languorous blonde. This woman appears to be a petite brunette.

Betsy!

So where is Dora?

The young pilot! The pierced ear and ponytail! Rev. Heedon?

. . . One moll is still better than none.

But it's not Betsy. Betsy is buxom. This woman has a somewhat flatter configuration.

Hark! Her voice echoes over the frozen wastes.

"Did you remember to take out the trash?"

It's . . .

I thought she was spending a lot of time in Luneberger Manor?

Antarctica? Not what it's cracked up to be.

§

May 10

Mildred does not like the way I am dressed. I point out that my costume fits my new resurrection personality. She disagrees. I ask what she proposes. She thinks I would look good in a long white robe, to match her nightgown, and offers to sew me one. I agree with her on the general subject of my wearing a long robe; as to the specific color, however, I dissent. She asks what I propose. I propose saffron.

May 11

Mildred wants an igloo. I point out that igloos are inappropriate in Antarctica. She says she knows it, but it's mating season, and what do I propose. I propose that our two parachutes, sewn together and properly deployed, would make an excellent residence. She wants to know who's going to clean off the penguin droppings.

May 12

Today I built my first igloo.

May 13

Tonight, a housewarming.

May 15

I'm going to be a daddy!

May 22

Twins. We name them Charisse and Cyrus.

Mildred straightened them out right away. She pointed out that we're the only resurrection bodies in Antarctica, so we have to set a Christian example for the penguins.

May 23

Mildred is worried. She thinks I should make her an honest woman. I remind her that "in the resurrection, they neither marry nor are given in marriage." She points out that this makes our children illegitimate. In Antarctica, I explain, being born out of wedlock is not frowned upon. It is looked upon as a natural part of resurrection.

May 24

Today Charisse and Cyrus taught the penguins to play games: William Tell, Twenty Questions, and Authors. They tried to get the penguins to put apples on their heads, but penguins are by nature a suspicious lot. Then they tried to teach them Twenty Questions, but apparently these birds have very little intellectual curiosity. That left Authors, a game that introduces them to the Classics.

May 26

It appears that the Ross Ice Shelf is now on the itinerary of the Major Cruise Line.

When the ship docked in our harbor today, it disgorged its flashlight-bearing passengers, in search of tourist attractions. The Disney people, however, have not yet erected a theme park around here, which means tourist attractions in this part of the world are severely limited.

As soon as the passengers disembarked, they flocked to the kids and penguins, tossed them popcorn, pulled out their flash cameras, and shot pictures of them playing Authors, using little shards of ice for cards and fish-oil candles for light. Then they looked around for other major attractions. They spotted Mildred and me, serenely sitting on the deck of our igloo in the light of the moon—Mildred working on a crossword, I working on Part II of my memoirs. They immediately flocked to us, tossed us popcorn, pulled out their cameras, and demanded that we pose.

Mildred and I obliged. She's always been a people person, and I've learned to do what I'm told.

A woman from Iowa said "Ew, don't they remind you of that famous picture?" and her husband said "Which one?" and she said "You know, the one of the couple with the pitchfork," and he said "Oh, you mean American Gothic," and she said "That's it, American Gothic, don't they just remind you of that couple?"

May 27

Does a resurrection body show up on film?

This is a question on which I have been meditating.

I don't know the answer. I didn't ask to see the pictures, and neither did Mildred. We're not vain people. Back in western Kansas we were taught the virtue of modesty.

May 29

Charisse and Cyrus took a ship back to America.

When they first broached the idea, Mildred was worried that the tourists on the ship would be a bad influence on them and try to sell them drugs, and that the ship would encounter storms as it crossed the wide Pacific, and that the penguins would feel abandoned by their playmates and would take out their frustrations on the parents by refusing to serve them their meals, that the kids would not settle down and get married, that America would not be hospitable to the offspring of resurrection persons, and that she and I would lose touch with them, perhaps permanently.

Charisse and Cyrus sought to allay her fears. "Drugs? what are drugs?" they asked. "What's the wide Pacific? The penguins can go back to rolling in the snow. America is said to be a very warmhearted country. We'll stay away from bad influences, we'll seek out nice young Christian people as our friends. We promise to write."

There was never much for the children to do down here at the bottom of the world. They had lots of time on their hands and very few hobbies. A deadly combination.

So the children left for America. I believe the plan is to give them jobs in a zoo. Probably in the penguin section.

"Where will they sleep? Who will cook for them? What will their salaries be? Who will pay for their college tuition? Will they be allowed to go to church regularly?" These were the questions Mildred asked the man.

"Don't worry," the man said. "That will all be taken care of. Your children will have the best care possible, the best beds, the best food. Their salaries will be commensurate with their skills and their good old American work ethic. My zoo will see to it that they get the best education possible. They will be allowed to go to the church of their choice, or, if they wish, to stay away from the churches of their choice, <u>Everson v. Board of Education</u> (1947). This is the American way."

"Do you promise?" said Mildred.

"Indeed I do," said the man. "I guarantee it."

So Mildred gave the nice American man a list of special instructions for the care and nurture of young resurrection bodies. Then tearful goodbyes were exchanged, and the children were on their way.

May 30

We're learning to cope with the empty igloo syndrome.

§

Selections from *The Teachings of Master Ed, Part I:*

In order to prosper in this region of the globe, it is desirable to have a resurrection body. Antarctica is death on regular bodies. Explorers with regular bodies have found this out the hard way. Men have perished in the Antarctic wastes, horses have perished, dogs have perished. Only penguins seem to have escaped the general slaughter.

Resurrection bodies can either fast or eat. Fasting is just like dieting, except that it leads to serenity. The eating is limited to items on the menu, which in this hardy clime is fish-intensive. Because fish is a Lenten food, and Lent is a religious season, the eating of fish, like fasting, also has spiritual benefits. So it makes no difference whether the resurrection body fasts or eats.

We choose to eat.

One might think that a constant regimen of posing, popcorn, and fish would become boring. Not true. It is an honor to be asked to adopt the pose that Grant Wood made famous.

In the period of time I have spent here, I have yet to be bored, despite the limited cultural possibilities Antarctica has to offer. This might be because I spent my regular life in Kansas. After Kansas, everything is an ecstasy.

It is amazing how many recipes there are for fish. In Craig Claiborne's New York Times Cook Book alone, for example, there are seventy-two pages of fish recipes.

All this is not to say that life here is nothing but a perpetual ecstasy. In fact, the word is serene. No boredom, an ecstasy or two around mealtime, and the rest is serenity: that is the substance of the Antarctic experience.

"You will achieve serenity." Charlie was right.

More should be said regarding serenity, perhaps.

In the state of serenity, REM (rapid eye movement) is held to a minimum.

There seems to be no difference between serenity as experienced by the male of the species and as experienced by the female of the species.

I have yet to see a serene child, however.

In the state of serenity, there is no need for nicotine and alcohol. Popcorn, yes. Nicotine and alcohol, no.

Serenity may lead to the loss of libido. Therefore, it should be cultivated with great caution.

I have come to recognize my vocation as a spiritual trailblazer. Soon there will be other spiritual beings, who will learn of my achievement of serenity and seek to follow in my footsteps. In time, Antarctica will be dotted with small colonies of spiritual seekers, who, tired of the life of grasping and striving, will become like their Master, Ed. Those small colonies will be known as "The Serene Ones." I will be their acknowledged leader and example. Our fame will spread throughout the globe. Thousands of like-minded spiritual beings will journey to this icy continent and seek to emulate our achievements.

ABC has heard of my spiritual achievements and is sending a television crew for an interview. The Mountain is coming to Muhammad.

What did Charlie say? "You will go on national TV."

Who will the interviewer be? This is the question of the hour.

I suspect it will be Barbara Walters herself. This is a big story, a big story indeed. "The Spiritual Achievements of Master Ed": the top brass at ABC know a human interest story when they see one, so it will be Barbara Walters. Of this I am certain.

Mildred, however, suspects it will be Ted Koppel. "He will ask tough questions. How do you know this? How do you know that? Why should our viewers believe you? Be prepared for Ted Koppel," she says. "Think of the questions he will ask. Think of your answers."

"It is going to be Barbara Walters," I retort. "She will ask questions along the lines of, How do you differ from Gandhi? from St. Francis? from Buddha?"

"Beware," replies Mildred with the wag of a finger. "Beware the Koppel skepticism."

"Even if it is Ted Koppel," I retort, "so what? His vaunted skepticism will be no match for my serenity."

"Don't say I didn't warn you."

§

KOPPEL: Could you tell us, Mrs. Budwieser, how you came to be on the Ross Ice Shelf down there in Antarctica? Is it true that you escaped from a mental hospital?

MILDRED: First off I'd like to say hi to everybody back in the good old U. S. of A. Hi, Deuces. Hi, Dr. Rex. I'm a lot better, thanks to Dr. Buller and finding out about my past lives. Hi, Thelma. All is forgiven. Your secret is safe with me. Hi, Rev. Gilltrip. Did I ever tell you how much I enjoyed your sermons? Hi, Carole. Keep up the good work [wink wink]. Hi, Dr. Digby. You should be ashamed of yourself, getting involved with an innocent young girl like Sue. There ought to be a law. Hi, Charisse and Cyrus. How are things working out at the zoo? Write, would you? Your old dad and I would sure like to hear from you.

KOPPEL: We're pressed for time, Mrs. Budwieser, I wonder if you could just answer my question.

MILDRED: I'm sorry, what was the question?

KOPPEL: Isn't it true that you escaped from a mental hospital?

MILDRED: First of all, it wasn't really a mental hospital, it was more like a rest home, and second of all, I didn't exactly escape, I just walked out the door, because the cake fell. She added a file to the recipe, Carole did, she doesn't cook much, she's too busy running around in German cars, which if you ask me is one of the reasons her marriage failed. And you have to understand it was Carole's idea, the file and the bars and the bedsheet and everything, I was just an innocent dupe—a four-letter word beginning with D. Also, it was probably in my horoscope for that day, I'm a Pisces, which is another reason I can't be held responsible.

KOPPEL: I'm afraid I don't understand.

MILDRED: Oh, did I mention I'm also a fictional character?

KOPPEL: What?

MILDRED: If you don't believe me, just ask Dr. Buller.

KOPPEL: Who?

MILDRED: Plus the fact that I have a resurrection body.

KOPPEL: I'm sorry, our audio seems to be malfunctioning. I thought I heard you say something about a resurrection body.

MILDRED: Right. Ed and I have resurrection bodies. Which proves there's a God, in case anyone in their right mind ever doubted it.

KOPPEL: I have to admit, I'm at a complete loss. Could you explain to your fellow Americans what a resurrection body is?

MILDRED: That's Ed's area of expertise. He's done a lot of reading on the subject.

KOPPEL: Mr. Budwieser, your wife—

ED: Strictly speaking, I'm not Mr. Budwieser, and Mildred's not my wife. "For in the resurrection, they neither marry, nor are given in marriage." Matthew 22:30, and so forth.

KOPPEL: Then whom am I addressing?

ED: You can just call me Master Ed.

KOPPEL: Mister Ed, could you tell us how you came to be on the Ross Ice Shelf down there in Antarctica?

ED: First I'd like to invite all like-minded spiritual beings to come down and join us. We are known as "The Serene Ones." I'll be happy to aid you in your quest for spiritual serenity. Just send $100 and a self-addressed stamped envelope to—

KOPPEL: We're pressed for time, Mister Ed, I wonder if you could just answer my question.

ED: I'm sorry, what was the question?

KOPPEL: Isn't it true that you escaped from a hospital?

ED: Not at all. It is true that I *left* a hospital. It is not true that I *escaped* from a hospital.

KOPPEL: Perhaps we have a definitional issue here. Most people would say that if you *left* a hospital without a signed release form, you *escaped* from that hospital.

ED: All I can say is, they tied a tag to my big toe. I just assumed that when they tie a tag to your big toe, you're free to get up and move about. Which is just what I did. A couple of very fine ladies came into my room and invited me out for a stroll. We walked down the corridor, hung a right, and found ourselves in the "Wheel of Fortune" studio. The puzzle was "Time is the great healer," which has always been my philosophy, and I solved it. I won a trip to Antarctica. Ascension Airlines flew me and my very fine ladies to this barren land, and I parachuted down, and here I am. I don't know what happened to my very fine ladies, incidentally. When I get to Heaven, that's the first question I'm going to ask.

MILDRED: You told me *this* was Heaven.

KOPPEL: I must say, Mister Ed, that the majority of Americans would find your story hard to believe.

MILDRED: The majority of Americans would find most of his stories hard to believe.

ED: The majority of Americans don't have resurrection bodies.

KOPPEL: Which brings us back to the question of resurrection bodies. But before we get to that question, we have to take time out for these important messages.

"You didn't tell me about the very fine ladies," says Mildred as soon as the television audience is out of earshot.

"You didn't tell me you'd escaped from a mental hospital."

"I didn't escape, Carole's plan fell through, like I just told America. Which floozies were they, besides Betsy?"

"They weren't floozies, the other one was Dora. What were you doing in a mental institution?"

"I was suffering from the Ophelia complex. I thought Dora ran off with the preacher?"

"That was a smokescreen, she just wanted to get away from Kirkland. What about the Ophelia complex, was that also Mabel's problem?"

"No, she was Lady Godiva in a previous existence. I want to hear more about your 'very fine' ladies."

"I thought you didn't believe in reincarnation. It's a long story."

"Quit changing the subject, I'm all ears."

One thing I have noticed about serenity is that it is not guaranteed. The moment you think you have achieved a serene mind, beware. The fact that you inhabit a resurrection body does not mean that you are safe from the ordinary passions and vicissitudes of life. Take Mildred, for instance. As soon as we are off the air, even temporarily, she loses her Antarctic serenity and we are back to Square One.

Never underestimate the abilities of Master Ed, however. I have become adept at dealing with this type of a situation. Though Mildred's serenity has abandoned her, mine has not. My three weeks on the Ross Ice Shelf have not been for naught. In the two minutes it takes for ABC to glorify the new Infiniti and to entice the cats and dogs of America with a new gourmet oat bran, I am able to transfer some of my hard-won serenity to Mildred. Master Ed at work.

KOPPEL: We're back, and Mister Ed was going to tell us about resurrection bodies.

ED: Studies have shown that a resurrection body weighs the same as a regular body, divided by 3.14159265, or *pi* carried out to eight decimals.

KOPPEL: Cut the statistics and get to the point.

ED: Resurrection bodies are much lighter than regular bodies, and they tend to be white. Also, you can practically see right through them. This is true of approximately 98.6% of resurrection bodies.

KOPPEL: Are you claiming that you and Mrs. Budwieser have RBs?

ED: Indeed I am.

KOPPEL: Then why do you show up on camera?

ED: The physics of it escapes me. But the important thing is not the *physics* of resurrection bodies. The important thing is the *fact* of resurrection bodies.

KOPPEL: And that fact is exactly what's under dispute here.

MILDRED: Why don't you just come down here, Mr. Koppel, and check us out? I challenge you to come down to Antarctica and see for yourselves what a resurrection body looks like.

KOPPEL: I may do that some day, Mrs. Budwieser. But for now, what I want is some *proof* that you and your husband have replaced your regular bodies with RBs. That's the issue, whether you really have RBs, or whether you are simply escaped fugitives from a couple of Kansas hospitals, causing severe environmental damage to the natural habitat of the Antarctic penguins.

MILDRED: Aren't we white?

KOPPEL: You certainly are, but that can be attributed to the Antarctic winter.

ED: Why don't you have your camera crew weigh us?

KOPPEL: I'm sure they don't have a scale with them, and besides, what would that prove? So you've lost a little weight, so what? That's to be expected in a frigid climate.

ED: What about our serenity? Have you ever seen this much serenity in ordinary bodies?

KOPPEL: I'm sure most members of our viewing audience would say hey, they're half frozen to death, why wouldn't they appear serene?

ED: And *I'm* sure most members of your viewing audience don't cultivate serenity. However, if they would just send me $100—

KOPPEL: I'm sorry, we don't have time to argue that point, we have to take a break. When we come back, we'll talk to a pair of distinguished guests in our KOOK studio in Kirkland, Kansas, Dr. Edward P. Rex and the Rev. Dr. Horace K. Gilltrip. We'll get their ideas on the infamous *American Gothic* couple down in Antarctica.

Charlie was right. "You will become a cultural icon."

§

The members of the ABC camera crew were very nice to us. *They* did not accuse us of causing severe damage to the natural habitat of the penguins.

This may be because they, unlike Ted Koppel, could see that we had resurrection bodies, and they knew that the resurrection body is unable to pollute. I do not know the reason. The important thing is, they did not repeat Mr. Koppel's unfounded charge. After the interview, they just took a few shots of the penguins serving us supper, offered us cigarettes, said thank-you-very-much, and left.

Before they enplaned, however, they whispered amongst themselves. They were about fifty yards off and we could not see them in the dark, but our finely-tuned ears were able to overhear some of their whispers.

The subject of their conversation was Mildred and me. "Should we take them back to America with us?" was the question before the house. "Have they been charged with any crime?" was one follow-up question. "Is there a reward for their capture?" was a second follow-up question. "Are they considered dangerous?" was a third.

No questions on the ability of a resurrection body to withstand the rigors of an Antarctic winter, no questions whatsoever.

Then the leader of the crew walked nervously back to the igloo on the deck of which we were serenely sitting and shone his flashlight in our eyes.

"Folks," he said, trying not to tip his hand on whether he considered us as resurrection bodies or as common criminals, "folks, we'd offer you a ride back to the States, but we're plumb full up."

"That's okay," I said. "We've got RBs, and one of our projects is to see if they're able to withstand the rigors of an Antarctic winter. Besides, Charlie promised me many adventures and a personal audience with God."

"Right," said the cameraman.

"Say hi to the kids, if you see them," said Mildred.

"Right," said the cameraman.

"Adios," said Mildred.

"Adios," said the cameraman.

"Adios," I said.

"Adios."

Then he went back to his crew. Again, we could hear them whisper among themselves. Phrases like *remarkable birds* and *good pets* and *stately servants* were in plenteous supply. Also, I distinctly heard one of them use the word *evidence.*

They did not bandy these phrases about idly, however. It has been said, "The philosophers have only *interpreted* the world. The point is, to *change* it." The members of the camera crew were no philosophers. They were persons of action. That is why, immediately after their whispered conversation, they swooped down on the evidence, captured a goodly number of them, put them in sacks, wrestled them aboard their aircraft, and took off.

Mildred and I considered the scene that had just transpired before our very eyes.

Charged with some crime?

A reward for their capture?

Considered dangerous!

Sometimes one must wonder about the advantages of going on national TV and becoming a cultural icon.

15

Loyalty

THAT NIGHT, in the midst of a deep and profound slumber, I dreamed an incredible dream.

I was at the foot of Mt. Kirkpatrick. An immense hand reached down from the 4,528-meter peak and presented me with two tablets of ice. Suddenly there was a great earthquake, and a mighty voice thundered forth from the very heart of the earth, instructing me to read the tablets. I awoke. The dream was as insubstantial as a penguin feather, but when I sat up in my bed I was holding two tablets of ice, untitled.

I turned on my flashlight and read:

Part One

Now it came to pass that on the next day, he took pity upon the remaining multitudes. And he came down from the deck of his igloo to be amongst them. Guiltless but with a heavy heart came he, to be a tutor of penguins.

And he opened his mouth and taught them, saying, I shall teach thee the beauties and the joys of the English language. And thus it was that on the first day he taught them the beauties and the joys of the English language, and numerous of its intricacies.

And he spake unto them also on the following day, saying, I shall teach thee the parts of speech, beginning with nouns. And he taught them nouns, and then he taught them verbs, and the rest. And it was the second day.

And he said unto them, yea, I shall go one step further and teach thee forbidden speech. And on the third day he taught them forbidden speech, which he did later count a mistake.

Then he further taught them, saying, Thou hast done right well. Thus art thou now prepared for the highest wisdom: thus shall I teach thee the Classicks.

And a young penguin which was in the back row spake, and in a very loud voice he cried out, saying, What the hell is a Classick?[1]

And he taught them the difference between the Classicks and trash. And it was the fourth day.

And on the fifth day, he read to them the greatest of all Classicks, which is called Romeo and Juliet. *And their hearts were much gladdened by his reading. For lo, they stood and faced him and flapped their tiny wings; and it was done in this manner even so, to show that they were greatly pleased.*

And on the morrow he rose up early and gathered them round about his feet and spake unto them, saying, Art thou ready to learn of prophecy, and of its fulfillment? And they spake as one, saying, Yea, Master, do as thou hast even now said. Thus it was

---

[1] *Other ancient authorities read, What . . . is a Classick?*

that he taught them the prophecies of old, and how those prophecies were being fulfilled in the latter times, yea, even in their very midst.

And there were many other things which he taught them on that sixth day, which, if they were to be recounted, would fill the pages of a large and wearisome book.

And it came to pass that on the seventh day he rested, even according to the established custom.

But Mildred betook herself on such an holy day to come down also to be amongst the penguins, and to read them another Classick, the which is called, "The Night before Christmas." And this also pleased them greatly, yea, even more so than Romeo and Juliet *did please them.*

Part Two

And on the beginning of the second week there was a great assemblage of all the penguins round about the deck of his igloo. And they called out unto him, saying, Master, come. And amongst the many penguins which were gathered in that place was there one exceeding small bird, which with a wee voice cried out unto him, saying, Wouldst thou be our Santa Claus?

Now as he was pondering this petition in his heart, a hue and a cry rose up in that place, and the feet of many penguins stomped on the ice which was there, and the voice of that exceeding small penguin became like unto the voice of a thousand penguins, and that one mighty voice called upon him, importuning him if he would not be their giver of gifts.

And lo, Mildred did then make intercession on behalf of the penguins which were there assembled, saying thus unto him, And shalt thou not humour them? For if thou canst indeed pretend to Shakespeare, peradventure canst thou not also pretend to Santa?

And he bethought himself, saying, even in his heart, This woman hath well spoken. Canst I not play Santa for these wretched and disheartened creatures? The talent is not indeed lacking, nor the will; but only the time, and the place, and the means.

Then spake he unto Mildred, asking of her, What indeed of the time, and the place, as well as the means?

And lo, she answered him right quickly, saying, The time and the place, as well as the means, are as follows.

Firstly, that the time needs be the month of June, and the twenty-fifth day, which is hard upon us.

Secondly, that the place needs be the Pole, which is at a great distance, to the South.

Thirdly, that the means needs be an expedition thereto.

But after these words had been spoken, immediately there did come unto his vexed spirit a great question, to wit, why these things must needs come to pass? And he importuned her, that she give him answers to such questions as he had.

Then, knowing with a woman's knowledge what it was that was in his heart, she spake thus. Every thing must needs be changed one hundred eighty degrees on this southernmost land, which is called Antarctica. For just as our winter is their summer, even so is our summer their winter. And just as we would not think to celebrate Christmas in the time of summer, even so neither would they.

And she spake further, saying, Certain it is that the boons must needs be at thy workshop, which is at the Pole at some distance, to the South.

Then she opened her mouth and continued in her speaking, explaining how it was that the expedition must peradventure travel by sled, and that penguins must replace dogs, and that abandoned camera equipment must replace sleds, and that abandoned fish bones must replace reins and harnesses; and that whale-blubber candles must replace the light of the sun; and furthermore, that twenty-pound test line must serve as the whip of the Master.

And she concluded her much speaking, saying, Go to, let us make ready for such a journey.

And behold, they went, and made them ready. But they did this thing with a heavy spirit, for it was a grievous and burdensome task, which would require much travail.

For they feared in their hearts lest the evildoers return, and do to them even as they had done unto those penguins which had earlier been ensnared and carried away.

After I finished reading this sign from on high, I wakened Mildred and showed it to her. I did not neglect to point out that she was also mentioned.

She rolled over on her side. "Let's talk about this," and she yawned, "in the morning."

What did Charlie say? "You will have many adventures."

§

June 15

It is a long way from the Ross Ice Shelf to the South Pole, a very long way indeed.

In preparing for an Antarctic expedition, one is well-advised to avoid the idea of passing the responsibility of lead penguin from one bird to another.

One may think, I have 4,207 penguins, approximately fifteen hundred of whom are adults; therefore I will pass the responsibility of lead penguin from adult penguin to adult penguin, until all adult penguins have had a chance to serve.

If this thought occurs, quash it. Antarctica is not a land that lends itself to the noble ideals of democracy and equality. Antarctica is a land that lends itself to one-penguin leadership. That penguin should be male. Your male penguin is adept at reading road maps and deciphering latitude and longitude. Your female penguin is incapable of these skills.

A thing I have discovered on this expedition is that a lead penguin should be a bachelor, or a widower. Your married male penguin, as the Apostle says, "careth for the things that are of the world, how he may please his wife." Because his wife is more interested in sightseeing than in keeping to the schedule, she will persuade him to take many side trips.

This is why we are currently one week behind schedule.

June 16

My new lead penguin is Clement. His former wife, Priscilla, was one of the unfortunates who was kidnapped in the incident involving the ABC camera crew. This makes Clement the functional equivalent of a widower.

After the kidnapping, there was talk of a rescue operation to extricate the unfortunate victims from the clutches of their abductors. The plan was for Clement and a select group of White Beret penguins to swim underwater to America, discover the location of the victims, storm the ramparts of the fortress in which the victims are being held against their wishes, perform a commando raid on that fortress, rescue the victims, hijack a Boeing 747, and force the pilot to fly the entire covey back to the Ross Ice Shelf.

I was all for this plan. Mildred was all for this plan. A substantial majority of the remaining penguins were all for this plan.

The plan was abandoned when Clement got cold feet.

I have put Clement in charge of the other 4,206 penguins, because his newly-found widower status will keep him on a direct course to the South Pole, and because I want him to have something to do to take his mind off his recent bereavement, and because I want to restore his confidence in his leadership ability.

Despite the protests from the other penguins, who have not forgotten his initial loss of confidence, I am determined to stick with my choice.

June 17

My new lead penguin is Homer. Homer is a skilled navigator, a confirmed bachelor, a trusted and loyal servant. He is known within the entire rookery as a penguin's penguin.

After the penguins balked at Clement's leadership and I reluctantly gave in to their wishes, I scrutinized the lists for some penguin to succeed him. In my mind, I eliminated all females, all unskilled navigators, all married men, all widowers, all distrusted and disloyal servants. Then I gathered the remaining penguins together and gave them all a multiple-choice test. Homer emerged as the champion.

The question may arise, What was Homer's score on the multiple-choice test?

Ten percent.

How many questions were there on the multiple-choice test?

Ten.

What was the question that won for Homer his position as new lead penguin?

"Who is the author of Romeo and Juliet? (a) R. F. Scott; (b) Roald Amundsen; (c) William Shakespeare; (d) Mildred Budwieser."

Homer is a fine lead penguin, a fine lead penguin indeed. He would be the perfect lead penguin, except that he has a gimpy leg, for which the camera crew must take full responsibility. During the unfortunate kidnapping incident, Homer tried valiantly to establish lines of communication between the perpetrators and the victims. "Come, let us reason together," he implored the two parties, and received a whack on the thigh for his efforts.

Despite this minor flaw, Homer has established himself as the leader of the penguin team. They are willing to put up with his handicap, and so am I.

It is his left leg. This may explain why we list somewhat to port in our pilgrimage to the bottom of the world. It may also explain why we have come full circle over the last two days.

June 19

My new lead penguin is Toto. Toto is a young male of two years—the penguin equivalent of a thirteen-year old human being. But his tender age should not be held against him. What should be borne in mind in judging the wisdom of my choice is that he is neither engaged nor married. This qualifies him eminently for the position of lead penguin.

"Toto?" said Mildred when I announced my selection. "Little Toto? You must be out of your mind."

"He is neither engaged nor married," I told her. "This makes him eminently qualified."

"You're thinking like a man."

"I am a man," came my sturdy retort.

"Yes, but what about tiny Toto?"

"I see many excellent qualities in Toto, not the least of which is a potential for strong, decisive leadership."

"He's barely out of diapers!"

"Think of it as a rite de passage," I said. "Think of it as an initiation into the virile world of manhood, an initiation through which the so-called 'boy' you disparagingly call 'tiny Toto' will emerge with flying colors."

Mildred shook her head sadly. Many of the other penguins followed her lead. Nevertheless, I persisted. Solid in my conviction that this decision would prove to be the correct one, and that I would be hailed for it in the end, I hitched up Toto and cracked my whip and cried "Mush!"

The first day is always the hardest for any lead penguin. Unaccustomed as they are to their new leadership role, they do not always cover the usual hundred miles. This is to be expected. They do not always lead their payload in a straight line. This is also to be expected. One must remember that they have a great deal on their minds: their new position of responsibility, the questions they missed on the multiple-choice exam, the hoots of the other penguins, whether a certain young lady is watching.

The question may arise, How many questions did Toto miss on his lead penguin examination?

The exact number is not important. What is important is that he came close on several of them.

Another factor that must be borne in mind is that your younger male penguin tends to playfulness. This explains why Toto has slipped out of his harness, why he has gathered the other young penguins around him, and why they are spending a goodly part of the time playing Fox and Geese.

June 20

My new lead penguin is Bernadette. She is a no-nonsense, get-things-done mother of twelve and grandmother of seventy-four.

Bernadette has led a full life. After her twelve children left home to establish coveys of their own, she went back to college and majored in military science, specializing in the tactics of the sea leopard. She minored in women's studies. She wrote her honors thesis on the subject, "Role Stratification in the Antarctic Penguin Army: A Case Study in Male Domination." After receiving her B.S. from East Ross Ice Shelf University she matriculated in West Ross Ice Shelf University, where she is currently a student assistant to Prof. Reginald Sopor, the well-known professor of political science. Her master's thesis was on the subject, "Role Stratification in the Third Division of the Antarctic Penguin Army: A Case Study in Male Domination." She is planning to write her doctoral dissertation on the subject, "Role Stratification in the Administrative Headquarters of the Third Division of the Antarctic Penguin Army: A Case Study in Male Domination."

Bernadette has an impressive resume, a very impressive resume indeed.

But that is not why I chose her to be my new lead penguin. I chose her because she is the de facto leader of a significant portion of the penguin rookery.

That is not the only reason, of course. She also scored ninety percent on the multiple-choice test I gave a selected group of female penguins, in the wakes of the so-called "Full-circle" and "Fox and Geese" debacles.

The question may arise, Which question did she miss?

She did not answer the question concerning the author of Romeo and Juliet. Instead of marking one of the four choices on that question, she wrote, "Does not apply."

You let her get away with that?

I considered disqualifying her for that impertinence, but Mildred spoke up in her favor.

We are now on schedule to reach the South Pole on Christmas Eve, June 24.

§

We have arrived at last, on schedule, just as I predicted.

My toy shop is standing at the ready. My South Pole elves are inside, waiting for me to enter and give the word: Load! They have polished the runners of my trusty sled, hitched up my trusty reindeer, and checked the hold for bombs.

I stride briskly to the door marked "Entrance 1," rap sharply, and wait impatiently for my minions to heed my knock and hurry to welcome me, crying, "Just in the nick of time! Not a moment to waste!" I can hear them even now, scurrying to and fro, preparing for my entrance, spirits quickened by the anticipation of my arrival. I glance at my watch. Five minutes before the hour of eight o'clock, post meridiem. I knock again. Come come! Up and about, minions! The Master is here. Tarry not. The hearts of four thousand and some odd penguins lie ready to be gladdened this joyous night.

??? There must be some mistake.

It is not my chief elf who opens the door marked "Entrance 1" and bids me enter. Not at all; it is a little red-faced balding man, clad in long johns, baggy pants, and suspenders, sporting a three-months beard, and holding a smoldering White Owl panatella in one hand and a brew of Michelob Light in the other. It is not a toy shop I have entered; it is a barracks, strewn with the apparatus of riotous living. And it is not a group of expectant elves who greet me; it is an international team of scientists, stationed here for the purpose of monitoring atmospheric changes and the depletion of the ozone layer.

They welcome me to this extreme region of the earth.

We exchange relevant information: names, nationalities, Social Security numbers, fish recipes, ribald stories.

We go on to discuss other important issues. U. S. policy toward China and Russia. The prospects for peace in the Middle East. Recent obituaries in *The Economist.* The expansion of the NFL into Australia. Whether there is life on Mars. The chemical composition of resurrection bodies. How to hit a knuckleball.

They speak of their families and loved ones back home. I speak of my charges outside.

They confide in me the problem of the loneliness of living in the remotest region of the globe, far from the accustomed amenities of civilization. I confide in them the problem of locating four thousand and some penguin-compatible Christmas gifts in the icy wastes of the polar basin.

We consider solutions to these problems.

We strike a deal.

They will invite my charges inside to warm their ice-glazed feathers. I will instruct my charges to furnish the evening's entertainment.

I return to the parking lot.

"Ed!" whispers Mildred. "Where on earth have you been? We've been waiting for two hours! It's freezing out here!"

"What's the hurry?" I whisper back. "They're only penguins, and you are equipped with a resurrection body that is operative down to -90° F. Besides, it's a full moon. Would you believe that gorgeous moon? Doesn't it remind you of our first—"

"The gifts, Ed, the gifts," she whispers. "They're waiting for the gifts. Plus, they want to see how you look in a red suit."

"There's been some kind of a mistake," I confide to her. "This is the South Pole. I was thinking it was the *North* Pole. Also, Christmas Eve is December 24. This is *June* 24."

"You agreed with me that the Antarctic calendar is one hundred and eighty degrees opposite the American calendar."

"I was in error."

"Tell that to the birds," she replies.

I turn around, raise my bright and shining arms, and address the multitudes. "Folks," I say, speaking through cupped resurrection hands. "If I could have your attention, please. There's been a slight mix-up."

I explain to them how Christmas became a holiday only in the third or fourth centuries of the Christian era, how it is truly significant only to those among us who have been baptized, how penguins are ineligible for baptism per se, how "Santa Claus" is a corruption of "St. Nicholas," and how the belief in a so-called

Santa Claus is a pagan excrescence that certain theologians wish to see excised from Christian hagiography.

It is a fine speech, a fine speech indeed.

"You promised," says Bernadette.

"We want Santa Claus!" cries a young penguin in the front row.

I break the sad news to them. "There is no Santa Claus," I inform them. "Santa Claus is not mentioned anywhere in the Bible. Besides, all the great thinkers tell us there is no Santa Claus. Voltaire tells us there is no Santa Claus, Sigmund Freud tells us there is no Santa Claus, W. C. Fields tells us there is no Santa Claus, Ronald Reagan tells us there is no Santa Claus—"

But other young penguins take up the cry: "WE WANT SANTA CLAUS!"

"According to Ludwig Feuerbach (1804-1870), the brilliant but obscure German philosopher, Santa Claus is a projection of purely human attributes, writ large upon an imaginary screen."

They all take to chanting: "WE WANT SANTA CLAUS!"

This calls for a change in strategy.

"Tell you what I'm gonna do," I say. "I'm gonna invite y'all into this here barracks, where you can warm the cockles of your hearts, meet lots of new and interesting people, and put on a top-flight show to prove once and for all that the penguin is one world-class bird."

This is not working. I am finding that the penguin is a very superstitious bird, particularly where religious holidays are concerned. They want their Santa Claus, and they want their Barbies and their Kens.

"I'll meetcha half way," I finally concede. "I'll try to scrounge up a Santa Claus suit, but there'll be no gifts."

"You promised," says Bernadette.

"'It is more blessed to give than to receive,'" I remind her.

"That's easy for you to say, you male chauvinist Yankee imperialist pig!" replies Bernadette. "You've got a resurrection body!"

§

A thing I have recently learned about penguins is that they are capable of sarcasm. Superstitious, true. But also sarcastic.

But the sarcasm of the lead penguin should not be overemphasized. What should be emphasized is the ability of the majority of penguins to know a good deal when they hear one. Not one minute after I offer to meet them half way, they are filing through Entrance 1 in anticipation of liquid refreshment and a chance to rub wings with an international team of scientists.

Things are going smoothly, smoothly indeed.

Problem number one is the Santa Claus suit.

The warehouse of the International South Pole Scientific Project is well-stocked. Tubes and beakers are in long supply, White Owl cigars are in long supply, candy bars, *Playmate* magazines, comic books, Monopoly games, long johns, baggy pants, and suspenders are in long supply. Smirnoff vodka is in extremely long supply.

Santa Claus suits, however, are in short supply, as are razors and aftershave.

Fortunately, however, red flannel shirts are an item that is in long supply, and they have one in my size. Also, one of the scientists sports a red stocking cap, which she lends me.

The penguins are pleased when I make my appearance.

There are some, however, who quibble. Bernadette is one who quibbles. "What about the beard?" she says loudly.

Perhaps I should not have shaved. Perhaps that was a mistake.

But I think quickly on my feet. "Remember me as I was just hours ago, white beard and all," I implore them. "Put that image together with what you now see, a merry fellow in a red flannel shirt and sporting a red stocking cap; that is the picture I wish to place before your imaginations."

"You had a gray beard," says Bernadette. "It wasn't white, it was gray."

"I am a relatively young Santa Claus," I reply. "When your grandchildren have children of their own—then I will sport a white beard. Then, and only then."

"Forget it," says Bernadette.

A thing I have recently learned about penguins is that they have no concept of entertaining the troops, no concept whatsoever. True, they are a gregarious bird, and true, some among their number exhibit a *joie de vivre*, but the concept of entertaining the troops is one that is foreign to their natures.

Perhaps I should have consulted with them. Perhaps I should have brought them into the decision-making process. Yes, that is definitely something I should have done. Forced entertainment is no entertainment at all: this is a basic principle of human motivation. Now that I think about this matter at greater length, I see the error of my ways.

The cause of my error can be traced to the fact that the penguin is a gregarious bird. I assumed that a gregarious bird, one who stays up half the night partying, is also a bird who offers great entertainment value for the dollar. This has turned out to be a mistaken assumption. I will not make that assumption again. I will excise it from the repertoire of my working hypotheses.

Problem number two is the entertainment.

Despite her quibbling and sarcasm, Bernadette is a very understanding penguin. She understands that my error was one of omission. She understands that I have put myself in an awkward position. She understands that a deal is a deal.

She offers to help me out of my awkward position. All I have to do in return, she says, is to admit that the question concerning the author of *Romeo and Juliet* is not an appropriate question to ask candidates for lead penguin in an expedition to the South Pole.

I admit to her that the question is inappropriate in that circumstance. I do so, however, with mental reservations.

"Fine," she says. "Now leave everything to me. We will perform a skit to end all skits."

"I will leave everything in your capable pinions," I reply.

Bernadette gathers the four thousand and some odd penguins in the corner of the barracks. She stands before a blackboard, mapping out the role of each individual penguin in the upcoming skit. They gravely nod their assent. She looks at me and whispers to them through pursed beak. They look over their shoulders at me and make penguin sounds.

The penguin sound is a sound that brooks no comparison with any other sound known to the resurrected ear. It is not comparable to the captious caw of the crow. It is not comparable to the gentle coo of the pigeon. It is not comparable to the sad dirge of the mourning dove, or even to the derisive hoot of the owl. Nor is it comparable to the joyous song of a western meadowlark across the western Kansas plain at sunrise. It is more chilling than any of these. It strikes terror into the hearts of all but the most intrepid.

But enough of the sound of the penguin. While Bernadette and her company plan their skit to end all skits, Mildred and I mingle with the scientists, who, in anticipation of an evening of live entertainment, have changed into more formal attire.

It's black bow ties and tails for the men, stunning low-cut evening gowns for the women.

"M'lord," says the smart young waiter. "May I bring you and M'lady cocktails?"

"Indeed you may," I reply grandly. "M'lady will have a vodka and tonic; and M'lord—he'll have the same."

The smart young waiter bows gravely and disappears through the crowd of mingled celebrities.

"Madame and Sire," says the host. "We are happy that you could grace us with your presence, as guests of the highest honor. If I may make so bold, let me introduce you to some of the more distinguished members of the international scientific community."

Introductions are made all around. "Sir Michael Skwiff of the Royal Society, I'd like you to meet the distinguished Dr. and Mrs. Budwieser, late of Kirkland; Dr. and Mrs. Budwieser, Sir Michael Skwiff."

"Ah yes. I before E except after C."

"Of the brewery billions, I suppose. Pleased indeed to make your acquaintance."

The smart young waiter appears with cocktails for M'lord and M'lady, who quaff them off in majestic fashion.

"Herr Hans Kelter of the Frei Universität of Berlin, I'd like you to meet Dr. and Mrs. Budwieser. They have resurrection bodies."

"Vell vell, ein paar uf scientific marfels!"

"It's nothing. Nothing. Really, nothing."

"Mme. Buveur, I'd like you to meet Dr. and Mrs. Budwieser. Perhaps you caught them on the Koppel show?"

"Of course. A first-class performance. Absolutely first-class. Stunning, I must say."

"Thank you. You are too, too kind."

Mildred is at her charming best. I am debonair.

Snatches of sparkling conversation:

"I can always be reached at the Hilton," I tell Simone.

"*Mais oui*," Simone tells me.

"So I says to the lady, I says. . . ."

The Chinese scientist nods agreeably.

"What I wanna know is, how much ozone do you folks really need down here?"

"*Aber ein' klein' bisschen*," replies Hans, indicating with thumb and forefinger.

"What about you, Boris, do you think the Fed should raise interest rates?"

"*Nyet*."

Meanwhile, the penguins plan their skit to end all skits. Theatrics is not natural to them, despite their gregarious temper, but they are going out of their way to fulfill my promise to the international team of scientists. This is out of gratefulness to me, gratefulness for all that I have done for them—gratefulness, and loyalty to their Master.

A thing I have learned on this expedition is that the penguin is a very loyal species. I used to think of the dog as the most loyal of species, and I still consider the dog the very acme of species, in the loyalty department. But I have had to place the loyal penguin on a level just below the dog. Where the dog is a perfect ten, one would have to give the penguin a nine and a half.

Loyalty to their Master is a fine trait to observe in members of the animal kingdom, a very fine trait indeed. A trait that deserves the gifts I bestow upon them: White Owl cigars for the men, chocolate bars for the women, and, for the youngsters, copies of *Romeo and Juliet.*

They bow and say their thank-yous.

§

It's finally time for the skit.

The penguins take turns mounting a makeshift stage and performing for the scientists, who show their delight and appreciation at every turn.

One young penguin takes to the piano and gives a farcical performance of chopsticks.

Another satirizes bodybuilder poses.

A third delivers a mock-heroic reading of scenes from "The Secret Life of Walter Mitty."

A fourth does an impersonation of W. C. Fields, as the Great Man in *Never Give a Sucker an Even Break.*

A fifth and sixth do a spoof on Don Quixote and Sancho Panza.

A seventh struts across the stage in an evening gown to the tune of "There She is, Miss Antarctica"—a good-natured parody of Mildred.

All this to the explosion of flashbulbs.

It is a stunning skit. It lacks a discernible theme, it is all nonsense, but it is nonetheless a stunning skit.

There is a curtain call. The performers take their bows. The scientists erupt in spontaneous applause. I am asked to come forward for a special presentation. Sensing the greatness of the moment, I rise and pick my way over the feet of the scientists, who touch at the hem of my Santa Claus suit as I make my way, modestly and unpretentiously, down the aisle and up the steps and toward center stage, bowing my head slightly and smiling faintly, with perhaps the hint of a twinkle in my grave, discerning eyes.

It is the kind of a moment toward which all human projects strive, the kind of a moment to which all human actions tend, the kind of a moment of which one can truthfully say, this, and this alone, is sufficient to justify one's very—

A thing I have discovered on this expedition is that the penguin can be a very deceitful species.

This does not apply to all known penguins, of course. But it certainly applies to Bernadette.

I do not believe that the other penguins, left to their own device, would have risen up against their Master, attacked an international team of scientists, rushed into the warehouse four thousand strong, made off with a year's supply of Smirnoff vodka, and escaped into the Antarctic wilderness, never to be seen or heard again. Left to their own device, the penguins would have continued to give the troops great entertainment value for the dollar.

Left to their own device, they would have made me proud to be their Master.

16

The Long Shining Tube

I RETURN TO THE LIFE OF MEDITATION. And as I meditate, I transcend myself. I view myself with the inner eye of wisdom, with detachment, as from a distance. . . .

The scientist is in his laboratory, alone.

He is feverishly busy: pouring foul-smelling liquids into beakers, adjusting laser beams, checking monitors, mentally advancing arcane postulates, entering complex data at the terminal, poring over printouts, stroking his handsome beard, pacing to and fro, mentally revising his postulates, inserting his intelligent, sensitive hands into the pockets of his white coat, taking them out again, returning them to his handsome beard.

He is the consummate synthesis of thought and action.

He is saving the world.

His colleagues have departed for points north, pleading loneliness and the rigors of winter in an icy clime. They have left him by himself, in the freezing and brutal night of Antarctica, to finish the sacred work to which only the most brilliant practitioners of their profession have been called.

Chilled and weary, he recalls *Hamlet*, Act I, Scene 1, ll. 8-9: "'tis bitter cold, and I am sick at heart." But he brushes off his fatigue with disdain.

He is the very embodiment of dedication.

The scientist was a child prodigy. By the age of two, he had mastered the periodic table. By three, he had discovered the principles of non-Euclidean geometry. At six, he wrote a paper for *The Bulletin of the Atomic Scientists* that made the scientific establishment sit up and take notice. At the age of ten, MIT awarded him a Ph.D. in theoretical chemistry, nuclear physics, genetics, and advanced mathematics, just for using the bathroom.

The story of how he earned this degree is the stuff of which legends are made. Wishing to remain anonymous, he slipped onto the MIT campus late one afternoon to "browse around," as he later self-deprecatingly put it. After a brief period of clandestinely watching four distinguished professors working at their blackboards, he went to the restroom and, while answering nature's call, penned, on the wall of the stall, a simple but elegant formula that integrated the formulae of those four professors. Immediately afterwards, the Dean, answering a call of his own, discovered this graffiti and called a special faculty meeting to try to decipher it. Just as the most eminent of the hoary professors was beginning to fathom its meaning, who but the *Wunderkind* strolled into the room. He advanced unassumingly to the blackboard and proceeded to lecture the MIT faculty on the significance and application of his innovative work.

He was instantly nominated for the Ph.D., by acclamation.

At the commencement ceremony, he was awarded his degree by none other than the redoubtable Einstein, who, called over for the occasion from the Institute for Advanced Study, gave a speech in which he likened himself to John the Baptist, preparing the way for one mightier than himself.

He inspects the telephones: hot lines to the President, to various prime ministers, to the Secretary-General.

He dials the President. He has an idea for streamlining the election process: have future presidents named by a committee of Nobel Prize winners, to be selected by him.

The President is watching a recently-released movie.

Annoyed by this slight, he dials his favorite prime minister. He has a plan for integrating the economies of eight third-world markets: teach their bankers the rudiments of yoga.

Mr. Prime Minister is intrigued by this idea, and promises to sleep over it.

He calls the Secretary-General. No plan this time, just a friendly chat.

Mr. Secretary-General apprises him, in detail, of the most recent developments in the Middle East.

He bends over the keyboard to put the finishing touches on a 14-page paper to be delivered at a joint session of the *Deutsche Philosophische Gesellschaft*, the Select Committee on Theoretical Physics, the Academy of Asian Wisdom, and the College of Cardinals.

Title: "The Field Theory of All There Is."

Subtitle: "A Sketch."

It integrates the central ideas of *The Critique of Pure Reason*, *The Special Theory of Relativity*, *The Tibetan Book of the Dead*, *Finnegans Wake*, and the Book of Revelation; it is composed in iambic pentameter.

He calculates that its subtlety and power will not be appreciated by a single human being for thirty-seven years.

His assistant, relaxing after a grueling day's work, is watching an old "Wheel of Fortune" on wide-screen television. She is also working on a crossword.

He sighs philosophically. Good help is hard to find.

The scientist considers the political, ecological, social, theological, cultural, and epistemological ramifications of startling the world with a letter to the editor of the *New York Times*, warning of the impending environmental apocalypse and suggesting a radical but eminently practical solution: the gradual replacement of the world's present population with resurrection bodies.

He decides, reluctantly, against this idea. Few would appreciate its beauty. There is, in the words of the redoubtable Keats, an "inhuman dearth of noble natures." These words put him in a pensive mood. He contemplates the human condition, sips his afternoon sherry, and levitates.

The voice of his assistant penetrates the field of his absolute consciousness. He stays her with a slight gesture of his hand.

"Where are the ice cubes?"

He considers this question from the political, ecological, sociological, theological, cultural, and epistemological points of view. He concludes that it is insoluble, given the present state of human knowledge. He puts it on his busy schedule, resolving to devote half an hour of significant thought to its solution.

"The ice cubes. Where are they?"

He casts a grave eye on her, regarding her as if she were but a bubble. The Wisdom of the East: Death does not touch the sage—he who looks upon the world as a bubble.

"HE SAID THERE WERE ICE CUBES IN THE REFRIGERATOR!"

§

Ice cubes? In the refrigerator?

Oh yes. Now I remember. She's referring to that last conversation. The one we had with the captain. Of the team of scientists. Before they took off for the winter.

The captain leaned out the door and offered us a ride. "There's lots of room on this here aircraft," he said. "You're more'n welcome to climb aboard."

"No thank you," I said. "We came down here to get away from the Kansas heat and humidity."

"Keep them resurrection bodies out of trouble," he said with a wink.

"Will do," I said.

"Say hi to the kids, if you see them," Mildred said.

"Happy to do that," he said. He was probably thinking, *what* kids?

"Sorry about the penguins," I said.

"Think nothing of it," he said good-humoredly, "penguins will be penguins."

"Bone voyage!" she said. "I know that phrase from crosswords."

"Happy New Year!" we took turns saying.

"There's plenty of vodka left," he said, waving goodbye. Then he added, as a joke, "and there're lots of ice cubes in the refrigerator!"

And now Mildred reports that she can't find the ice cubes. "I don't suppose there are any outside?" This is not a joke. It is an order, disguised as a question.

But joke or no joke, I go out for ice cubes. I roll my resurrection eyes at the ozone-depleted heavens, but I put on my Santa Claus cap and grab a flashlight and go out for ice cubes.

§

One of the well-known facts about the South Pole is that the pole itself resembles a red, white, and blue barber-shop totem, topped off by an aluminum globe about the size of a basketball. I look around for this totem, theorizing that the best ice cubes will be found in the adjacent area.

I find, however, that there is no such totem. Instead, there is an unmarked manhole cover, from which steam is arising.

I think I should go get Mildred. She's probably also been under the impression that the South Pole resembles a totemized basketball.

I return to dispel the widespread myth.

"What does this have to do with ice cubes?" she wants to know.

The ice cubes!

"Well?"

"I regard this as a significant discovery," I reply.

"I send you out for ice cubes, and you come back talking about a manhole cover."

"It has steam rising from it," I explain.

"Steam?"

"S-T-E-A-M."

"A manhole cover, with steam rising from it." There is unbelief in her voice—unbelief, and ridicule.

"*Hot* steam." A subtle distinction.

I persuade Mildred to go out and cast her eyes on my discovery. She is skeptical, but she has faith in my ability to recognize the difference between a barber-shop totem and a manhole cover.

I shine my flashlight on the steaming lozenge.

"I've got to hand it to you, Honey, you weren't dreaming," she compliments me. "Not this time."

"Let's see what's under it," I suggest.

"Do you think it's safe?"

Safe? Perhaps she has hit upon a significant question. Suppose there is a nuclear power station down there in the earth's plumbing? Suppose there is a cauldron of volcanic activity? Or suppose there is a gang of terrorists, stewing up a brew of mischief? The possibilities are daunting.

But back in Kirkland the Budwiesers were always known as risk-takers. When the Deuces played poker, I was always the one who took the art of bluffing to its highest level. When Mildred watched "Wheel of Fortune," she always urged the contestants to go for the large capitalization slices, which were located in the dangerous territory near the BANKRUPT.

This is not to say we didn't respect the law. Despite the fact that we were an audacious duo, we were fundamentally law-abiding. There were a few traffic tickets, but they were always for parking in the handicapped space. No moving violations whatsoever. We always kept our adventurous spirits within the parameters of our duties as law-abiding citizens.

I know of no Antarctic law prohibiting the displacement of manhole covers, so I daringly bend down and prepare to remove it.

"Let me help you," says Mildred. "Last time you bent over like that, you were laid up for two weeks."

"That was pre-resurrection," I remind her as I grasp the edges of the sizeable lozenge with my powerful post-resurrection hands and attempt to dis—

But now is heard a faint, distant sound. I abandon my labor and look about to locate its source. Its source, barely visible in this twilight hour, is a helicopter, looming mysteriously over the horizon.

Just in time. They've come to alert us to the dangers that await under the manhole cover.

And now the helicopter is coming nearer . . . and now it is descending, quickly at first, then more slowly. It is beginning to kick up the dry snow and make . . . a whirlwind! the time-honored indication that God is about to reveal His message to a waiting world.

And what did Charlie say? "God will answer your most burning questions!"

"Speak, Lord," I cry, "for Thy servant heareth!"

"Yoo-hoo!" shouts Mildred into the twilight. "Over here!"

The copter lands. The rotors cease their toil. A dim but imposing figure emerges from the doorway.

I fall upon my knees, prepared to adore—

"Who's that with him?" asks Mildred.

I look up.

A second figure? That means it's probably not God. It must be Dora and Betsy. That's even better!

I stand up and begin to move toward them.

They've come to explain, to apologize. Perhaps there was a problem with the parachute straps. Perhaps the wind currents wafted them to a distant shore. Perhaps the engine of that frail craft sputtered to a stop, leaving them to plummet into the ocean, from which they have only now been rescued. Perhaps Pete Principal and the pilot—

But there are more than two figures—there are now three, four, five . . . six figures, arrayed in a spread formation and coming toward us.

Other resurrection bodies!

They saw us on "Nightline" and have finally come to join me. They hunger for the supreme wisdom and seek spiritual instruction from the acknowledged source of transcendental knowledge. They have come to be initiated into the mysteries of resurrection life. They yearn for serenity.

I sit down on the manhole cover, adopt the lotus position, and prepare to meet my disciples.

"Why're they crouching?" inquires Mildred. "Don't they want us to see them, or something?"

Crouching?

The police!

They caught us on "Nightline" and have come to apprehend us and charge us with escaping from the hospitals and polluting the natural habitat of the Antarctic penguins. I am not guilty of these charges, of course. I have the perfect alibi. They tied a tag to my big toe. This left me with the impression that I was free to get up and move about, to leave the premises or not to leave the premises, as I so chose. Mildred also has the perfect alibi. She is not responsible for her actions.

In no time at all I am up and about and grasping the edges of the manhole cover.

Mildred, however, is sanguine about the situation. She continues to peer at the approaching figures. "Why're they carrying nets? Don't they know there're no butterflies down here?"

Nets!

I swiftly remove the large iron lozenge and scramble down the hole. She follows me.

I make sure to put the cover back where I found it.

Charlie was right again. "You will have many adventures."

§

This escalator operates briskly and efficiently. I would not recommend it for children. It is not a plaything. You cannot run up it and hope to reach the top. Once you have committed to the DOWN mode, you cannot retrace your steps. It is like a ski slope in this regard.

There is no ski lift to get you back to the top, however. Escalators generally come in pairs, DOWN and UP. This escalator is an exception to that rule. It moves DOWN, and DOWN only. As far as the resurrection eye can see, it's DOWN. It reminds me of the Atlanta airport.

I was once in the Hartsfield International Airport. It was not of my own free will; it was by accident. I was flying to Dodge City for a job interview, and I ended up in Atlanta by mistake. I'm not saying it was my fault. I'm saying it was pilot error. Pilot error, as well as widespread passenger error. I was in the situation of being the only person on that plane who had the correct destination, Dodge City. Everybody else was flying to Dallas.

When I got to Dallas, I tried to rectify the airline's mistake by having them fly the plane to its original destination. All I got for my troubles was a one-way ticket back to Kirkland. The ticket agent was very nice, but stubborn. He would not admit that his airline had made a mistake. Even after I informed him that I wasn't planning to sue, all I wanted was to hear him say it was his company's mistake, he would not admit the error. They don't like to admit it when they're wrong. It would open up a Pandora's box.

When I got on the plane heading back to Kirkland, it was the same thing. Pilot error, widespread passenger error.

When I arrived in Atlanta, I headed straight for the ticket counter. "Straight" in Hartsfield International Airport involves a dip or two. This airport is built on the principle of the Great Chain of Being. Many levels. Talk about irony! One of the great modern airports, and built on a medieval principle. First you descend to Hell, then you ascend to Heaven. It's done with escalators, the modern version of angels.

The ticket agent in Atlanta was not as friendly as the ticket agent in Dallas. She said it was my own fault. She wondered how everyone else could be so wrong and I could be so right. She wondered this publicly, with a certain level of sarcasm in her voice.

We had a lengthy discussion on the subject of lawsuits. This did not daunt her; it only increased the level of sarcasm.

I pointed out to her that she was a poor representative of Atlanta. Also, a poor role model for the youth of America. These were harsh words, but the situation called for them.

Half an hour later, I had had it up to here with pilots and passengers and ticket agents and cops. So I caught the first bus back to Kirkland. That's how I got to see Appalachia and Philadelphia and the stockyards of Chicago and Omaha.

As it turned out, I didn't take the Dodge City job. It was associate sales representative for a major publishing firm. The job was to spend a summer selling books in the airports of western Kansas. Bibles, I believe.

It was not an attractive job. There was a great deal of travel involved. Besides, I'm not sure I would have been a very good Bible salesman. If they had wanted me to sell the tragedies of

Shakespeare, I'd have been a world beater. But that publishing firm specialized in Bibles, as I may have mentioned.

I didn't take the job. This was because of the travel. As I heard Mildred put it to Thelma Blossum, she didn't want to have to spend half her summer tracking me down.

She wouldn't have needed to worry. The man in Dodge City said I was overqualified. It had nothing to do with the fact that I was two weeks late for the interview, which he could understand. He said the long and the short of it was, I was too smart for my own good. He also said they were looking for someone with a little more experience, someone who knew his way around the block.

Yes indeed. Riding this escalator down to the center of the earth takes me back to my adventures in the Atlanta airport. Mildred says it takes *her* back to the adventures of Alice and the Mad Hatter.

§

I keep thinking about the long shining tube.

Maybe Mark Ecclebury was right, what happens when you leave the standard world is that you go down a long shining tube until you come upon a scene right out of a Matisse painting. He missed the part about the resurrection body, but otherwise he was absolutely correct.

I'll have to send him a postcard congratulating him on his mystic knowledge.

No—it was probably just a lucky guess.

I keep waiting for this tube to shine. It's a tube, no doubt about it, and it's certainly long, but I'm still waiting for the shine to appear.

I point out this defect to Mildred. She says it hasn't been polished lately. She says if you leave chrome out in the steam without polishing it regularly, what you get is flat-looking chrome.

She's looking around for a suggestion box. "Watch the chrome. It's flat. Leaves a bad impression. Polish it once in a while. I recommend a soft, dry cloth." These are the thoughts she's writing down. I know from experience. I swear, that woman composes notes for suggestion boxes in her dreams.

There are no suggestion boxes on this escalator, however. Maybe when we get all the way down to the Matisse, she'll spot one. I'll be cavorting around the meadow, tripping the light fantastic with an assortment of wood nymphs, and she'll be looking around for a suggestion box. When she finally finds one, she'll deposit the note about the chrome. Then she'll write another note telling them to put their suggestion boxes in high-traffic areas.

Speaking of traffic, there's doesn't seem to be a lot of it around today. Mildred points out that we haven't run across a single soul, with or without a resurrection body.

"Maybe Sunday is their slow day around here," I suggest. "Maybe they have blue laws prohibiting travel on Sunday."

"Or maybe it's Ascension Day and everybody else is on an escalator going UP."

"No," I assure her. "Ascension Day is on a Thursday."

"Maybe they moved it to a Sunday. That would be just like the theologians, to move it to Sunday. Monday would have been better. It would have given us another three-day weekend."

We should have paid more attention the morning in Sunday School when they covered the topic of Last Things. But we were young at the time, and when you're young, you tend to think of First Things. The first thing I was thinking about was my book.

The one that was going to make it to the top of the charts. The one on the symbol of the feather in the poetry of Emily Dickinson. Mildred says the first thing she was thinking about was Cyrus. She remembers being pregnant with him that morning. He was making his presence felt, she says, which meant she was enjoying the kicks and had her eyes closed and wasn't paying much attention.

Regular attenders of Sunday School are well-advised to remain awake and alert and lively when the topic of Last Things is being considered. Special attention should be paid to the section on eligibility requirements:

1. The first requirement for access to a quality afterlife is a valid death certificate. Your survivors can obtain copies of such a document through your funeral director, or from the health department of the county in which you were residing at the time of decease. Have your loved ones ask for ten to twelve copies initially, though they may later need more. Some of these copies should be sent, together with copies of your marriage license or licenses (if applicable), to the appropriate insurance companies and mutual funds. Several should be taken, in person, to the nearest Social Security office (to avoid disappointment, call ahead for an appointment). These, however, are not the copies that will concern you specifically. It is the remaining copies you need to worry about. Three of them should be sent to your lawyer, who will know what to do with them. One should be sent to your family minister, priest, rabbi, imam, or other religious leader. And one should be attached firmly to your coffin or urn.

Note, however, that in some states the death certificate may be waived. Kansas law, for example, stipulates that the function of this important document may be filled by a simple but legible toe tag.

To summarize this point: the first requirement for entrance into the glories of the resurrection life is death.

2. The second requirement is either faith, or good behavior, or a combination of the two, depending on the religion with which you happen to be affiliated. If you are in doubt regarding the details of this requirement, check with your minister, priest, imam, or rabbi. In some cases, you may wish to consult a guru. Better yet, use one of your accumulated sick days and spend it in the downtown library. At the computer prompt, punch in SUBJECT, then type the name of your religion. If for some reason you are not computer-literate, you might browse through the old-fashioned card catalog, or, if members of the library staff appear to have time on their hands, just ask one of them for his or her help.

Once you have retrieved the book describing the doctrines and practices of your religion, read it. Then simply follow the directions. If you find them ambiguous, poorly written, or difficult to follow, you might consider changing denominations. It is important that you feel comfortable in your chosen faith.

In the unlikely event that you are not a member in good standing of any organized religion, join one. Call or write the Tipper Analytical Services for a free brochure, which will give you the current rating of the religions, according to (1) degree of difficulty and (2) truth in advertising.

To summarize this final point: the second requirement for entrance into the joys of the resurrection life is adherence to the doctrines and practices of the religion of your choice.

I think I see the end of the tube. . . .

Yes, absolutely, the end of the tube!

It looks like . . . I can't see too well without my glasses . . . and the steam makes it difficult. . . .

17

Online to God

OH.

Mark was wrong. It's not a Matisse.

From this altitude it looks like a mid-sized Middle-American city, sprawled over a broad and level plain. Wide streets, laid out with rectangular precision. Exactly four shopping centers and eight plywood-steepled churches per square mile. Houses everywhere, reflecting every taste and pocketbook. There are white bungalows, tan bungalows, grey bungalows, basic bungalows, hump-backed bungalows, added-on-to-bungalows, bungalows with back yards the size of postage stamps, bungalows with back yards the size of a small vegetable garden, bungalows with back yards large enough for a chain-link fence and a dog run, bungalows with a used car parked in the driveway, bungalows with both a used car and an old Winnebago parked in the driveway.

As we descend the escalator, Mildred notices that most of these bungalows and yards are neat and well-maintained. Some, she points out with a sigh, are not. Every town has to have a few atheists.

We continue to go down. We spot a sign on an S&L; it reads 117°. The dog days of summer: hot and humid. Which would explain the steam.

The streets are abuzz with old '80s K cars, teeming with serene people. No, not serene. What's the word? Austere? Or maybe just bored. The typical vehicle contains two or three passengers. The driver is a balding man dressed in a polyester suit. The navigator is a middle-aged woman whose hair has spent the night in tight curlers. And in four out of five instances, there's a back-seat passenger. Invariably a silver-haired great-grandmother. They're all sitting up straight. Except for the elderly woman. She's leaning forward. Probably giving her son-in-law advice on the art of living.

So it's definitely not a Matisse. No cavorting nudes. And absolutely no *joie de vivre*.

The escalator deposits us on a side street lined with modest tan bungalows. We strike out on foot in search of further adventure.

The first person we encounter is a woman in her late sixties bearing a striking resemblance to Thelma Blossum. She is accompanied by a German shepherd, pulling a little red wagon laden with a batch of identical packages. She and her dog come up to us, smiling and wagging their tails. She shakes our hands and shoves a package into Mildred's eager palms. "I'm the Welcome Wagon," she beams. "Welcome to Kirkland South!"

§

She found us a room at Motel 2.

The first thing Mildred asked our Welcome Wagon was whether she knew of an affordable motel. Mrs. Welcome Wagon just happened to know of one in our price range. In fact, she brought us all the way over here and checked us in and then invited herself up to the room. Then she plunked herself down on the only available bed to introduce the contents of the Welcome-to-Kirkland-South propaganda while her dog sniffed around for illegal substances. She pointed out the best bargains in fast foods and indicated which stores currently had Ridiculous Sales and gave us the inside information on which preachers in which of the numerous churches kept their sermons down to twenty minutes. When she finally left, she made a further appointment. "Just to check up on you, see how you're getting along in Our Fair City," explained Our Lady of Perpetual Smiles. Then she was off in search of other prey.

Motel 2 is apparently named for the number of rooms. A kitchen and a bedroom.

Resurrection bodies have no need of bathrooms, in case the reader missed that point.

The kitchen cabinets are well-stocked with decaf and coffee mugs, and the Freon-impaired refrigerator is loaded with cans of warm 3.2 beer. The kitchen itself is a veritable gambler's nest: the table is already set up for a Friday evening of friendly cards. The only things lacking are the players. They're probably listed in the Welcome package.

The bedroom is decorated in muddy browns and faded oranges and dull greens and furnished with garage-sale knickknacks. Mildred is delighted. It also contains one queen-sized bed. In fact, Motel 2 comes fully equipped: besides the refrigerator and table and the bed, there's a chest-of-drawers, a phone, and cable TV. There are even a computer and a printer.

Mildred opens the chest-of-drawers and practices the art of rummaging. "Look!" she says. "A gift! For you!"

She waves my gift over her head like an Olympic torch. It's a Classic. A Gideon Bible.

She keeps rummaging. "More gifts!"

It's a flower-decorated nightgown for the lady and a pair of bright-grey pajamas for the gentleman.

We've had a long day. It's already past six o'clock. We slip into our thoughtful gifts and stretch out on our new bed. Armed with my remote, I turn on the TV and begin to surf the channels. Mildred picks up the phone and places a call to the front desk for a tub of buttered popcorn and the daily crossword.

The local PBS station is holding a fundraiser. A bald little man with a nonstop voice and a terminal smile broaches the subject of guilt. He follows this gentle reminder with a recommendation that we purge ourselves by pledging to join. They have various membership categories, he explains, one for every pocketbook and degree of public spirit. Besides enjoying the advantage of a guilt-free existence, he promises, we will forever and ever have access to quality programming. He is handed a list, from which he reads the names of persons who in the last half hour have heeded his call for repentance. Their reward: footage of a pride of lions prowling the Serengeti in quest of edible zebra.

I switch channels.

Half a dozen men and women are sitting around on an expensive sofa. The men have well-greased pompadours, the women could be models for Maybelline. Their smiles rival that of the PBS salesman. They are all sharing conversion experiences and praising the Lord for a wide assortment of benefits. Periodically their leader turns and peers directly into the camera. He asks us members of the viewing audience where we prefer to spend eternity. There's still time, he encourages us; the votes have not yet been counted. Then he gives us a number to call.

The idea seems to be, the more money you send, the better your chances of getting into the best places.

"It's exactly like regular life," observes Mildred. "You get what you pay for."

The front-desk clerk brings the popcorn and crossword. Mildred settles down for a short evening. I switch channels.

A big brassy woman in her late thirties with rainbow-colored hair is purchasing a vowel.

I quickly change channels.

"Don't you want to watch the Wheel?" asks Mildred.

I explain my belief that the program is rigged.

The American Movie Channel announces an oldie but goodie. *The Secret Life of Walter Mitty*, starring Danny Kaye in the title role.

"'An unassuming middle-aged man has dreams of greatness,'" reads Mildred from the TV schedule. "'But life gets in the way.'" She pats me on the hand "It should be right up your alley."

This opinion does not satisfy my appetite for surfing.

"What's the matter, don't you like Danny Kaye?" asks Mildred.

I don't have time to answer. KKLD is interrupting its regular programming with a late-breaking story. "This just in. Police report that a RV has run off a cliff. The driver has been taken to Kirkland South General, where he's listed in serious condition with possible brain damage. The name—"

I quickly change channels.

"Don't you want to hear who it is?" my former wife inquires.

"I have a low tolerance for tragedy."

"I thought that was your specialty?"

"That was pre-resurrection."

We are back to PBS. The Serengeti lions have apparently finished their feast and are yielding the remainder of their time to

"Masterpiece Theater." We catch the lead-in: the camera panning across all the old Classics—Dickens and Company. There is, however, a new host. Hostess, to be exact. An attractive young woman, fashionable wire-frame glasses, exaggerated shoulder pads. Could be mistaken for Ms. Penni Mode. The program tonight, she announces, is a twentieth-century Classic: *Fahrenheit 451*. Adapted for the post-modern world by a Ms. Candi Greene.

It's back to the button.

"Candi Greene," says Mildred. "Doesn't that name ring a bell?"

I confirm her hunch, and it's on to "General Hospital."

Today's episode features a bedridden couple. The woman is giving the man a backrub. "Carole and I don't seem to be getting along too well these days," says the man. "That time of life for her, etcetera etcetera—not that there's anything wrong with a few biological changes, it's all part of growing . . . older." "More mature," the woman corrects him. "Yes," he agrees. "More mature . . . more adult." Then he changes the subject. "Speaking of Carole, I'm always struck by how well you maintain your youthful, ah, appearance." At this point he turns over, sits up, and embraces the woman. "I can't see why Ed would want to keep away from somebody like you," he whispers.

"She reminds me of you, in some ways," I say to Mildred. "I mean that as a compliment."

"I was going to say she reminds me of Mabel."

"Well, you *are* identical twins," I remind her.

Mildred agrees with this observation. "I'm sleepy," she suddenly announces. She removes the remote from my grasp and shuts off the TV.

"I was trying to figure out who that guy reminds me of."

"Probably Romeo," she yawns.

"No, someone in my *last* life."

Mildred does not answer. Instead, she puts her unfinished crossword and #2 pencil and empty tub of popcorn on her night stand. Then she turns over on her side and goes to sleep.

But I remain awake for a while, lying there in my grey pajamas with grey piping and grey buttons, watching the last sunlight filter through the Venetian blinds and onto the mud-brown wallpaper, thinking of who that man reminds me of.

Digby? . . . No. Couldn't be.

§

It is the middle of the night. I am still awake, staring at the ceiling, thinking about Charlie. What was his last promise? "God will answer your most burning questions."

I sift through the ashes of my burnt questions and come up with a short list:

1. Where am I?
2. Why am I here?
3. What is the meaning of my life?
4. Was I really Shakespeare in my next-to-last existence?
5. What can I hope for?

I poke Mildred with my elbow.

"Hmmm?"

"God will answer my questions," I whisper.

She sits up. "What?"

"God will answer my most burning questions. That's what Charlie promised. So far, everything Charlie promised has come true."

"Charlie?"

I explain about Charlie, in twenty-five words or less.

And what does she say? "Well, why don't you call?"

"Who? Charlie?"

"No. God."

"What's His number?"

"Isn't it listed in the Yellow Pages?"

I fumble around for the phone directory. It's in the chest-of-drawers, right next to the Gideon Bible. "What should I look under?"

"Try 'Churches'," she suggests.

"Which one? They list lots of churches."

"Try 'Protestant'."

"There's no heading called 'Protestant'."

"Here, let me see that directory. You're looking like a man . . . Protestant, Protestant . . . here's one—'A full-service church.' They have nurseries for all services, a mom's day out, interpreters for the hearing-impaired, a championship softball team, a preschool for the children of working mothers, a youth group, a straight singles fellowship, a gay singles fellowship, a family counseling center, an aerobics class for grannies, and immaculate restrooms."

I call the recommended number and get a recorded message from the Rev. Dr. F. N. Gamus, advertising the services of his corporation. He appears to be especially jubilant about their mom's day out and their interpreters for the hearing-impaired. He ends with a Thought for the Day. *Be Happy*. No mention of God. Just *Be Happy*.

After a severe bout of meditation on the Thought for the Day, I turn to Mildred and ask for other suggestions.

"Try U-P-S-T-A-I-R-S."

I dial UPSTAIRS.

"You have reached the Bandero residence," answers a male voice. "I can't come to the phone right now, but at the tone, please leave your message."

I leave my message: "I think I'm in love with your wife."

"Who was that?" Mildred is all ears.

"That," I reply, "was God."

"I didn't know God had a wife," says Mildred sarcastically. The sarcasm, however, is laced with anger and pain.

We engage in a discussion of the Divine Family Tree and whether the number four fits into the Trinity and the literal versus the symbolic interpretation of Scripture. The conversation soon wanders to the subject of coveting one's neighbor's wife. I end up admitting that it wasn't really God I was talking to, it was someone whose name I didn't catch, and I didn't know him, how could I, it was a wrong number, and besides, I wasn't really in love with his wife, it was just a temporary infatuation. She suggests that I never let it happen again. I promise, with mental reservations, and turn the conversation back to the subject of God.

"Okay, okay," I say. "*Now* what number should I dial?"

"1-800-463, of course."

"Four six three?"

"G-O-D."

I follow her directions to the jot and tittle.

A female voice answers: "I'm sorry, but that number has been disconnected."

I replace the receiver and sit on the edge of the bed, placing my head between my hands.

Mildred is curious. "What'd He say?"

"He said He's dead."

Mildred sits up and frowns. “But I talked to Him just last night,” she insists.

“Did you ask Him a burning question?”

“Of course.”

“What did you ask Him?”

“If He could spare a Jenn-Air stove.”

“What’d He say?”

“He promised to work on it. So He’s definitely not dead.”

She’s right. He’s probably just temporarily incapacitated. Pleased that the situation is not grave, I lie down, turn over on my side, and put in a full night of sleep.

§

“I’ve got it!” exclaims Mildred. “E-mail!”

I wake up. “What?”

“E-mail. The modern way to get in touch with another person.”

I roll over. “What’s e-mail?”

“It’s what you send through computers.”

I’m skeptical. How does Mildred suddenly know so much about computers? She spends half her life balancing the budget without the aid of even a calculator, and suddenly she’s knowledgeable about computers?

“So how do you suddenly know so much about computers?”

“I spent over forty days inside one.”

“Sure,” I say sarcastically. “When?”

“Between Easter and the day you landed on Antarctica.”

How does this woman suddenly know so much about my post-resurrection itinerary?

“Tell me about e-mail,” I request.

She explains the concept of e-mail to me, in user-friendly terms. Half an hour later I am sitting at the computer, against my better judgment, taking my first computer lesson from a middle-aged woman with only an A.A. in Dental Hygiene who claims to have spent over forty days inside the machine that is responsible for ruining more of America's young minds than any other device, with the exception of the condom. Suddenly my former wife of thirty-some years is bandying about phrases like "electronic mail" and "log on" and "upgrades" and "laser printout," and she's typing abracadabra like "bsbuller@aol.com," which, she explains, is the up-to-date and patriotic way to log on to the mind of God.

Then she places me in front of the computer with my list of questions and instructs me to "log on." Half an hour later, I am reading a miraculous printout of a catechism, consisting of my questions and God's answers:

1. Where am I?

I believe the technical term is Hell.

But I thought Hell was horrible. This isn't great, but I somehow had the idea Hell was a lot worse.

The negatives have been blown out of proportion by the clergy.

2. Why am I here?

Because it pleased me to put you there.

Your ways are past finding out—is that what you're saying?

No, we just came up with a clever plot line.

We?

I have a story consultant. And a client.

Could you name names?

They wish to remain anonymous.

3. What is the meaning of my life?

I'll let you figure it out for yourself. That's half the fun, isn't it? Locating the patterns, tracing the plot, working out the theme, the images, noting the contrasts and parallels between the major characters, etc., etc.

4. Was I Shakespeare in my next-to-last existence?

Yes.

Really?

Sure. But keep in mind that every aspiring writer since 1616 has been Shakespeare in a previous existence. That's what writing is all about, doing Shakespeare all over again. In fact, I'd estimate that well over 90 percent of the reading public has been Shakespeare in a previous existence.

One more question, then I've got to get back to work.

5. What can I hope for?

Immortality.

Immortality?

Isn't that the goal of every fictional character?

§

Mildred is in her element. Happy as a lark. She's gone shopping. But not in the simple sense of shopping. In the sense of mixing with the multitudes and taking one of her surveys to find out what the general population likes best about this place, whether most of them think it measures up or whether they're like her husband, victims of excessive expectations.

Hell, is it? I have to admit I'm disappointed. You spend your whole life working for a Matisse, and all you get is a Bosch. . . .

Maybe I should sue?

I have a good case. (1) No warning label, and (2) contradictory instructions.

Life should come with a warning label. If they can put it on the cigarettes you used to smoke, they can put it on your cradle: "THE SURGEON GENERAL HAS DETERMINED THAT LIVING CAN BE DANGEROUS TO YOUR GOALS."

Also, the instructions are inconsistent. Here you are, faced with the scriptures of the six or seven major religions, a couple dozen minor ones, several dead ones, countless primitive ones, as well as the ethical teachings of Plato and Aristotle, not to speak of Confucius.

I've got them on both counts. Now all I have to do is find myself a good lawyer.

I go out on the street and hail a passing pedestrian, as they're called, who's sporting a high-dollar business suit and tie and carrying a leather monogrammed briefcase.

"I'm looking for a lawyer," I say.

"Be with you in a minute," he says, gazing past me at an ambulance that is rushing to the scene of an accident that has just marred the idyllic landscape.

He hustles over and helps the young blonde victim through a trying period in her life. He takes her injured hand and places his card within it. Such care! Such compassion! Such humanity! I can't believe my luck. First, that I've found a lawyer on the first try, and second, that he's such a fine specimen of the human spirit.

After the ambulance removes the object of his devotion, my new friend returns to me, pulls a legal-size pad out of his or her briefcase, and speaks.

"Have you admitted to anything?"

"I haven't done anything wrong."

"That's beside the point. I just want to make sure you haven't admitted to anything. Have you admitted to anything? Yes? No?"

"Let's go with No."

"Great. We've got us a case."

"But you don't even know what I have in mind."

"A lawsuit, right?"

"Yes, but who am I going to sue?"

"Some Higher Power, right?"

"How did *you* know?"

"People like to go after the deep pockets, and who has deeper pockets than the Higher Powers?"

This guy makes good sense!

"So, which Higher Power are we talking about here?" His question. He's standing at the curb, licking on the point of his pencil, getting ready to write everything down. I have to be careful what I say.

"God," is what I finally say. "That is, if He's still classified as a Higher Power?"

"Oh, certainly. The latest *Fortune* lists Him as Number One among current deities, in terms of net worth."

This is just about the best news I've heard since Easter Morning. Not only is God still able to exert influence over the day-to-day running of the world, but He's maintained his Number One ranking in spite of a flurry of late activity on the part of His competitors. The bottom line is, He remains ultimately responsible.

"Now," he continues, "let's make us a list of complaints."

Which is exactly what we do. We make a list of the ways God's creation has failed to meet my expectations, beginning with the death of Henry Constant and ending with Motel 2, paying special attention to the toe-tag incident. I do not neglect to mention being accused by Ms. Penni Mode of being a dead white male ("Possible slander," he agrees) and being replaced by Ms. Candi Greene ("How do you spell that?") and being forced to resign my position as a role model for the youth of America and Digby's bad financial advice and being made the butt of the Deuces' crude jests ("Mental anguish") and being the innocent victim of Rev. Heedon's ill-considered interpretation of the Eleventh Commandment and investing in the flawed Winnebago ("How do we get around *Caveat emptor*?") and being abandoned by Dora in my hour of need ("You got her present address?") and Betsy Bandero's ill-timed phone call and the fact that my own son was not there for me when I needed him, as well as the ridicule I was forced to endure upon announcing my past life as Shakespeare ("Hmmm") and the blizzard that interrupted my pilgrimage to the West Coast ("Sounds suspicious") and the failure of the wonder drugs and of the medical profession generally ("Malpractice!") and being threatened by Rev. Gilltrip ("Malpractice?") and Nurse Comfort's matter-of-fact attitude toward my impending death. Nor do I neglect to mention Charlie's promises and how they were kept in letter but not in spirit ("You got that all on tape?") and the forty-day wait and being ignored by a former student and being transported in a decrepit airplane and prematurely ejected from same ("Just an ejection? Not a crash?") by my two attractive molls and being surprised on the Ross Ice Shelf by the unplanned appearance of Mildred ("Bait and switch") and being subjected to ridicule by Ted Koppel ("Another deep pocket") and then being put in the demeaning position of having to play Santa to a gaggle of ungrateful penguins and being left to my own devices by the team of international scientists ("Leaving the scene of an accident") and hounded by the police just because of a trumped-up charge of environmental damage ("Slander again") and then being forced against my will to scurry down a poorly-maintained one-way escalator.

It is when we reach the bottom of the escalator that we begin to encounter difficulties. My attorney of record starts to play devil's advocate. "This is what it'll look like to a jury," is a sentence that is suddenly in vogue. Also, "There's the problem of lack of evidence."

"But what about *this*?" I produce the printout of my conversation with God and thrust it into his evidence-deprived hands.

He mulls.

He mutters.

He speaks: "What's the precedent?"

"Precedent?"

"For a character suing his author."

"What!"

He looks at his watch. "Never mind," he says.

"But . . . I've got a resurrection body!"

"Take my advice, sir. Put on some weight. Get a tan. Pump a little iron. Work on that window-pane body."

He begins to move on. "Hey," he says. "Gotta go. I'm due in court. A whiplash case."

"But—"

"Tell you what," he says, breaking into a canter, "I'll get back to you."

"What about Mildred?" I cry after him. "*She's* a witness!"

I can see his head bobbing up and down as he disappears into a gathering crowd of curiosity seekers. "Looks to me," he yells over his briefcase-free shoulder, "like the lady's involved in this thing up to her eyeballs."

About the Author

Paul Wiebe grew up in the Idaho outback. Early on he found that the life of irrigating potatoes, driving trucks, repairing fences, digging ditches, chasing mad steers across the open range, and castrating the occasional boar was not to his liking.

This discovery led him to the halls of higher education. Bethel College (Kansas) granted him a B.A; the University of Chicago eventually presented him with a Ph.D. and sent him away to Wichita State University. There he taught religion and literature and performed the tasks of his chosen profession—translating and writing books on the theory of religion, composing footnotes for journal articles, and arriving late at the meetings of those committees he could recall having been assigned to.

But his mastery of the academic proprieties was never more than tenuous. Thus it came as no surprise to his colleagues and students when he resigned his tenured position and, in an attempt to recapture a vanishing sanity, took to writing comic novels. Besides *Dead White Male,* they include *Benedict XVI, The Church of the Comic Spirit,* and *Christian Bride, Muslim Mosque.*

Wiebe now lives in Southern California with his wife and pet mockingbird.

www.ingramcontent.com/pod-product-compliance
Lightning Source LLC
Chambersburg PA
CBHW071239170626
46809CB00001B/8

* 9 7 8 0 9 7 1 8 5 9 9 2 0 *